SHE WAS SHROUDED IN SCANDAL

Since her husband's tragic death in the Peninsula, Carlotta Ennis had hoped to attract a wealthy husband in Bath. Instead she made the ruinous mistake of loving a rake who was willing to seduce her, but not to marry her. Now that she has been so thoroughly compromised, she is certain no decent gentleman will ever marry her . . . until James Rutledge returns home from the war and offers his hand—though Carlotta is convinced it is out of duty, and not love.

HE RESCUED HER HONOR

After Carlotta's husband gave his own life to save him in the heat of battle, James had vowed to return the man's gift by providing for his wife and son. Though the lovely widow agrees to become his bride, James believes it is his fortune alone that she desires. Yet as near tragedy sends Carlotta into his arms, it also propels her to confess her deepest secrets. Will James let her dark past come between them, or listen to his heart's undeniable truth . . . that he's fallen in love with a fallen woman?

Dear Romance Reader,

In July of 1999, we launched the Ballad line with four new series, and each month we present both new and continuing stories set everywhere from medieval England to the American West—the kind of passionate, romantic stories you love best, written by the most gifted authors. At the back of each book, we tell you when you can find subsequent books in the series that have captured your heart.

This month, rising star Cheryl Bolen offers the third installment of her atmospheric *Brides of Bath* series. What will happen when a man driven by honor loses his heart to **A Fallen Woman**? Next, the always talented Tracy Cozzens explores **A Dangerous Fancy** in the next entry of her *American Heiresses* series as a proper young woman, who has caught the eye of the Prince of Wales himself, discovers that a roguish commoner might be her unlikely savior—and the kind of man who could win her love.

The fabulous Pat Pritchard continues her *Gamblers* series with the second of her incredibly sexy heroes. A U.S. Marshal posing as a hardened card-player has no time for romance—until he meets a woman who makes him feel like the **King of Hearts.** Finally, promising newcomer Kate Silver whisks us back to the glittering French court of Louis XIV in her brand-new series . . . *And One for All.* When a Musketeer in the King's Guard learns that his comrade may not be all "he" seems, he must promise to keep her secret, **On My Lady's Honor**—unless passion sweeps them both away. Enjoy!

Kate Duffy
Editorial Director

The Brides of Bath

A FALLEN WOMAN

Cheryl Bolen

ZEBRA BOOKS
Kensington Publishing Corp.
http://www.kensingtonbooks.com

ZEBRA BOOKS are published by

Kensington Publishing Corp.
850 Third Avenue
New York, NY 10022

All Kensington titles, imprints, and distributed lines are available at special quantity discounts for bulk purchases for sales promotion, premiums, fund-raising, educational or institutional use.

Special book excerpts or customized printings can also be created to fit specific needs. For details, write or phone the office of the Kensington Special Sales Manager: Kensington Publishing Corp., 850 Third Avenue, New York, NY 10022. Attn. Special Sales Department. Phone: 1-800-221-2647.

Zebra and the Z logo Reg. U.S. Pat. & TM Off.

First Printing: August 2002
10 9 8 7 6 5 4 3 2 1

Printed in the United States of America

*This book is dedicated to my firstborn, Johnny,
who has brought his father and me
nothing but joy and pride.
I love you, son.*

One

She knew they were gossiping about her. As soon as Carlotta Ennis had glided into the sedately gay Pump Room, the snickering women's voices had risen to a crescendo. *Never mind them,* Carlotta told herself as she regally strolled to procure her cup of the medicinal water.

While she waited for the attendant to fill her cup, Carlotta heard a distant female voice. "Will you look at how low her neckline plunges!"

No doubt, Carlotta was the subject of such outrage. The lady under discussion stood up straighter and tugged at the bodice of her purple velvet gown, a sly smile playing at her lips as her neckline fell even lower. Flaunting convention had always been as much a part of Carlotta's persona as the velvety timbre of her seductive voice.

She took her water and began to drink. Surely the water would do her good. She had not been here—nor anywhere in this watering city—since the unpleasantness with Gregory.

"Nasty-tasting, is it not, Mrs. Ennis?" a gentleman's voice asked her.

She swallowed the water, silently agreeing with the man's accurate description, returned her cup to the liveried attendant, then turned her gaze upon the gentleman who had spoken to her. It was Sir Wendell Anthrop. She guessed him to be roughly three decades her senior—in his mid-fifties. What he lacked in hair he more than made up for in girth.

"Yes, it is quite revolting," she answered, "but as I have been in poor health of late, I thought it would do me good to drink the abominable restorative."

She felt his eyes sweep over her from the top of her head to the tip of her toes, with a perceptible lingering over her full bosom. "I am sorry to hear you've been unwell, Mrs. Ennis," he said, his steely eyes pensive. "I knew the Assembly Rooms have seemed wretchedly empty without you." He moved closer, possessively placing a hand on her elbow. "May I have the pleasure of walking with you this morning?"

It was a welcome sign. A man of decent birth was not ashamed to be seen with her. It would do her good to allow Sir Wendell to see her home to Queensbury Street.

Before they left the Pump Room they strolled the lofty chamber from one end to the other, Sir Wendell pausing frequently to speak with acquaintances who icily ignored Carlotta's existence.

It had not always been this way. Not so very long ago she had been as vital a part of Bath society as the Master of Ceremonies himself. Women vied to befriend her; men made fools of themselves to attract her attention. And Carlotta had thrived on their adulation.

Despite the drone of voices and the soft orchestra music, Carlotta and Sir Wendell were easily able to converse on banal topics such as the fair weather and the actors performing at the theatre.

After leaving the Pump Room they joined the flow of people funneling onto Milsom Street. The streets were far more full than the last time she had ventured out—when Gregory had been with her. But, then, this was the season for Bath. That is why Sir Wendell was here. He could afford residences in several cities. Unlike Carlotta, who was forced by pecuniary circumstances to live in Bath year round. She craved the shops and the assemblies and theatre—all of which were far cheaper in Bath than in London.

As they strolled along Milsom Street, she avoided looking at the milliners and mantua-maker shops where her accounts were sadly in arrears, fearing the shopkeepers would recognize her and run from their establishments, demanding that she settle her bills. She read the sign for Bingham Butchers and colored, remembering the extent of her unpaid bill there. At least Peggy, her cook, housekeeper, maid, was the one who had to patronize the butcher. Bless poor, devoted Peggy.

Carlotta and Sir Wendell turned on to George Street and spoke again of the weather and mutual friends and the musicians who were performing currently in the city.

"It would give me the greatest pleasure if you would accompany me tomorrow evening to the musicale," he said, giving her hand a firm squeeze.

A pity Sir Wendell was old and fat. Though not in the least attractive to her, he was a man of consequence in Bath. Allowing him to escort her in society would reintroduce her in an agreeable manner. "The pleasure would be mine," Carlotta said, gazing at him through heavily lashed eyes.

Perhaps the man could even be her savior from economic woes. Despite the fact that she was not attracted to him, she could entertain the idea of being married to Sir Wendell. As the wife of such a wealthy man, she would be able to pay off all the tradesmen she owed, she could help Gran—and best of all, she could bring her little boy to live with her at long last. Yes, she could marry the man for incentives such as those. She knew better than to hold out for love. Her love had been lavishly spent on a man who wanted no part of it.

Sir Wendell appeared to puff up with self-importance and proceeded to regale her with trivial observations of Bath. She caught herself not attending his words, for each street brought memories of Gregory. Thank God he had gone home to Sutton Manor. She did not think she could bear to see him with that young wife of his.

She fought back tears when she saw the tearoom where Gregory had taken her for refuge during blustery winter days. How she had loved to sit there, warming her hands around a cup of steaming brew and gazing into his honeyed eyes. She grew weak just remembering the effect his crooked grin had on her. Surely it was a sin to love a man as totally as she had loved Gregory. Even Stephen Ennis—the husband whose son she bore, the man who had given her his name and earned and deserved her ceaseless love— had received but a trickling of the affection she later laid at Gregory Blankenship's shrine.

"I believe this is your residence," Sir Wendell said.

She had not realized they had reached Queensbury Street, and to assure herself, she looked up to see the familiar little row house. "Thank you, Sir Wendell, for seeing me home."

The man grabbed her hand much as a thief would steal a chop of mutton. And he held it firm, his eyes devouring her bosom. She was uncomfortable and wished she had a shawl to drape over her breasts. Before Gregory, she never would have been visited by such shame. She allowed a stab of anger at herself and of resentment toward Gregory.

"I must say I was happy to learn that Blankenship has left Bath and taken up residence at Sutton Manor for I've always had a tendre for you, Mrs. Ennis."

Carlotta's heart began to drum madly as he squeezed her hand even harder and leered at her with a lecherous grin. "That is too kind of you, Sir Wendell." Why did she say that when the man repulsed her? Avoiding contact with his puffy green eyes, she set one slippered foot on the first step to her house.

His grip on her hand tightened. "You know I am a very wealthy man." He moved closer and spoke in a husky, low voice. "I'm noted for my generosity, especially to the women I . . . ah, protect."

Her stomach flipped. The despicable man wanted her for his mistress! She had to get away from him. Her other foot now moved to the first step.

His gaze was once more on her bosom. "I am prepared to settle you with five hundred a year, my dear Mrs. Ennis."

She twisted her hand free and whirled around, fairly flying up the steps, not deigning to reply to the obnoxious man.

"How dare you turn your back to me!" he shouted. "All of Bath knows you were Gregory Blankenship's fancy piece!"

She came to an abrupt stop and turned to face him, anger flashing in her eyes, scorn in her voice. "You, sir, are not Gregory Blankenship." Then she turned back and hurried up the steps.

"What's the matter," he bleated viciously, "is five

hundred pounds not enough? How much did Blankenship pay for your services?"

Despite the tears which blurred her vision, Carlotta's hand found the knob and she shoved the door open, slamming it behind her and hurrying up the stairs to throw herself on her bed for another good sob. Thank God Gran wasn't here to see her shame.

She had only cried twice in her life: when Stephen Ennis died and when Gregory Blankenship left her. But during the year since Gregory left she had turned into a watering pot. She not only had lost the man she loved recklessly and hopelessly, she had also lost her last semblance of respectability.

James Moore, now the Earl of Rutledge, was born under a lucky star. From his earliest days he had known it. He had been a great favorite with his nurse and had been blessed with good health. His strong body had not only resisted disease and infirmity but also gifted him with uncommon skill in rugby and cricket and any manner of gentlemanly sports. His extraordinary abilities distinguished him through Rugby, Sandhurst, and in the Light.

He had been the only young man in his lodgings at Sandhurst not to succumb to a deadly fever that claimed many of his classmates. When he was a soldier in the Peninsula, his noble Captain Stephen Ennis saved James from almost certain death—at the cost of his own life. From Waterloo, he emerged unscathed. While later serving in India, he received the news that an uncle, whose existence he had been unaware of, had died and left his fortune and title to James.

At the age of seven and twenty, James, whose father had been a gentleman farmer of modest means, found himself master of Yarmouth Hall. Now, he settled back in a comfortable leather chair, propped his boot-clad feet on the massive Jacobean desk, and surveyed the jewel-toned leather volumes that stacked row upon row two full stories up to the paneled wood ceiling far above. Bindings of red, emerald green, and lapis blue wrapped around the cavernous room. James wondered how many of them his uncle had read.

A shadow darkened the west doorway, and he turned to see Adams.

"Your lordship has a visitor," the tall, stiff, gray-haired butler announced.

The lord quickly dropped his feet to the Turkish carpet, hoping Adams had not witnessed his uncivilized behavior. James was not at all used to having a butler or to being master of any place, much less a four-hundred-year-old ancestral home of nearly one hundred rooms. He was not sure how he was supposed to act. And, truth be told, he was a good deal intimidated by the overbearing butler. A haughtier man he had never beheld.

"Pray, who is it?" James asked.

"A Mr. Jonas Smythe." Without saying another word, Adams conveyed his distaste for the unfortunate Mr. Smythe.

"Show him in," James said.

The Bow Street runner had not been expected back so quickly. It had been less than a week since the man had been hired. James stood and greeted Mr. Smythe, then asked Adams to close the door.

As Mr. Smythe had done at their first meeting, he lowered his stooped-over frame into a chair facing the desk James sat behind. "Have you a report so soon?" James inquired.

"Yes, milord." The bearded man withdrew a small notebook from the pocket of his red vest. "I believe I have all the information you requested."

James's anticipation heightened as he watched the man thumb through the Occurrence Book.

Mr. Smythe leafed through a few sheets of paper to refresh his memory, then spoke without consulting his notes. "Let me jest give ye the lay. Mrs. Ennis stays year-round in Bath on a right respectable street, Queensbury by name. Seems like a dull sort of place. I'm from Lunnon meself, and I like a bit o' bustle." He looked down at his book once more. "Well, like I was tellin', she rents lodgings in a town 'ouse. The rub is the lady can't get the dibs in tune. She owes everyone, gov'nah. Quarterly income won't cover. 'Tis only sixty pounds. Too bad Mr. Ennis was put to bed with a shovel."

James was almost relieved to hear Carlotta Ennis was in financial difficulties, for that meant he could have the pleasure of assisting her. It was a small price to pay for what her husband had done for him. And until James was assured of the happiness of Captain Ennis's family, he could never sleep well in his silken canopied bed at Yarmouth Hall.

"Tell me," James said, "did you see Mrs. Ennis?"

Mr. Smythe looked up from his notebook, snapping it shut. His pudgy fingers twirled his mustache, and his drooping eyes glimmered. "As fine a looking woman as ever there was."

James nodded. *Yes, that would be Carlotta Ennis.* "I thank you for the information, Mr. Smythe. My man of business will settle your bill if you will have my butler direct you to the morning room." James pulled the bell rope.

The runner stood and handed James several pages of paper from his notebook. " 'Ere's the official report with all the proper documentation, yer lordship."

Once the man was gone, James perused the report. How different Carlotta Ennis's life would have been had Captain Ennis lived. And it was James's fault she was a widow. He felt bloody bad about it. He always did when Lady Luck smiled upon him while trampling another.

Oddly, as he read the report he thought he smelled lavender, Carlotta Ennis's scent. It was as much a part of her as her glossy black hair. He vividly pictured the captain's elegant wife. Lavender and purple gowns of the latest fashion had softly molded to the smooth curves of her taller than average body, scarcely covering her full breasts. She carried herself so regally, she seemed almost ethereal. Her rich black hair—seldom covered with bonnet or hat—swept back, with wispy curls tumbling about her perfectly chiseled face. He'd always thought her cold, perhaps because she brought to mind a statue of a Roman goddess. Even her smooth skin reminded him of flawless polished marble.

Only her smoky lavender eyes showed any warmth.

He was somewhat piqued that the report had not mentioned the son she bore in Portugal in 1812. For it was the boy who troubled James the most. The poor lad would be raised without a father. The corners of James's mouth tugged downward as he remembered his own fatherless childhood. He had been the only one in his class at Rugby who had no male parent to visit him on Father-Son Day. But it was not that one day every spring which blemished his otherwise satisfactory childhood. It was not having a father to teach him the ins and outs of riding and shooting and angling, or to teach him the correct way to tie a cravat. It was having to become the man of the family when he was but four years of age. It was his self-imposed sense of isolation that permeated his childhood. He was different. He had no papa. Who could expect him to know what other lads—lads who had fathers—knew?

James turned his thoughts once again to Captain Ennis's son. James wanted to buy the lad's first horse and teach him to ride. They could go angling, and he would instruct the boy on how to shoot. If the little fellow needed help with his Latin or his sums, James wanted to be the one to provide it.

He pulled the bell rope again, and when Adams appeared he told him to inform Mannington to pack his things. "We go to Bath inside the hour."

Surrendering an arm or leg to a sawbones would have been more pleasant than facing Captain Ennis's widow. For she knew James's insubordination had caused her husband's death.

Two

The knocking persisted. It was no use pretending she was not at home. Mrs. McKay knew Carlotta's every move and had likely witnessed her parting from the odious Sir Wendell earlier in the day. Carlotta suspected the woman's only entertainment derived from poking her hawk-like nose into her tenant's affairs. The woman's nosiness was exceeded only by her gall. She would solicitously inquire on the quality of the previous night's turbot after watching Carlotta's maid return from the fishmonger's. And she would brazenly ask Carlotta how so-and-so was getting along, though her only acquaintance with so-and-so was through the keyhole of Carlotta's door. Of course, it had been some time now since Carlotta had entertained visitors.

After shoving her sewing in the drawer of her work table, Carlotta rose, crossed the faded carpet, and opened the door to her landlady.

Without being asked, Mrs. McKay strolled into the room, sighing deeply.

"Won't you sit down?" Carlotta asked.

The plump, redheaded matron sat on the settee Carlotta had just vacated, a frown on her well painted face. Carlotta seated herself on the edge of a nearby armchair, her stomach tumbling over the dreaded confrontation.

The landlady mopped her aging brow with a hanky. "I don't get up those stairs as well as I once did."

Carlotta nodded sympathetically.

Mrs. McKay's ample bosom lifted in an exaggerated sigh, and her face folded into a pained expression. "I had hoped it would not come to this, Mrs. Ennis, but if I cannot soon obtain the last quarter's rent you owe, I am going to be forced to evict you."

Now it was Carlotta who sighed. Where did the money go? She had never had much of a head for numbers and was hopeless with managing money. If she had it, she spent it. Every last farthing.

As of late, she had tried her best to economize—really, she had. She'd not gone to the milliner's in a year. Of course, she had not needed to. She still possessed an extraordinary wardrobe. White champagne gave way to cheaper wine, then to tea, and now she drank only one cup a day. She had switched from candles to the cheaper tallows and could barely afford any coal. Green peas were so dear they were only a memory, as was the generous settlement from Gregory.

Her fine carriage had been sold—at a huge loss. And what good was her elaborate wardrobe when she had nowhere to wear the ball gowns with trains, the morning dresses and promenade wear in every color of the rainbow—with hats and shoes to match each.

She had sold off all the jewels Gregory had given her, except for the diamonds. Within the next fortnight, they, too, would be gone. Then she would have nothing left of Gregory, save the emptiness in her heart.

"If you could but wait until the first of next month," Carlotta said, "you'll receive what is due as well as an advance on the next quarter."

The worry lifted from the elder woman's face. "If you can assure me, then that would be fine and good. A lady of quality such as yourself is precisely the type of tenant I wish to have, but I do have my own bills to see to."

"I understand perfectly, Mrs. McKay," Carlotta said. "Since . . . since I've been ill, I've acquired a great many debts myself, but I assure you that you're at the top of my list, come the first of the month." Unlike the promises she made to the other tradesmen, this one she meant to honor. She simply had to keep a roof over head. Nothing could be worse than returning, as an unmarried woman, to Gran's house and burying herself in dreary Yorkshire.

Mrs. McKay stood up, crossed the carpet and patted Carlotta's shoulder. "There, there, Mrs. Ennis, all will come about—once you get your health back." Her eyes traveled the length of Carlotta. "You look poorly. You've grown ever so thin."

Carlotta nodded. She couldn't deny the woman's words. Indeed, she had lost her appetite—and so much more.

"If I might be so bold as to make a suggestion," Mrs. McKay began, "if you'd sack your young woman, you'd have ever so much more money."

Sack Peggy! Carlotta would beggar first. Since she'd rescued the starving thirteen-year-old Peggy from the London wharves upon returning from Portugal, Carlotta had formed a bond with the frail young woman that was as irrevocable as the tides. Peggy had served Carlotta alternately as abigail, cook, and housekeeper during feast and during famine.

A huge lump formed in Carlotta's throat as she remembered Peggy vowing undying loyalty while inarticulately telling her that their relationship had been the only constant in the maid's dreary life.

"That is completely out of the question," Carlotta said to Mrs. McKay. "I am all that Peggy has in the world. I could never sack her."

The old woman shrugged. "I'll just let myself out," she said meekly.

After her landlady left, Carlotta went directly to her bedchamber, donned her pelisse, and decided to take a walk. A walk along the Royal Crescent would do her good. She had spent far too many days prostrate on her bed, crying over a love long lost and never to be resurrected. Buttoning her pelisse, closing the door behind her, and descending the stairs, she left the precarious security of Mrs. McKay's chambers to ponder her hopelessly befuddled circumstances.

The few pounds she received each quarter from her late husband's estate did not go very far. First, she had to send half of it to Gran. The other half would not even cover half her bills. And never was there a penny left. What was she to do?

Carlotta had always thought she would marry again. Indeed, she had never believed Gregory when he insisted he would never wed her. *I'll bring him around,* she had thought with as much confidence as foolishness.

Now she knew her beauty was no longer enough to secure a husband. Now that she had tarnished herself. The best she could hope for was to be set up as some peer's ladybird. No, she could never allow herself to sink that low. She had loved Gregory fiercely enough to ruin herself—but to coldheartedly make an *arrangement*? She shuddered.

She took a deep whiff of the fresh air. She had kept herself cooped up long enough. Despite her recent misery, Carlotta would rather live in Bath than anywhere else. Yorkshire farm life had been fine for a youngster—including her own son who was being raised there—but for a woman who had seen the world and relished living in the bustling city of Bath, Yorkshire countryside seemed as lifeless as a tomb.

With the verdant hills as a backdrop, Carlotta headed down Royal Avenue toward the Royal Crescent, but could not help but sink deeper into hopelessness, for there were no solutions for any of her problems. It would be easy for her to wallow in self-pity. After all, she had become a widow at nineteen when her husband—the third son of an earl—was killed in The Peninsula. Then four years later she had recklessly fallen completely in love with Gregory Blankenship, who would not offer marriage. Not to her, anyway. Tears pricked her lids as she thought of how he'd turned to his best friend's young sister for a bride. It wasn't fair.

But Carlotta had seen enough of life to know unhappiness did not last forever. At the end of every storm, a rainbow bridged the way to a new and better day. Surely her rainbow was due. Throughout the valleys and peaks of her life, poetry had always sustained her. Now the words of Robert Burns brought solace. *Come grow old with me. The best is yet to be.* She refused to give in to gloom. Somewhere on this earth there was a man with whom she would grow old—and reap her elusive happiness.

When she returned to her lodgings, Mrs. McKay met her at the Queensbury Street door, her eyes glowing triumphantly. "You've had a caller while you were out, Mrs. Ennis. I've asked Lord Rutledge to await your return in my parlor."

Lord Rutledge? Carlotta did not know anyone by that name. A puzzled look on her face, Carlotta followed her landlady into the parlor.

He stood when she entered. He was quite young—about her age, she guessed. From the top of his sandy head to the tips of his well-polished Hessians, Lord Rutledge personified sturdy good looks. He wasn't as handsome as Gregory—but, then, no one was. Lord Rutledge did possess a tall, athletic body, wore well tailored clothing, and shot her a grin that was as familiar as it was friendly. Where had she seen this man before?

"Lord Rutledge?" she said tentatively.

He stepped closer to her and swept into a bow. "Perhaps you would know me better were I in red regimentals. I am James Moore."

How could she not have recognized the man whose disobedience had cost Stephen's life? He obviously enjoyed prime good health and discreetly displayed wealth, while poor, dear Stephen lay buried in foreign soil these six years past. Surely the man did not expect her to bear his company. What could she possibly have to say to him? *Life appears to have treated you well, my lord? Please leave my house because you are not welcome here?* She glanced from him to an obviously besotted Mrs. McKay and decided to tolerate him for a short period. She could not cause a scene in front of Mrs. McKay. It wouldn't do to get thrown out of her lodgings.

As soon as she had realized who he was, her entire demeanor had stiffened unnaturally. When she finally spoke, she could barely conceal the iciness in her voice. "Won't you come upstairs and have tea, my lord?"

James had expected a cool reception. He had deserved it. Actually, he had expected far worse. At least Mrs. Ennis had not bounced him from her residence. "I should be delighted," he said.

Facing the lovely Carlotta Ennis for the first time in six years left James feeling like an awkward schoolboy at his first dance. She was as beautiful as he remembered. Still smelling of lavender and filling out the bodice of her lavender silk better than any woman he'd ever known, she had become slimmer, and something about the hollowness in her delicate face testified to a sorrow for which he felt responsible.

Not without pleasure, he left behind the talkative Mrs. McKay, who now probably knew far more about him than Stephen Ennis's widow did, and he followed Carlotta up a dark, wooden staircase to the second floor.

In her lodgings there, Carlotta addressed a youthful maid. "Please prepare a pot of tea, Peggy."

It seemed to James the maid directed a scolding glance at her mistress. Was tea such an extravagance? James wondered.

He surveyed Mrs. Ennis's parlor. Furnished in the fashion popular a generation earlier, the room definitely did not measure up to what Carlotta must have expected when she had married the son of an earl. It pained James to see her living here in a house she did not even own.

She came back and sat on the faded brocade sofa across from him, then addressed him in a voice devoid of emotion. "Has an infirmity brought you to Bath, my lord?"

"No, Mrs. Ennis, I enjoy excellent health and was fortunate to escape unscathed from Waterloo."

Since she made no response, he continued. "Actually, you are the reason I am here."

She raised her brows. "Me?"

"You and your son. I am responsible for the two of you. Now that I've inherited, my fondest desire is to be of service to you."

Her hands fisted in her lap. "I want nothing from you, and my son wants nothing from you."

He had known this would be difficult, but he hadn't expected her harshness could wound so deeply.

Her maid entered the room and set a tray of tea cakes with a pot of freshly brewed tea on the table in front of them.

Carlotta busied herself dispensing the sugar and pouring his tea. Even in her somewhat shabby surroundings, Carlotta Ennis was the most elegant creature he'd ever known. Her gilded porcelain teapot and floral cups were opulent yet dainty, like the woman who possessed them. The roses in her carpet bespoke her femininity though not nearly as thoroughly as her graceful person.

He tried not to stare at her lovely breasts—though it was not without difficulty. Therefore, he fixed his vision on her delicate hands as she prepared the tea. His gaze moved to her aquiline profile. Only stray flyaway tendrils of silken hair humanized an otherwise marble-like statue of perfection.

His mouth went dry, his voice hoarse. "Whether you want my assistance or not, Mrs. Ennis, I shall remain in Bath until such time as I determine I am not needed."

The teacup clattered to the saucer as Carlotta directed an irate glance at James. "Stay in Bath if you like. It's nothing to me."

He spoke almost to himself. "I've asked myself a thousand times, why Captain Ennis—a husband and father—and not me."

The anger seemed almost to drain from her graceful body as she shot him an arrogant look. "It must be as Lord Byron says. 'Heaven gives its favorites early death.' "

James lowered his head. "Indeed. There was never a finer man than Captain Ennis."

She handed James his tea. "And nothing you ever do will bring him back."

"I'm neither fool enough to believe I could replace a husband and father, nor unconscionable enough not to try to help. May I see your little boy?"

She stiffened. "He doesn't live with me."

Her words were like a blow to him. "Then . . . where is he?"

"In Yorkshire with my grandmother. Since she had four sons and also raised my brothers, and since she lives in the country, I believe Stevie is better off there with her than he would be with me."

"I had hoped to . . ." he trailed off. How could he tell the boy's mother he had hoped to help raise the lad? "I suppose your grandfather is most happy to have a lad about."

She coughed. "Unfortunately, my grandfather died before Stevie was born."

"Then Stevie has no men to influence him?" James's agitated voice did not conceal his disappointment. By Jove, the boy needed a man, he thought angrily.

Her eyes lowered as she shook her head, and for the first time he detected emotion in her demeanor. Was it guilt?

"I've brought the lad a gift," he said, reaching for a package he'd placed at his feet. "It's a toy sword, an exact replica of the one his father used in the Light."

She made no move to accept it. "And will you tell my son that because of your negligence, his father is dead?"

He swallowed hard, letting the package drop. "I had hoped not to dredge up the past but to ensure hope for the future."

Anger flashed in her eyes. "Stevie and I want nothing from you, my lord."

He got to his feet. "Nevertheless, I will make myself available to you. I mean to be of assistance to you and the child, and I shall wait until the day I can. Every day I will sit within my carriage in front of your residence. You will learn to depend upon my reliability." He spun away and headed for the door.

"I think not." Carlotta spat the words at him.

He had not been gone five minutes when Mrs. McKay trudged up the stairs to Carlotta's chambers and pounded on the door.

"Yes?" Carlotta said, opening the door and gazing into her landlady's excited face.

This time Mrs. McKay made no move to cross the threshold. "I want to thank you for coming up with the money earlier than promised," she said in wheezed gasps. "No one's ever paid me a year in advance before."

Carlotta had no idea what the woman was talking about. Had she gone delusional? Then, in a burst of sudden revelation, Carlotta knew. "Lord Rutledge?"

The cagey woman nodded. "Such a fine gentleman to come all the way to Bath to repay the debt he owed your husband."

Mrs. McKay had obviously been waiting, ear to her door, for James's departure so she could gloat about his generosity. Glancing over Mrs. McKay's shoulder, Carlotta impatiently asked, "Was there anything else, Mrs. McKay?"

"Mercy me, no. I've got to go take the waters."

Carlotta watched her landlady hold tightly to the rail as she ambled down the poorly lit stairway, the slender Peggy pausing at the landing for the heavier woman to pass. Peggy flattened herself and smiled and seemed about to burst with excitement. Once she was face-to-face with her employer, she began to squeal. "Oh, madam, you won't believe our good fortune!"

Oh, but Carlotta could. "You've been to the greengrocer's?"

Peggy nodded, her broad smile revealing an airy gap between her front teeth.

"And our bill has been settled there."

The girl's green eyes widened. "However did you know?"

"I expect you'll find all our bills have been paid. It seems Lord Rutledge is settling a large debt he owed my late husband."

"The gent who had tea with you?"

Carlotta nodded as they entered the parlor, shutting the door behind them.

"You should see his fine carriage, ma'am. It's even nicer than Mr. Bl—"

"Peggy," Carlotta snapped, "I should like you to learn if my suspicions are correct. Go to all the tradesmen and find out the extent of our debt. I believe Lord Rutledge will have preceded you."

"What a fine lord he must be!" Peggy said, turn-

ing on her soft kid slippers—a hand-me-down from
Carlotta—and leaving the rooms let by her mistress.

Carlotta needed to be alone to ponder the afternoon's events. Seeing Mr. Moore—who was now
Lord Rutledge—steeped her once again in the agony of grief, coldly reminding her of the words she
would never be able to utter to the noble Stephen
Ennis.

She pictured the nervous Lord Rutledge and now
that he was gone, she could admit a peculiar admiration for him. Not many men would have the courage to try to make amends. And she'd been quite
brutal to him.

If only she'd had more time to prepare for the
meeting with him. As it was, his sudden appearance
plunged her anew into the despair she'd experienced six years ago. The day she'd lost Stephen.

Without being aware of her actions, Carlotta
moved to her bedchamber, removed the pelisse she
was still wearing—then collapsed on her bed as tears
cascaded down her cheeks. She felt as alone as she
had that fateful day in Portugal. Perhaps she
wouldn't be so lonely if the boy were with her. And
if the boy were with her . . . mayhap through him
she could gain absolution from his father. No doubt
from the heavens that so favored him, Stephen
looked down on the son who bore so strong a resemblance to him.

Three

The following morning Peggy answered a knock and faced a manservant presenting a lace-wrapped nosegay of colorful blooms. "From my master to your mistress," he said. "And please tell Mrs. Ennis my master awaits her command from his carriage below."

Peggy all but flew to the little round table where Carlotta was taking her breakfast beside the window. "It's just as I told you, ma'am. He's such a fine lord." She handed her mistress the flowers, but Carlotta took no interest in them.

"Put them in water, if you will, Peggy."

"Yes, ma'am, but I gots to say my piece, seeing as how he's gone and paid all your debts. Lord Rutledge is your guardian angel, if you asks me. As fine a lord as ever there was. He's waiting in his carriage below just so you can command him."

Carlotta continued to peruse her morning paper. "I fear it will be a very long wait, indeed." She pretended not to see the frown on Peggy's face as the young servant left to fetch water for the flowers. In Peggy's absence, Carlotta stole a glance through her lace curtains at the carriage below. She was not so unaffected as she liked to appear.

By the time she had finished her breakfast, another knock sounded at her door. *So he'd already grown impatient.* With a smug expression on her face, she crossed the room and swung open the door, only to gaze at a smiling and panting Mrs. McKay. Carlotta's gaze moved down to Mrs. McKay's nonexistent waist, where a small nosegay was pinned. *Why, that cad was playing all his trumps!*

"Won't you come in?" Carlotta asked.

Sighing, Mrs. McKay waddled over to the sofa and plopped on it, removed her handkerchief, and wiped her brow while her gaze traveled the room until she spotted Carlotta's flowers in a vase on the tea table. Her smile lost a trifle of its brightness.

"Lovely flowers you're wearing," Carlotta said to her. "Lord Rutledge must have been quite taken with you."

Mrs. McKay straightened and stretched out her neck, lifting one less roll from her sagging chin. "I daresay it's you he's smitten over, Mrs. Ennis. His man tells me his poor master won't move that fine carriage until he can do so with you."

Carlotta lowered herself into a chair facing her landlady. "I assure you he's not smitten over me. He merely wants to be of service to me—to repay my husband's generosity to him."

"I understand he's been most generous to you."

"To the tradesmen I owe, you mean," Carlotta said, her eyes narrow. "News travels quickly in Bath, does it not?"

"A businesswoman must stay well informed."

"Of course."

"And as a businesswoman, I have no objection to Lord Rutledge's carriage being in front of my establishment. I couldn't pay for better advertising. Why, half of Bath will be desirous of living here now—so close to nobility, you know."

"I daresay you're right."

"But I do feel sorry for Lord Rutledge," Mrs. McKay said. "Couldn't you take a ride with him or something?"

"I could."

"But?"

"But I'm still rather vexed with him over something that happened in The Peninsula." No use tarnishing the man's reputation here by telling the woman how wretched that something was. He wasn't actually a bad man. He deserved a new start. As did she, she thought bitterly.

Not without effort, Mrs. McKay brought herself to a standing position. "I know it's none of my concern, but he's such a fine man . . ."

A wicked little smile flashed across Carlotta's face. "When he suitably demonstrates to me his reliability, I shall let him off the hook."

Mrs. McKay, her eyes narrowed, nodded solemnly and left the chambers.

"Peggy! Come help me dress. I believe I'll take a walk."

When she left the house, Carlotta did not spare a glance at Lord Rutledge's carriage, but from the corner of her eye saw him disembark. She kept on walking, having no idea where she was going. After a minute she realized someone was on her heels, and she knew very well who that someone was.

He did not wait to be addressed. "Ah, Mrs. Ennis, how lovely you look today," he said as he drew abreast of her. "I would ask if you minded if I tag along, but I fear I know the answer."

Her mouth scrunched into a half-concealed smile.

"I am told the waters at the Pump Room can cure whatever ails you," he said. "Mrs. McKay tells me you have not been well."

"Therefore, you think I should allow you to accompany me to the Pump Room?" she said, malice now gone from her voice.

"Most definitely."

She continued walking toward the abbey court. "I must warn you, my lord, about the water at the Pump Room. It's quite dreadful tasting." It was as close as she could come to offering a truce.

"I believe I'll forgo the water, then, since I enjoy remarkably good health," he said.

They passed the lending library that was patronized by a steady stream of well-dressed customers entering and exiting. Carlotta sighed inwardly. Her subscription there had lapsed, another casualty of her reduced circumstances. But then, she thought hopefully, Lord Rutledge had probably settled that debt, too.

When there was a lull in passing horses and hay carts and sedan chairs borne by sturdy Irishmen, they crossed the street. Then she summoned the courage to remark on Lord Rutledge's kindness in paying her debts. "This is difficult for me," she began, "but I would be remiss not to thank you for your generosity in settling with my creditors."

"No thanks needed. 'Twas a debt I owed Captain Ennis."

A debt that mere money could never repay. Her lips thinned.

As they walked along, she wondered how the man had learned of the tradesmen she owed. Had he hired a Bow Street runner? However he had learned of her present whereabouts and pecuniary difficulties showed a great deal of determination. The least she could do was to allow him to try to assuage his conscience with benevolence toward her. He could clearly afford it.

And she clearly needed it.

The Pump Room was not at all the crowded chamber centered around a rusty pump that James had envisioned. Though over a hundred people mingled within the vast, high-ceilinged classical Roman chamber, it easily held them all with room to spare for strolling.

"You must sign the book," Carlotta urged him.

"What book?"

"The one that announces all new arrivals. Perhaps one of the soldiers you served with will see it. Do you not find there is something quite gratifying in meeting those we knew in The Peninsula?"

"Indeed, madam." He caught her lavender scent when she moved closer to him, and memories of Portugal flooded him. Memories of the peaceful refuge found in Mrs. Ennis's lively quarters there. No matter how bleak were the regiment's days, evening card games hosted by the beautiful Mrs. Ennis had suffused him in warmth.

With her at his side, James strode to the podium where the book stood unguarded. He perused the names in the book, looking for others who had served in his regiment. Not seeing any familiar names, he took up the quill and carefully signed his name and the address of his hotel. Then he shot a concerned glance at Carlotta. "Will you not take the waters? After all, you could use a restorative."

Her long black lashes lowered, and she nodded.

He accompanied her to the station where cups of water were drawn from an urn plastered on the wall, and he watched as she drank. She seemed so delicate and frail—altogether different from when she'd been a happy wife.

When she finished, he tucked her hand into the crook of his arm and began to stroll about the room, a jauntiness in his step to match the tempo of the soft orchestra music. Unsure of the precarious state of his favor with the widow, he was reluctant to initiate conversation. They walked without talking at all, and when they had nearly completed a turn about the room, her soothing voice anchored him to their setting.

"Even though it's the height of the season," she said, "I see no one I know. You remember Captain Harrison's wife from The Peninsula?"

He nodded. He remembered Felicity Harrison's flaxen fairness, so perfect a contrast to Carlotta. The soldiers had dubbed them the Goddess of Day and the Goddess of Night. Carlotta, of course, was the Goddess of Night.

"A pity you won't be able to see her," Carlotta said. "She, too, lives in Bath but is presently in London with her new husband, who's a nabob. You remember Colonel Gordon?"

He quickly gazed at every tall man in the room—and there were many. "He's here?"

"Hardly. He's dead."

"No great loss, I should say. Never cared for him," he murmured.

"And with good reason. We learned much later he killed Captain Harrison on the battlefield because he was in love with Felicity."

James's mouth dropped open. "He murdered Captain Harrison?"

"Indeed, he did. In fact, he deliberately injured himself so he could escort Captain Harrison's widow back to England. The man was obviously deranged. He did terrible things, but he's dead now."

They strolled past the musicians. "How did he die?" James asked.

"Felicity's new husband—before he was her husband—rescued her from the colonel, who was abducting her, and the colonel was killed in the ensuing fight."

He shook his head. "It sounds like something out of one of those Minerva Press novels women are so fond of."

"Yes, indeed."

A moment later, he asked, "Did Mrs. Harrison ever have any children?"

"Not with the captain. She and the nabob have a daughter."

" 'Tis good Captain Harrison left no children behind. A boy needs a father." As they came back to the pump, he asked, "Is your Stevie like his father?"

Her voice was soft and mellow when she answered. "He is very much his father's son. He's enamored of all things military, and he looks exactly like Stephen."

"I should like to write him a letter telling him what a fine and brave officer his father was."

Her face grew solemn. "Stevie would like that."

Even though she had been unwell and had lost weight, he had no doubts that Carlotta Ennis was the loveliest woman in the room. What surprised him was the lack of suitors flocking around her. Her recent illness must have secluded her for a considerable period of time. Another piece of luck for him, no doubt.

"I hope I'm not tiring you," he said.

"It's actually good to be out and about again."

"I understand there's to be a Shakespearean production at the theatre tonight." He stopped short of begging her to accompany him. He wanted to gauge her reaction first.

"Edmund Kean's to portray Hamlet, is he not?" she asked. "I've never seen him, though I would like to some day."

"It would be my greatest pleasure to take you, madam."

She looked up into his face, her eyes a smoky lavender. "I don't know . . . I've been avoiding the night chill for so long now."

"Mrs. McKay was remarking to me how much recovered you are."

Carlotta shrugged. "Perhaps I could go to the theatre, to see Kean, of course."

After two turns around the room, he suggested they return to Queensbury Street. "I should not want to tire you, else I would have to forgo the pleasure of your company tonight."

As they walked back up Milsom Street, he saw a fair-haired lad on a pony and thought of Stevie Ennis. "Look, that boy must be the age of Stevie," he said.

Her gaze swung to the boy, her eyes flinching. "I daresay he is," she said in a morose voice.

"Does Stevie have a pony?"

"I . . . I don't believe so, though he's horse mad."

"I would like to select a gentle mount for him."

"You've spent quite enough." Carlotta did not look at him. Her mind was too full of her new-found good fortune. Lord Rutledge's generosity seemed an answer to her prayers. She must do whatever she could to stay in his good graces.

And she dared not allow him to learn of her indiscretion. The earl's guilt could not be counted upon to keep propelling him to acts of benevolence.

What would he do if he learned of her sullied past? Carlotta bit her lip. To settle her debts so promptly, he very well could have employed a runner. What else did the Bow Street spy tell Lord Rutledge?

Turning onto Queensbury Street, she continued to think about Lord Rutledge. Several times now he had spoken of Stevie. The man clearly wanted to meet her son, perhaps even to sponsor the lad—which meant that Stevie could be her ticket to economic freedom. There was no telling how far Lord Rutledge's generosity would extend if Stevie lived here in Bath with her.

She really ought to send for the boy. But she had no money with which to hire a nurse or to pay for his fare on the post chaise. Then, too, the lad was too young to travel alone.

"I truly wish you could meet my son," she said.

"As do I."

"If I were not so . . . so financially strapped, I would have him."

"A boy should be with his mother."

"How I wish I could have him!"

"Would it be presumptuous of me to send my man to Yorkshire—in my chaise—to get the boy and bring him to you?"

Her heart tumbled. She had never before had the responsibility of the boy. What did one do with a small lad? She pushed the brief stab of remembered fear away. Surely a nurse would be engaged. Carlotta could not be expected to know about such things. However, if she did have Stevie, Lord Rutledge was sure to assume some of the responsibility for him—and indulge them both, to boot.

Her lip trembled as she turned toward the earl. "Oh, my lord, nothing could be more wonderful, but I cannot afford a nurse for him."

"But I can. It's my responsibility—to repay your husband."

"I shall write to my grandmother today," she said decisively. "When can they expect your man? And what's his name?"

"Mannington. He should be able to be there late Friday."

They stopped in front of her house. "The boy is apt to be frightened of traveling so far from home with a stranger," James said. "Tell him he will have a pony of his very own when he arrives in Bath."

"That should make him very happy, indeed."

Their night at the theatre proved enchanting to James. He'd had no difficulty procuring an excellent box. And the woman who sat beside him stunned him with her beauty. He had almost lost his breath when he called for Carlotta and gazed upon her magnificence. A regal purple gown of soft silk clung to her graceful body, barely covering the ivory smoothness of her full breasts. Her glorious black hair was swept back, with soft curls spiraling loosely along her graceful neck. And, as always, she smelled of lavender fields.

"Have you seen Kean perform before?" she asked, turning to face him.

"Once. At Drury Lane. He gave an impressive performance as Othello."

"Really? Kean's a superior talent. I daresay he could play any role convincingly."

When the curtain rose, Carlotta directed her full attention to the stage, while the play held little of James's attention. Like a child awaiting Christmas, he bubbled with anticipation. Just being with Carlotta had filled him with purpose and contentment,

and his delight would swell tenfold once Stevie arrived. He had sent to Yarmouth for the boy's pony.
He grew anxious to see Stevie's reaction to it.

And now that it was certain he would be staying
in Bath for some time, he would need to let a house.
A hotel was no place to entertain a child. He would
also purchase a chessboard so he could teach the
youngster to play. And he would buy tin soldiers.
Armies of them.

Throughout the first three acts, James made a
mental list of all the things he needed to buy for
the boy.

When intermission came, Carlotta had no desire
to leave the box for refreshment—which surprised
James. Women generally enjoyed fluttering about,
talking to other women. But not Carlotta. She
seemed to have few friends. Of course, Felicity Harrison was out of the country . . .

Carlotta turned to James, excitement in her normally seductive voice. "Do you know, I have never
seen *Hamlet* performed before. It's really quite so-
bering. And I must say Kean is even greater than I
expected."

"A fine actor, indeed," James agreed.

"When I was a girl, my brother and I used to
perform all the Shakespearean plays, and I loved to
play Ophelia."

"Then you must have had a dramatic flair."

She smiled, her lashes lapping against the satiny
skin below her eyes.

"We shall have to perform some lighter plays with
Stevie when he comes," he suggested.

"I cannot wait."

The theatre lights dimmed, and the curtain lifted
on Act Four. During the final two acts, James found
himself making myriad plans for Stevie. He would

teach him to ride and to fish. They would explore the Roman ruins and perform plays and rollick in the park. He would tell the lad about Waterloo and present him with the epaulets he had worn there.

Throughout his musings, James would steal glances at Carlotta, her perfect profile evoking thoughts of a Roman goddess. Ah yes, he remembered, the Goddess of Night. And he was stirred by her provocativeness.

When the play was over and the actors took their bows, James could scarcely believe the time had passed so quickly.

Carlotta turned to him, placing her gloved hand on his, her lilac-gray eyes sparkling. "Thank you for bringing me tonight. It was wonderful."

He stood and offered her his arm. "The pleasure was mine entirely."

During the short carriage ride to Queensbury Street, James faced Carlotta. Even in the dim light, her beauty shone. "Mannington departs at dawn in this carriage," he said.

"I cannot believe I will see my baby next week," she said, her voice a whisper of the night. "Thank you."

" 'Tis nothing. I happen to be a very rich man."

"I would say you're my rainbow."

Her rainbow? Whatever did that mean? He pondered it for a moment, then he understood. Or thought he did.

Four

Lord Rutledge had caused Stephen's death. And she vowed to make him pay for it. If she played her hand shrewdly enough, the earl would indeed be her rainbow. The man's guilt drove him relentlessly to try to win Carlotta's forgiveness. Of course, she could never forgive him, but she could *pretend* to absolve him of guilt . . . while accepting any generous offering he might happen to throw her way.

The very thought of having Stevie here, though, sent her heart racing. She had no experience at being a mother. Stephen had been killed when Stevie was but one month old. Carlotta was still recuperating from her lying-in when she had plunged into a deep and devastating grief. Scarcely a month before she had lost her husband, her only brother had been slain in battle. Then she had lost Stephen, too. The only time she'd had sole responsibility for her babe was when she had sailed home to England with him. As if sensing his father's demise, Stevie had cried incessantly, and nothing she did would satisfy him.

By the time she reached London—and Gran's comforting presence—Carlotta had been content to turn over the babe to Gran's care.

Even when her grandmother returned to Yorkshire.

Thank goodness Lord Rutledge stood by, willing to offer assistance with her son. Let him have the responsibility for the boy! Clearly, the man desired to bring Stevie to Bath, and by having him here Carlotta could better manipulate Lord Rutledge . . . and his hefty purse.

She looked around her shabby drawing room. Perhaps Lord Rutledge would even wish to provide a finer place for the lad and her to live. A smile curving her lips, Carlotta vowed to see that he did.

The day Mannington left, James found himself wondering each hour how far his valet had gone and when he would reach Yorkshire. Time after time he would count on his fingers the number of days he calculated it would take before he could expect to see Stevie Ennis. He tried to picture the lad as a miniature version of his noble father. Captain Ennis had been possessed of a head of light brown hair that had likely been blond when he was the boy's age. Therefore, James imagined the boy with hair the color of newly minted gold. Would the absence of his parents have rendered the lad solemn? Such thoughts twisted at James's heart. He pledged to do everything in his power to compensate the boy for depriving him of a father.

More than once James winced from guilt. For it was he—and not the slain captain—who was deriving immense satisfaction from Stephen Ennis's lovely wife and he who hoped to become a father to Captain Ennis's young son.

He hoped his manipulations could result in Carlotta becoming a true mother to her son. A frown pierced James's countenance as he momentarily wondered again at the deprivation of a mother who could relinquish her ties to her only child.

James had much to do to compensate the boy. In his entire life James had never been driven by such purpose. Not when he had risen to the top of his class at Sandhurst. Not when he stood near the victorious Wellington at Waterloo. Not even when he had inherited the earldom. But now—now that he was supplanting Stephen Ennis—James was bursting with plans and hope and eagerly looked forward to each new day.

This day he wished to accompany Mrs. Ennis to the Pump Room. He liked to think that her health was being restored by his attentions, but it would not hurt her to take the water there. He would try anything that might restore the rose in her pale cheeks.

As he walked beneath fair skies to her lodgings, James stopped and bought her posies and purchased a smaller bouquet for her landlady.

"Oh, your lordship, you're much too kind," the rotund Mrs. McKay soon squealed with delight as he presented them to her when she answered his knock.

" 'Tis small repayment for your many kindnesses to Mrs. Ennis," he answered as he turned away and mounted the stairs to Carlotta's rooms.

Oddly, whenever he was about to behold Mrs. Ennis, James's stomach behaved in a most peculiar manner, not unlike one who feared falling on his face in front of the queen.

Carlotta's maid answered the door, dipped him a curtsey, and bade him to come in. "Allow me to fetch me mistress," she said, scurrying through a door to the bedchamber.

As he took a seat on the faded sopha, it occurred to him these skimpy lodgings were not only unfit for the beautiful, cultured Carlotta Ennis, but they were also completely unfit for little Stevie. The boy would have to have a nurse and nursery and room to play. This place was most inadequate. What had he been thinking of to contemplate his own relocation when it was the lad's mother's relocation which mattered most? James fleetingly thought of how disappointed Mrs. McKay would be to lose her most respectable tenant; then he remembered he had paid her a year's rent in advance—money she was free to keep. He smiled. She would not be too disappointed.

That peculiar feeling in his stomach returned as beautiful Carlotta gracefully swept into the room. She wore a sprigged lilac dress and looked rather like a young girl—not a widow closer to thirty summers than to twenty.

"What a pleasant surprise to see you, my lord," she said, offering him her hand.

He stood and bent to kiss it, stirred by her lavender scent. "Oblige me by allowing me to escort you to the Pump Room. The waters there should be beneficial to you—given your recent ill health."

Her brows lowered almost imperceptibly as a flash of some emotion—was it fear?—flitted across her lovely face, to be replaced immediately with dancing eyes and a happy voice. "How very kind of you to be concerned for me," she said, slipping her arm through his, "but what I really need is sunshine. Please do me the goodness of escorting me to Crescent Fields."

"Whatever you desire, my dear Mrs. Ennis. Shall you need a bonnet?" Though he did not discuss it,

James was keenly aware of Mrs. Ennis's avoidance of the Pump Room.

She turned to gaze at him with those sultry eyes of hers. "I never wear one."

Of course. Her lack of headwear had not gone unnoticed by him. "Another example of your distinctive style, I should say."

Her lashes lowered. "Then you've noticed."

"That you wear every shade of purple known to man?"

She tossed her head back and laughed. "I've never been a slave to fashion. My philosophy is to wear what looks best on one." She leveled a serious gaze at him. "Hats look hideous on women."

"I must admit," he said, opening the exterior door for her, "I'd much rather gaze upon a lady's shimmering hair than a hat."

She looked up at him. Almost seductively. "I daresay a man thinks of how much he would like to run his fingers through a woman's hair." Then she swept through the doorway.

He swallowed, breathless at the thought of running his hands through Carlotta's glossy black hair. Now he understood. Carlotta did not dress to please other women. She dressed to please men.

Once they were on the pavement, she looked up at him and smiled. "I could scarcely sleep last night, my lord, for my anxiousness to see Stevie. To think, by this time next week my little lamb will be with me!"

He filled with pride and, smiling, squeezed her hand that rested on his arm.

"There's just one thing," she said hesitantly.

His brows lowered at the tinge of worry in her voice.

"I fear my lodgings are not adequate for a rambunctious lad."

He patted her gloved hand. "Not to worry your pretty head. We'll have to procure more suitable lodgings for you—and the nurse we must hire."

She spoke in a voice barely above a whisper. "You are aware of the fact I have no money?"

"And you must be aware of the heavy debt I owe your husband, the lad's father." *Your husband.* It had been some time now since James had thought of Carlotta as belonging to Stephen Ennis. James was suddenly imbued with a bitter jealousy toward a man long dead, a man buried beneath Portuguese soil. "Allow me to let a house for you. In what area should you desire to live?"

She did not hesitate. "This side of the river, I should say. Everything is so much more at hand here."

"I shall make inquiries today. Perhaps tomorrow we can look at some houses." He stopped abruptly. "That is . . . I shouldn't want anyone in Bath to get the wrong idea about us. Perhaps you would prefer to go without me."

For the second time that day, she tossed her head back and laughed. Then, as quickly as she had erupted into laughter, she stopped, and a melancholy look crossed her face. "I'm hardly a maiden, my lord. Having no husband, it's only natural I should ask a gentleman to help me in matters of tenancy."

"Yes, of course." How helpless poor Carlotta was. James vowed to expend all his resources to relieve her of worries.

Few words were exchanged during their walk to Crescent Fields, and it occurred to James that not once since he had been in Bath had Carlotta spoken to a friend. Not that first day at the Pump Room, nor the night at the theatre, nor today—though they had passed dozens of people. Did she have no friends? Being of good birth and being the widow of an earl's son, she quite naturally should have easily slid into an exalted position in Bath society. That she had not must be a testament to her sadly reduced circumstances. Circumstances he took sole blame for.

The following day they went house hunting. The first one they looked at, on Camden Crescent, Carlotta dismissed as being too shabbily furnished. The town house on Avon Street faced a fish shop, which would not do at all for Carlotta. "I daresay I'd never sleep a wink for smelling three-day-old fish," she declared. The third one, a beautifully furnished town house on Monmouth Place, met with her approval.

"Lord Rutledge," she said in front of the agent, "you'll simply have to make all the arrangements for me. I'm hopeless with anything financial." Though she no longer possessed a good name she needed to protect, Carlotta wished to prevent James from discovering that fact. She looked at the agent. "Lord Rutledge served with my late husband and is a dear friend of the family. I declare, I don't know what I'd do without him."

After making arrangements to meet with the agent later that afternoon, James escorted Carlotta back to Queensbury. Her step was lighter than it had been in an age. In her deepest gloom, she had always held hope. " 'Oh, wind,' " she said wistfully to the skies above, " 'if winter comes, can spring be far behind'?"

James was silent for a moment. "May I hope your recitation of Shelley is fraught with symbolism?"

She met his gaze and nodded, then slipped her arm through his. "I can see that we shall get along beautifully, my lord. I love a man who knows his poetry."

When they turned onto her street, he cleared his throat. "There's one other thing I want to discuss about when the lad . . . your son comes."

"Yes?"

"I've been thinking. Everything will be so new, so unfamiliar, to him. I shouldn't like to throw too many new people, too many new experiences, at him at once. We should give him time to adjust to us."

What was he trying to get at? She looked quizzically at Lord Rutledge. "Yes?"

"I think we should allow him to become used to me and to being with you before we thrust a new nurse on him."

Good grief, would she have to have sole responsibility for the boy? "But, my lord, I'm hardly experienced with lads."

"Peggy can help you, and it's not as if I won't be around—every minute you'll allow me. I like to think I'm good with children."

"I'm sure you're wonderful," she said. If only *he* could take complete responsibility for the lad. "How . . . how long before we can . . . before the little darling adjusts to his new home? Before we can procure his nurse?"

There was no hesitation in his voice when he answered. "When I'm assured he's comfortable with you, if you must know."

So he's aware of what an unnatural mother I've been. No matter how inflamed she was, she must not allow him to believe her an unfeeling mother. "Of course you're right, my lord. Stevie likely will be nervous at first—what with the new surroundings and everything." She dared not tell Lord Rutledge the boy had never been completely comfortable with her.

"When I was nearly the same age as he," he said in a low voice, "I was sent to my grandmother's during my mother's bereavement, and I still remember how frightened I was to be removed from everything familiar and thrust into a completely alien environment."

She looked up into Lord Rutledge's handsome face. It seemed queer to think Lord Rutledge was ever a boy. He was so . . . so large and manly . . . and virile. Certainly not one given to fears. Stephen had told her James was a fine and brave soldier. This sensitive side of him—something she would never have suspected—was even more admirable than his generosity. Of course, he was flawed. He had allowed her dear Stephen to die because of his negligence. He *would* do well with the boy, though. She had no doubt Stevie would get on with him.

Before the week was out, James helped Carlotta move her pitifully few belongings into the town house on Monmouth Street. The following day, Stevie arrived.

Five

The sight of Stevie oddly stirred Carlotta. He had changed vastly in the two years since she had last seen him. Then, baby fat rounded his cheeks and the lisping four-year-old had more closely resembled a toddler than a young boy. Now, he was a miniature of his father. His thin, stern face looked far older than his six years.

Memories of the boy's father flooded her. She remembered how he had looked that night her brother introduced him to her at Almack's. He had worn his red military jacket with its shining gold buttons, a gleaming sword at his side. One look at him, and her heart was captured. She thought, too, of the heartache of his untimely death. But most of all, she remembered how proud Stephen had been when she bore him a son. Tears filled her eyes. She felt traitorous for sitting in her gilded drawing room that was being paid for by the man responsible for poor Stephen's death.

Forcing a smile, she moved to Stevie, her arms outstretched. "My darling son, how good it is to see you! And how you've grown!" She stooped to gather him into her embrace.

He stood rigid, his arms at his sides, a hint of a

smile tugging at his lips as his mother affectionately greeted him.

Holding him at arm's length, she directed a mock scowl at him. "No kiss for your mama?"

A full-fledged smile altered his small face as he moved to her and pecked her proffered cheek.

She took his hand and walked him down the hall of their town house. "You must come sit on my lap and tell me what you've been doing."

They entered the gold drawing room, and she sat on a silken settee, beckoning for him to sit on her lap.

He stopped three feet short of her. "Will I not muss your gown?"

"Oh, fiddle! You're much more important than any old dress." A smile on her face, she patted her lap.

He sprang to the proffered seat.

Her arms encircled him. "My goodness, lad, you've grown so thin. I declare, I'm going to have to fatten you up." Though she tried to make light of his thinness, it disturbed her. He had been nothing like this the last time she had seen him. Was something wrong with the lad? Instantly, she grew angry with her grandmother. Why had Gran failed to notify Carlotta of a condition which might affect *her* child's health? Had there not been enough food? she wondered with a stab of fear. At the first of every quarter, Carlotta religiously sent half her meager funds to Gran.

By the expression on his face, Carlotta realized her words had disappointed him. She gave him an affectionate squeeze. "I daresay your papa was also thin when he was your age. You're so very much like your father."

"How am I like my papa?"

She hugged him to her. "Well, first of all, you're the very image of him. Your face is but a younger version of his face, and your hair is just a shade lighter than his was when I met him. He was somewhat on the slender side, too, but he became more muscular with age."

Stevie's eyes brightened at that comment. "I should enjoy being like my papa when I grow up."

"I'm certain he would have liked that."

"Tell me again about his bravery." He pronounced *bravery* like bwave-awee. His pronunciation made her smile and caused an unexpected stab of sadness. She had missed so much of his life.

"Better than that," she said. "There's here in Bath a former soldier who served with your papa. He wants to tell you all about your father. His name is Lord Rutledge, and he is very much looking forward to meeting you. He's also bought replica swords and toy soldiers and even a very special present for you."

"It must be the pony!" he shrieked.

"You'll have to wait until this afternoon, love," she said. James had the ridiculous notion that the reunion between mother and son should be private. Had she a say in the matter, Lord Rutledge would be sharing this very settee with them right now. She really was at a loss for what to say to a six-year-old lad.

"I know you were very sad last year when your nurse got married. What was her name?"

"Sah-wa."

"Oh, yes, Sara!"

"She's got a baby girl now," he said. "I got to go visit them."

"Did you now? And how do you like babies?"

"I like them very much."

"It seems just yesterday you were a wee one," Carlotta said wistfully. She swallowed. Her son had become a person, and she had missed everything. "And look at how big you are now!"

He grinned up at her.

"I believe it's time I introduce the master of the house to my maid and the other servants."

That afternoon James, laden with packages for Stevie, arrived. Not only was the boy delighted with all that Lord Rutledge brought him, but he shed the reticence he bore with his mother and readily laughed with James, who had a talent for saying what pleased a child of Stevie's age.

As much as Carlotta wished to dislike James for what he had done on The Peninsula, she seemed unable to do so. He was so very selfless—and quite charming.

As soon as James presented Stevie with the toy soldiers, the two of them spread out regiments on the Turkish carpet and completely forgot Carlotta's existence.

For the first half hour, she watched them play, though she was bored beyond bearing. Finally, she excused herself and went to her room and allowed herself the luxury of reading a new volume of poetry which Lord Rutledge had presented her the day before.

She smiled as she remembered how sweet he had been when he had offered it to her.

"I saw this at the booksellers and immediately thought of you—knowing how much you love poetry, that is," he had said shyly.

Not only was it a volume she had wanted to read,

it was also beautifully bound in fine green leather
with an ornate, gold-scrolled cover.

She had handed it back to him. "Please, my lord,
could you personalize it on the flyleaf for me?"

He looked embarrassed, but nevertheless took up
the quill and wrote: *For Mrs. Ennis, with deep affection,
the Earl of Rutledge, October 11, 1817.*

After reading the verses for more than an hour,
she went back downstairs, and from what she could
tell there was no difference from when she had left.
Only now Lord Rutledge and the lad were making
mock artillery noises—which caused her to burst
out laughing.

James sat up ramrod straight and shot her a quizzing glance. "Pray tell, what do you find so humor-
ous, Mrs. Ennis?"

"Why, it's the authenticity of your artillery noises,
Lord Rutledge!"

" 'Tis just one of my hidden talents," he said with
a wink and a smile.

Stevie looked up shyly at his mother. "I say,
Mother, I love my sap-wize."

"Oh, dear," she answered, "I daresay Lord Rutledge's other surprise is even better than the toy
soldiers."

The boy's green eyes widened as he leaped to his
feet. "The pony!"

James got up and gave the boy a hand. "I'd almost
forgotten. Your surprise awaits outside." Then
James addressed Carlotta. "I beg that the servants
not disturb the soldiers. Stevie and I will finish this
battle after dinner—if that is agreeable to you?"

Carlotta shrugged. "Of course it's acceptable to
me." Better Lord Rutledge than her. She would
have absolutely no idea how to go about staging a

battle with toy soldiers! A pity Stevie hadn't been a girl.

The three of them hurried outside where a groom stood holding the reins to a bay pony.

Stevie's eyes darted from the pony, back to James. "Uncle James?"

Uncle James? Surely the boy was not going to address the man responsible for his father's death as his *uncle!* Lord Rutledge had some gall!

"She's yours, Stevie," James said.

Carlotta's anger was short lived when she saw the broad smile light Stevie's thin face as he ran toward the animal and lovingly ran a hand over its flank.

Carlotta moved to Stevie and put a hand on his shoulder. She was thoroughly cognizant that Lord Rutledge—her benefactor—was scrutinizing her motherly behavior. "What shall you call her, my love?"

"I believe I shall call her Bwownie."

"Because she's brown," Carlotta finished.

"I hope your wife approves of the name," James said, deadpan serious.

Stevie began to giggle. "Silly, I don't have a wife. I'm only six years old."

"Only six?" James winked at Carlotta. "And I took you for a short man." He scooped a still giggling Stevie up and set him on the pony. "Have you ridden before?"

The boy's voice was shaky when he replied. "Not by myself."

Carlotta realized her son was frightened and came to place a gentle hand at his waist.

James took the reins. "I'll walk beside you and hold the lead line," he said, "until you feel safe enough."

Carlotta watched the two until they turned at the

end of Monmouth Street. She could just as well have been in Portugal for all the notice they took of her, but she truly did not care. Her only concern at the moment was her guilt over admiring Lord Rutledge so greatly when he was the one who had caused Stephen's death. What would Stephen think about his son calling James *uncle*?

Moments later, at the opposite end of her block, Carlotta saw Stevie and the pony trotting toward her, Lord Rutledge leading the pair. When they drew up to Carlotta, James proposed that the three of them walk to Sydney Gardens. "I daresay it will be easier for Stevie to ride at the park, it being away from the busy traffic on the streets of Bath," he said.

After James instructed the groom to bring the pony along to the park on the opposite side of the River Avon, the threesome took off walking. His mother on one side of him, Lord Rutledge on the other, Stevie skipped happily along.

During the walk, Carlotta noted the look of utter contentment on Lord Rutledge's face. She was at a total loss to understand how one six-year-old boy could bring such obvious joy to a man of eight-and-twenty years. However, hers was not to question why but to relish the bond between man and boy, a bond that freed her.

Lord Rutledge, unlike her son, did not forget Carlotta's presence but continued to address her in respectful tones and to introduce her into his and Stevie's conversations. "Your mama won't wish you to ride off where she cannot see you." Or, "Your papa was very happy to have a son—and a beautiful wife." He would also direct comments to her. "I hope it didn't alarm you too much when I put your son on top of the mount. You looked rather nervous."

" 'Twasn't me so much as it was the look on poor Stevie's face which set my heart racing," she replied.

When they got to Sydney Gardens, James hoisted the boy once again on the pony's back and explained how to handle the reins. When he finished, he asked, "Do you think you'll be able to handle Brownie all by yourself now?"

Stevie nodded confidently.

"Your mama and I will still stroll beside you." James gripped the line to ensure the lad's safety as he and Carlotta began to walk next to the boy.

"Be assured," James told Carlotta, "the mount was selected for his gentleness. He'll not run off with your son."

For the first time in her boy's life, Carlotta felt completely responsible for him and found that she was unable to remove her gaze from him.

"How did you find the volume of Coleridge?" Lord Rutledge asked her.

She looked up at him with shining eyes. "Masterful. A sheer delight to read. I cannot wait to be able to reread it."

He chuckled. "Perhaps you'll be able to do so tonight. When Stevie and I continue our battle."

"You're much too kind. Surely, Lord Rutledge, you cannot possibly enjoy playing war with a mere slip of a child."

He patted her hand. "Oh, but I do."

"I must say Stevie does seem to have taken to you, *Uncle*. Would that he were as enamored of me as he is of you!"

"It's as you've said before. I have much more in common with him than you. That's not to say the lad isn't completely devoted to his mother."

She smiled. "I'm completely indebted to you, my lord, for being the means by which I have my Stevie restored to me and for making my son so completely happy."

"It's I who am indebted to you." A croak splintered his low voice when he spoke. "Thank you for allowing me to repay my enormous debt to Captain Ennis in the only way I know."

His words threatened to destroy her composure. Instead of graciously accepting what he said, she bristled over his reference to his debt, to his culpability in poor Stephen's death. Most of all, shame washed over her. Shame that she could gratefully accept this man's money as well as his constant presence. When this man was responsible for Stephen's death. Poor Stephen, whom she'd never loved as recklessly as she had loved Gregory Blankenship. Poor Stephen, who had worshipped her and who deserved better.

Six

It was only with a great deal of difficulty that Carlotta could keep from bursting into laughter when James, spread out on the Turkish carpet with Stevie and his soldiers, said to the boy, "Captain Ennis, there's a letter from your mother."

Stevie refrained from looking at Carlotta when he replied, "What? From my beautiful mother? It is to be hoped no ink from her plume messed her lovely gown."

The little scamp *would* think of messes! Carlotta's dancing eyes traveled to the spilled gravy on her son's linen shirt, a remnant of the dinner he had so recently shared with Lord Rutledge and her. The idea of allowing a youngster at their table for the evening meal was rather novel to her, but the earl had insisted that Stevie not be foisted upon servants until he was more comfortable in his new surroundings.

She continued with her embroidery as she sat near the fire some ten feet away from the battle being waged by her son and Lord Rutledge. For the past several months she had been endeavoring to train herself in discipline, a virtue she had never possessed. Tonight, she would not allow herself the luxury of rereading Coleridge until she finished the piecework she had begun two weeks previously.

The monotony of the sewing allowed her to reflect on the Earl of Rutledge. Her thoughts flitted to the previous day when she had thanked him for taking so active an interest in her son. "A lad needs a father—or a father figure," she had said.

"He also needs a mother," Lord Rutledge had said, his flashing gaze alighting on her.

The earl knew her entirely too thoroughly. How he had learned, she could not even guess. He alone knew what a wretched mother she had been all these years; yet, until this moment, he had refrained from lecturing her on her many shortcomings. Especially her shortcomings as a mother.

So content was she in her own domestic setting this night, she soon forgot all about Coleridge. Warmed by the fire in the hearth and happy to emerge from her recent solitude, Carlotta relished every minute she spent in the cozy drawing room with her offspring and the Earl of Rutledge.

As she ran her needle in and out of the linen, she pondered Stevie's words. *Beautiful mother.* Throughout her life, she had basked in her blatant beauty, but now such a description seemed oddly cold. Was her beauty all she had to recommend herself to her son?

A pity she was not more like Lord Rutledge, who had such a facility in relating to lads. Without moving her head, she stole a glance at the earl. "Fire the cannon," he ordered. Sitting there opposite Stevie, he looked as large and as powerful as a cannon mounted on a caisson. The earl's pantaloons stretched across his muscled legs that trailed into a pair of shiny black Hessians. His shoulders strained against the well-cut, chocolate-colored coat that narrowed at his trim waist. When he leaned over the rows of miniature tin soldiers, his cork-colored hair spilled over his pensive forehead, causing Carlotta's breath to grow short. Why had she never before noticed how startlingly handsome Lord Rutledge was? Could it be she was finally able to judge a man on his own merit—and not upon how he compared with the physical perfection of Gregory Blankenship?

Then she chided herself. *This is the man responsible for poor Stephen's death.* Her face grim, she returned to her embroidery.

Her thoughts focused on the perceptible distance she had always kept between herself and Stevie. Even now, he was some fifteen feet away from her and could not have been more detached had she been in The Colonies.

"Perhaps you should move closer to the fire, dearest," she said to her son.

He kept on playing. *God in heaven! Was her endearment so alien to him?* "My love, come sit closer to the fire," she repeated. "I worry you will take a chill."

He looked at his mother, a wistful, puzzled look on his thin face. Then, he dutifully began to move his soldiers. "To the south, men!" he said in a commanding voice.

" 'Tis actually west," Lord Rutledge playfully corrected.

"March westward, men," Stevie amended, his voice still authoritative.

Carlotta could not help but chuckle as her glance met the earl's. He smiled, too.

She watched as Stevie moved his columns of soldiers closer to her. His columns were not lined up as straight as his opponent's, a fact that sent another smile to Carlotta's lips. She seemed to be doing a lot of smiling of late. Since Lord Rutledge had come to Bath.

When Stevie's move was complete, he cast a shy glance up to his mother.

"That's much better, love," she said softly. The words were no sooner out of her mouth when her glance lit upon Lord Rutledge's smiling face. She looked away quickly.

Soon the males were thick in the heat of battle as Carlotta changed to green thread, her thoughts mulling over her long-ago decision to send Stevie away. At the time, she had been convinced it was the right thing to do. But now she wondered if she had made a grave mistake. Would her son ever think of her as anything but a beautiful woman who wouldn't want to muss her gown? Would he ever be as close to her as he was to the man who had deprived him of his father? she wondered bitterly.

Being a parent was exceedingly difficult! The problem was, one never knew if one were doing the right thing. Success—which would be years in the proving—was imperfectly measured by the worth of another human being. A most heady responsibility, to be sure.

Assaulting her piecework with green embroidery threads, Carlotta listened contentedly to Stevie and Lord Rutledge and their frequent laughter.

And despite their comforting presence, she felt as if she did not belong in this domestic scene. She had not earned the right to be here. Would she always be such an outsider?

She flung her embroidery aside, dropped to the carpet on her knees, and scooted toward her son. "I believe your reinforcements have finally arrived, Captain."

For as long as she lived, Carlotta would never forget Stevie's broad answering smile.

* * *

James poured more wine into Carlotta's glass, then planted his booted feet into the brittle grass and leaned back to watch Stevie play below in the roofless Roman ruins at the bottom of the hill they sat on.

"I declare, I get tired just watching Stevie!" Carlotta said. "How can he unleash such energy after so big a meal?" She turned to James. "Forgive me for not telling you sooner how very good the picnic you provided was."

" 'Twas rather filling," he answered.

"I believe I could lie back and fall asleep right here on the hill," she said.

Completely unsummoned, the very thought of Carlotta lying beside him caused James's mind to spin—and his body to react. He had been with Mrs. Ennis and Stevie every day now for the past two weeks, and the more he was with her, the more he questioned his own motives in wanting to help her and her son. For James had come to realize he eagerly looked forward to every moment he spent in Carlotta Ennis's presence.

He even began to wonder if he might have coveted Captain Ennis's wife while the good captain was still alive. Until the past few days, James had never dared to direct his thoughts along so sinister a path, but now he doubted his own altruism. Could his desire for Carlotta Ennis have been festering all these years?

Could that be why no other woman had ever been able to capture his heart? Had he always obsessed over the raven-haired widow with soft violet eyes?

His heartbeat growing erratic, James allowed himself to glance at Carlotta as she swallowed a sip of wine, unaware that he was watching her. After their

nuncheon, she had unbuttoned her lavender me-
rino pelisse. The roundness of her breasts claimed
his attention. They would be soft. Like Carlotta. The
new Carlotta who was becoming more gentle and
loving with each passing day.

She set down her glass and looked at him. "Think
you Stevie is ready for a nurse now?"

He stiffened. "No," he said sharply. For some odd
reason, Mrs. Ennis deferred to his judgment and
adhered to his decisions. He rather liked that.

"Why?" she asked softly.

How could he tell her he did not want the apple-
cart upset? He had never been happier than he had
been these past two weeks. The three of them had
been like a family. Like a family he had craved since
he was a small child. "I still believe the boy needs
time to get used to you. You've got many years to
make up for."

It pained him that Carlotta Ennis, his paragon,
had formerly been a somewhat unfeeling mother,
but he took peculiar pride in her metamorphosis.

She reached out and briefly stroked his forearm.
"You are right, of course. You're always so devilishly
right, and you know me too devilishly well!"

He reeled from her soft touch. He grew aroused
and had to tear his eyes away from her. The sounds
of Stevie's childish voice singing wafted up to them.
James had to wipe Carlotta and her dizzying touch
from his mind. "The boy seems happy."

"Yes, he does. I'm so grateful to you, my lord."

Despite her words, James detected a hint of in-
sincerity in her voice. Carlotta was grateful he had
rescued her from the near-squalor of Mrs. McKay's
dwelling. And she was thankful that through his efforts she had become reunited her with her son.

But still, he knew, she held him accountable for her husband's death.

For as long as he drew breath, James would feel his guilt. Because of his disobedience, Stephen Ennis had died. And in dying, he had saved James's life. No day ever passed that James did not think about the captain and feel remorse. He had lived while the captain—who left a wife and son—died. Surely there had been a reason for sparing James. For years he had kept the pain bottled inside of him, but he could no longer suffer silently. Like steam under a kettle lid, he needed release.

"As you know, Mrs. Ennis," he began, his heart thudding, "my negligence caused your . . . your husband's death." It was as painful for him to think of her as the wife of another man as it was to remember the man who had been her husband.

She nodded, her beautiful face solemn.

"It's time I tell you about it."

She shook her head. "I don't think I can bear it."

He closed his hand over hers. It felt so small. "Please," he said.

Their eyes met and held.

"I need to talk about it," he said in a throaty voice.

She could not remove her gaze from him. "You've never asked anything of me before," she said pensively. Then, she nodded. "Go on."

He cleared his throat. "One of the first things a soldier learns is that when a comrade falls in combat, you don't stop. You keep fighting."

Absently twirling her now-empty wineglass in her hand, she nodded.

"But I disobeyed orders to keep marching . . ." his voice faltered. He coughed, then sat up even straighter and looked into her eyes. "Harold Dutton had been with me ever since Sandhurst." His voice choked again.

Carlotta nodded solemnly.

"When I heard him cry out . . ."

"You quite naturally went to help him," she said, her voice barely above a whisper, her eyes misty.

He nodded, then glanced away from her. "Captain Ennis saw what was going on and ordered me to advance. I disobeyed."

Tears began to fill her eyes. "I think I know what happened next," she said softly. "You were a great favorite with Stephen. He disobeyed his own orders by going back for you."

He met her somber gaze and nodded. "And with his back to the enemy, he caught a musket ball that would have hit me."

She said nothing for several minutes. The only sound was the whistle of the wind and Stevie's voice lifted in play. Finally she spoke. "It's good that so many years have passed. I can be more objective now that I can no longer remember the sound of Stephen's voice. Now, I think, I cannot hate you for causing Stephen's death. He was as culpable as you." With a pang in her heart, she realized her words were true. The bitterness she harbored for the earl slid away. A false laugh broke from her throat. "The both of you were most likely too soft to be good soldiers."

The wind picked up. Blue tinged her fair skin, and she rebuttoned her pelisse. They sat silently for several minutes, listening to Stevie playing below. "I'm thinking of William Blake," she said, almost as if she were unaware of James's presence.

" 'Tiger, tiger burning bright . . .' " he began.

She shook her head. "No. Not that one. This

one: 'When the voices of children are heard on the green, and laughing is heard on the hill, my heart is at rest within my breast and everything else is still.' "

He was very nearly overpowered by the rush of emotion which consumed him. Never before had he felt himself surrounded with such overwhelming beauty, beauty that fogged his senses and robbed him of speech.

As he sat watching her—a lump forming in his throat—he realized the wisdom of her decision not to wear hats. The sun glanced off her radiant black hair. She was so beautiful it hurt to look at her.

"A pity it would be were the sun to freckle your fair face," he said.

She tossed her head back and laughed. "I never freckle. I daresay, I must have gypsy blood in me!"

They smiled at each other. "You've never told me about your own father," she said. "Were you close to him? Is that why you want to nurture Stevie?"

He shook his head. "My father died of fever when I was four. My entire childhood was spent wishing I had a father like the other lads."

"I'm surprised to learn you had no father. You're so very . . ." Her voice trailed off. "That is, you're quite manly. Stephen said you were as fine and brave a soldier as he had ever commanded."

James smiled. "Not having a father made me work harder than the other boys who profited from their father's coaching." He hesitated a moment. "I was fortunate that I was blessed with athletic abilities—the only thing I ever got from my father," he said wistfully.

"I think I'm beginning to understand why you didn't want Stevie to be raised as you were."

He nodded.

"I never missed not having a mother," Carlotta said, "even though mine died bringing me into the world. My grandmother did an excellent job of taking the place of my mother—though she was probably a bit overindulgent. She was my father's mother and had always longed for a daughter."

An older, overindulgent grandmother would explain Carlotta's former self-absorption, he thought, glad that she was becoming a true mother at long last.

The wind grew more fierce. "I'm afraid Stevie may not be dressed warmly enough," she said.

James nodded and stood up. "I'll fetch him. It's time we headed back to Bath."

It was time he removed himself from Carlotta and what she was doing to him. He did not know how much longer he could be around her and not try to ravish her.

On the carriage ride back to Bath, Stevie bounced back and forth between his mother's bench and James's, and the child did most of the talking. When they reached Carlotta's house on Monmouth Place, James helped them disembark, then walked them only as far as the door. "I regret to say," he said, "I have pressing business back at Yarmouth Hall. I leave in the morning and will be gone for a few days."

Stevie pouted. "I wish you didn't have to go."

James looked from Stevie to his mother.

"We shall miss you very much," she said.

By the look on her solemn face, James believed her.

All the more reason to remove himself from her disturbing presence.

Seven

The first day Lord Rutledge was gone, Carlotta did not want to get out of her bed. She had been so gay these past few weeks, eagerly looking forward to each new day, looking forward to being with him. Lord Rutledge had indeed been a rainbow after the greatest storm of her life. Without the earl, though, one monotonous day now would be much the same as another.

She forced herself to climb from the bed and summon Peggy to help her dress.

"Which dress shall ye wear today, Mrs. Ennis?" Peggy asked cheerfully.

Carlotta shrugged. What difference did it make what she wore? Only Peggy and a six-year-old child would see her. Curiously, her heart sank. "I don't care. You pick one."

Peggy cast a puzzled glance at her mistress. "Methinks Lord Rutledge would wish to see ye in lavender today." A smile on her youthful face, the maid swung open the door to the linen press and selected the lavender sarcenet morning gown.

"It doesn't matter what his lordship wishes," Carlotta said in a forlorn voice, "because he's left Bath."

Peggy spun back toward Carlotta, her face

crunched in disappointment. "When does he return?"

Carlotta shrugged.

"Oh, madame, it's sorry I am to hear that, for Lord Rutledge has been so very good for ye. I'll be worried now that ye will return to your moping ways, like when Mr. Blankenship left." She assisted her mistress into the selected gown.

Carlotta laughed without mirth, as Peggy began to brush out her hair. " 'Tis not the same, Peggy. There's nothing between Lord Rutledge and me."

Peggy shot Carlotta a questioning glance. "Ye are trying to convince yerself, but ye can't fool Peggy."

"It's the truth!" Carlotta insisted. "He's . . . he's only interested in the boy."

"Then yer as blind as a bat if ye believe that! I seen the way he looks at ye. He's lovesick. And if ye asks me, I'll wager he's left Bath because he doesn't think he has a chance with one as beautiful as ye," Peggy said as she fastened a pin in Carlotta's swept-back tresses.

"I'm heartily sick of hearing about my beauty," Carlotta snapped. The earl had most likely left because he had come to realize how fully her inner beauty was at odds with her outward beauty. She wanted to throw something at the looking glass she sat in front of.

After breakfast, Carlotta lingered over her tea, gripping her purple Kashmir shawl to her. It seemed to her that Lord Rutledge must have taken the sun with him, for deep gray blanketed the cloudy skies. She had neither the desire to leave Monmouth Place nor to mount the stairs to the nursery where her son was likely playing with his soldiers. It was so very gloomy a day.

Unaccountably, memories of the things she had

done with the earl and the topics they had discussed intruded on her thoughts. She wondered what they would be doing now, were he still in Bath. No doubt, they would have been gay no matter how dreary the skies outside. She could not imagine being with Lord Rutledge and not being happy. He filled whatever room he was in with good humor. And so much more, she thought forlornly.

He had brought purpose back to her life. He'd given her the desire to get out of bed in the mornings and to care about her appearance. He had restored her son to her, and he had been full of sage advice. And though he was a gentleman, he always spoke his mind, even when his words would offend.

Sitting next to the candle which illuminated her drawing room this dreary day, she worked at her embroidery—the piecework she still had not finished. She was anxious to finish so she could allow herself the luxury of rereading Coleridge.

The very thought of Lord Rutledge giving her the precious volume sent her pulse racing. How thoughtful he had been, and how very well he had come to know her. No man had ever understood her as he seemed to. She blushed to think at the age of five and twenty, she had already been intimate with two different men, and a third—whose knowledge did not extend past the bedchamber door—most certainly knew her better than the others.

Her heart drummed. Was it his knowledge of her wickedness that had driven Lord Rutledge away? He was no fool. He knew she had been a wretched mother, and he had been responsible for nudging her out of her indifference. Had he also learned of her greater shame? After all, he *had* lived in Bath. She blinked away the tears which threatened.

She had already lost so much in the past year.

Her thoughts drifted to that soul-deadening moment when she had realized that Gregory would never offer marriage. She had not even been angry with him, for he had told her before he ever bedded her that he would never offer marriage. Yet she'd been so blinded by her love of him she had foolishly believed she could change him. All that had changed was her respectability.

And now, were she to lose Lord Rutledge, too, she thought she would undoubtedly die.

She had come to crave just being with him, having someone to talk to who withheld judgment.

Then she remembered her physical reaction yesterday when he had placed his big hand over hers. The memory caused her to whimper. She set down her embroidery and sat there in the dimness, picturing Lord Rutledge as he had looked, his long legs stretched before him after they had partaken of their nuncheon. He was possessed of a very fine face, especially when he was pensive. And the sound of his laughter filled her own soul with happiness.

Though she had wildly and recklessly loved Gregory Blankenship, she had not the respect for him that she had for James Rutledge.

And she had likely lost him forever.

James sat at his desk on the ground floor of the wainscoted library at Yarmouth Hall, watching rain trickle against his foggy window. He had been unable to concentrate on the columns of figures in the ledger his steward had given him. He wondered how he had managed to conduct business at all these past few days with his steward and his secretary and his housekeeper when all the while his every thought centered on Carlotta Ennis.

By removing himself from Bath, he had wanted to purge himself of his obsessive desire for her. More than that, this self-imposed exile was his way of punishing himself for having craved a woman who belonged to another. For he had come to realize he had always been in love with Carlotta Ennis. His Goddess of the Night. Even when her husband had been alive.

James was so disgusted with himself, he questioned his own sincerity in befriending Stevie. Had that, too, been done in order to be close to the lad's ravishingly beautiful mother?

He heard a rapping at his door and looked up to see his secretary stroll into the vast room. "I have some correspondence which needs your signature, my lord," Fordyce said. The young man drew up in front of his employer and handed James a stack of letters. "If I might be so bold as to suggest you move closer to the fire. It's deuced cold here by the window, my lord."

"The cold suits me," James said grimly, dipping his quill into the ink and penning his signature on one page after another, glancing over each before he signed.

When he finished, he handed them back to his man of business. "Be a good man and tell Mrs. MacGinnis not to bother with dinner tonight. I'm not hungry."

Once Fordyce had left the chamber, James poured himself a glass of port. So what if it was but two in the afternoon? He sat back in his leather chair and took a long drink. What had come over him? he wondered. He'd always been a man's man, interested in masculine pursuits. Yet now all he could think of was a violet-eyed widow and her small, dependent son. The pair of them elicited in him a sense of protection. He thrived on supporting them in any way he could, be it by paying their lease or just by being there with a helping hand.

But how could he allow himself the intoxication of being near her when he'd adulterously coveted her all these years?

He took another sip and closed his eyes as the port warmed its path down to his gut. Against his will, he pictured Carlotta. Carlotta lying on silken sheets, her black hair draping across her breasts. Breasts that begged to be taken in his hands—and in his mouth. He saw her heavily lashed eyelids drop seductively as she lifted her face to his.

Enraged with himself, he threw his wineglass against the bricks of the hearth.

One dreary day succeeded another. Carlotta finally finished her piecework and reread her slim volume of Coleridge so many times she committed the verses to memory. Oddly, every line brought to mind the noble James Rutledge and reminded her of how truly she missed him.

She had not left Monmouth Place since she had last seen him. She had not taken a single meal with Stevie, nor had she actually sat down at the table for a meal herself. It was as if Lord Rutledge had stolen away with her appetite, too.

After a week had passed, she told herself he was never coming back.

As a tribute to her fondness for him and for what he had done for her and Stevie, Carlotta flung aside her poetry and mounted the stairs to her son's nursery. Just because the carpet had been ripped from beneath her feet was no reason to penalize the boy. He had to be feeling Lord Rutledge's loss as keenly as she. The two had been extremely close. She scorned herself for not having thought of Stevie's bereavement.

With each step she took, her excitement grew. Her lips curved into a smile as she climbed past the second floor. She had missed the little fellow. Hang Lord Rutledge! She no longer needed him to show her how to be a mother. He had opened her eyes to her son's worth. Now she could proceed without his guidance. She would see that Stevie's happiness was not thwarted—with or without Lord James Rutledge!

As she neared the top floor, where her son's nursery was located, she heard muffled sobs. Clutching at her breast, she flew to the door and flung it open. Had something happened to her son? she wondered, her heart beating erratically.

There sat her son, huddled in a corner of the chilly room, his thin legs blue from the cold, his thumb shoved into his little mouth, big tears puddling on his face. Thankfully, she saw no blood.

Eight

Carlotta flew across the nursery's wooden floor and fell to her knees in front of her son, drawing him into her arms. "Stevie, my love, what's wrong?"

"I'm afwaid to be up here by myself."

She held him tightly against her, gently stroking his quivering back, her eyes filling with tears.

Memories of her own fears when she was no older than Stevie rushed over her. She'd been terrified to be in her own chamber without her nurse—even during the day. It was so vast and dark and frequently cold—a testament to her grandmother's thriftiness. Yet she'd never told anyone of her fright. She had merely huddled in a corner and cried. Like Stevie.

Her child's suffering was like a raw wound in her heart. "Oh, my love, I'm so sorry. I didn't realize . . ." She gathered him closer to her, the tears now running freely down her cheeks. "I give you my word, you'll never be left alone again."

She scooped him up in her arms and carried him downstairs to the drawing room. There, she sat beside the fire and settled him on her lap as she began to read him a children's book.

Soon Stevie was giggling over the talking animals in the book, and there was no sign of the tears that had so recently ravaged him. As they sat reading, a hazy sun broke through the clouds.

"Go get your coat on, sweetheart," Carlotta said to him, swatting at his bottom. "I'm taking you to the Pump Room." Her stomach dropped perceptibly as she thought of the icy reception she was sure to get there. But as long as Lord Rutledge wasn't around to see her shame, she could suffer it. Stevie had always expressed an interest in drinking the miraculous water there, and she would devote this day to making her son happy, to making him forget his distress.

Once he was at the Pump Room, though, the water did not hold as much interest as the orchestra which played on a balcony high above the lofty chamber. Stevie craned his little neck to watch them. Carlotta soon realized the lad had never before seen musical instruments being played.

"You'll strain your neck," she cautioned, taking his hand and moving forward. "You must be a gentleman and escort your mama around the room. It's what one does when one comes to the Pump Room."

Stevie wrinkled his brow as he concentrated on being a gentleman. He took long strides as he clutched his mother's hand.

"I believe all the ladies in the room will be jealous of me," she said with mirth, "for I most undoubtedly have the most handsome escort of all."

He was unable to the hide the smile which slid across his face, though he tried to act like a grown-up man. "Wemembah when Lord Wutledge said he mistook me for a short man?" He giggled.

Carlotta burst out laughing. The earl was so very good with children.

"I've missed his lordship," Stevie said solemnly.

Her thoughts exactly. "I have, too, darling, but

he has a big estate that demands his attention. We can't have him all the time."

"I wish you'd marry him so we could always be with him."

The smile vanished from her face. As highly as she regarded the earl, she had not once considered herself suitable to be his countess. A conquest of such grand proportions had never even crossed her mind. Yet the very thought of it set her insides trembling.

Not only was he not married, he had also remarked frequently on her beauty. And how could she forget that he had spread his protective cloak around her, smothering her in his care? Yet she had not once considered him a suitor.

Her heart drummed. It was because she was so ruined. She was not fit even to give thought to such a misalliance. The earl deserved far better.

And, of course, Lord Rutledge's only interest in her was as the wife of Stephen Ennis and the mother of the fallen captain's young son. That was all.

Stevie looked up at her strained face. "Am I not escorting you properly?"

She squeezed his hand and looked down at him, her face lifting into a smile. "You're doing wonderfully. I am, indeed, the luckiest woman in the room."

The smile stayed on her face. Despite her ruin and despite the respectable people in the room likely scorning her, Carlotta believed what she had just told her son. Oddly, showing Stevie off to all of Bath filled her with the most glorious sensation, a sweeping pride like she had never known.

As she and Stevie were taking their leave of the Pump Room, Carlotta's eyes met those of Miss Arbuckle, a most worthy young woman of gentle birth, and Carlotta nodded to her.

A wide smile brightened the plain Miss Arbuckle's face. "This must be your little boy!" Miss Arbuckle said, walking up to them. "I'd almost forgotten you were a mother."

"Allow me to make you known to my son," Carlotta said with pride before she made the introductions.

"I declare," Miss Arbuckle said, looking at Stevie, "everyone is talking about what a fine boy you have there."

"I'm most blessed," Carlotta said in a low voice, her smile reaching her eyes as she took and held the hand of the generous Miss Arbuckle.

Of course Miss Arbuckle, being a maiden, had not heard of Carlotta's shame. Nevertheless, the young woman was virtuous and kind. "It's so very thoughtful of you to take notice of my little lamb," Carlotta said, beaming down at her son. "And it has been a pleasure seeing you again."

Her hand still in Carlotta's, Miss Arbuckle said, "You must call on us. It's been a great while since we've had a chat. I do hope you are better now. You look your former radiant self."

"You're much too kind," Carlotta answered in a soft voice, her lashes sweeping downward.

"And bring your boy. Mama's always had a preference for lads, which I daresay is a good thing, given that she had four sons and only one daughter."

"Please extend to your mother my wishes for good health," Carlotta said as she and Stevie left the chamber.

Carlotta felt feather light. She was bursting with pride over her beautiful child. She'd just conversed with a most respectable lady. The sun had broken through the clouds. All in all, it was a lovely day to be alive. And she owed all this pleasure to one small boy.

"You've been such a good escort," she said to Stevie, "I'm going to take you to the sweet shop and allow you to buy a comfit."

He, quite literally, smiled from ear to ear.

That Sunday she took Stevie to services at Bath Cathedral. Ever since she had allowed herself to be Gregory Blankenship's whore, she had quit going to church.

For the lad's sake, she had to start back.

He behaved well, appearing to listen to the priest. Even though the ceremony was tediously long, he did not get too fidgety.

When they left the cathedral, she was prepared to receive the cut direct, but several persons of her acquaintance actually nodded at her. She smiled back and even managed to introduce some of the matrons to her son.

She began to feel less ashamed. Perhaps not *all* of Bath knew that she was ruined. After all, Gregory was not one to brag about his sexual conquests. He was, first and foremost, a gentleman. And, secondly, he had no need to boast. Women making fools of themselves over him was an everyday occurrence. Had been since he discarded leading strings.

Her thoughts flitted to the day he had told her he was marrying Glee Pembroke. It was as if he were cutting Carlotta's heart from her chest. *Why not me?* Carlotta had asked in anguish. He had mumbled something about it not being a real marriage—that he was only marrying Glee in order to receive his inheritance, that he wanted to keep Carlotta for his mistress.

At that moment Carlotta's disgust with herself

pinnacled. For that is when she finally came to the realization she was nothing more than a whore.

Carlotta had known Gregory had at last fallen in love when his young wife became pregnant—after the marriage, of course, because Glee was the daughter of a viscount, a most respectable girl, to be sure. And nothing Carlotta had seen since could convince her otherwise. Gregory Blankenship had succumbed to a wisp of a girl. Who happened to be of noble birth.

This Sunday, despite a chill that hung in the air, Carlotta took Stevie to see the concert at Sydney Gardens. He remembered instantly this was where he came to ride his pony.

Looking up at his mother, he said, "I miss Bwownie. Almost as much as I miss Lord Wutledge."

She set her hand on his tiny shoulders and spoke with sympathy. "I know, my darling. I miss him, too."

Throughout the concert, Stevie sat mesmerized, watching the musicians with fascination.

When the concert was finished, Carlotta said, "I think Brownie needs exercising. Don't you agree?"

Stevie's face brightened. "Today?"

"Why not?"

For the next few days, Carlotta's every thought and every move had but one purpose: to make Stevie happy. They went to the sweet shop each day. She read every children's story she had to him; then, she went to the booksellers and bought more. She took him to the Wednesday night musicale, though he was the only child in attendance. She marched him to the Pump Room every morning for his healthful water, and she allowed him to ride his pony daily.

She made good, too, on her vow that he never be left alone again. She had Peggy begin sleeping in the boy's room every night and made sure he was never left alone in the nursery.

That she took him where no other children went did not cause her a moment's consternation. Let them say she was indulgent! As far as she could tell, he behaved with the greatest propriety for a small boy, and as long as he did, she would continue to indulge him. After all, he was rather special. Why, anyone could look at him and see that!

As she watched her son on his pony one afternoon, she had to admit Lord Rutledge's efforts to teach Stevie to ride had been quite successful. The boy sat confidently in his saddle, the sun catching his golden locks, his lips tightened with concentration. She now felt confident enough to allow him to ride without a groom running along beside him. She felt so confident, she had brought a volume of poetry she had borrowed from the lending library. She planned to sit on a bench and read while keeping an eye out for Stevie as he and his pony trotted around the perimeter of the park.

But she found herself unable to watch Stevie and read. A nagging fear for the boy's safety kept tugging at her, forcing her to watch him constantly. Tucking the book under her arm, she crossed the park and began to walk beside Stevie.

"You don't have to worry about me," he told her. "Lord Wutledge taught me to handle a horse."

She could not stifle her laugh. He tried to sound so grown up when he looked so very small—even on a pony that in no way compared to a horse!

It was while she was smiling up at her son, her hand settled on the back of his saddle, that she saw the shimmering eyes of Lord Rutledge watching her.

Nine

"My lord, you're back!" Carlotta said to him. The smile on her lovely face convinced James his return did not displease her.

He closed the gap between them and bowed before her, then took her hand to dutifully brush his lips across. It seemed to him she had grown even more beautiful during his absence. Not only that, but his Goddess of the Night looked almost virginal in her orchid muslin dress.

Stevie brought Brownie to a stop and spoke excitedly. "See, Mama, I told you he'd come back!"

James looked up at the boy's happy face, and he felt strangely exhilarated by the enthusiastic welcome given him by Carlotta and her son. But he could not allow them to see his vulnerability. "I trust you've been exercising Brownie regularly?" he said to Stevie.

The boy's eyes darted to his mother, then back to James. "Now that the weather's turned nice, I have."

James set a hand across the lad's thigh. "Good lad." Then he met Carlotta's gaze. "The weather was bad here as well after I left?"

He and Carlotta fell into step behind Stevie and the pony as they trotted around the park.

Carlotta laughed. "I declare, my lord, I was convinced you had taken the sun with you."

Patting her hand, he tucked her arm into his. "Yarmouth was wretched." *Anywhere without Carlotta was wretched.* Even after he had discovered she was an imperfect being, he still hungered for her. He'd grown to realize he needed her as the flowers need sunshine.

"May I hope you successfully concluded your business there?" she asked.

He nodded. "I see you and Stevie have prospered without me. My plan has worked."

She whirled to face him. "What plan?"

"My plan to force you to take responsibility for your son." He watched as the color drained from her face. He should not have been so mercilessly blunt.

Her lashes dropped. "Your plan worked," she said softly. "A pity you know me so dreadfully well. A woman should like a man *not* to know all her glaring faults."

She had used the words *man* and *woman* in the same sentence. Could he hope that she was beginning to think of him as a man? Not just as her benefactor. Not just as Stevie's mentor. But as a flesh-and-blood man. If that were the case, then these past eleven days of misery without her had been worth it.

"I'm only joyful that in some small way I've been instrumental in bringing the two of you closer," he said. "It's what's right, Carlotta."

Her eyes flashed.

Good lord! He had called her Carlotta! How could he have dared take such a liberty?

"It's I who is most joyful, my lord," she said humbly. "Now I realize how empty my life has been these past six years. How very much I have missed." She stopped and gazed into his eyes. "I am immeasurably indebted to you for restoring my child to me." Her voice cracked. "I deeply regret the years of his precious life I have not been a part of—years I can never recapture."

"Life's too short to dwell on the past. Think only of the future, Carlotta."

She sniffed and laughed alternately. " 'The best is yet to be.' "

It was good to have his lordship back, Carlotta mused as she finished her last morsel of sweetmeat after dinner. She watched him as he explained to Stevie how soldiers in The Peninsula had their meals served.

She had grown to enjoy having Stevie at the dinner table, despite his table manners, which were considerably lacking. A pity he would one day have to return to taking his meals in the nursery. One simply did not foist messy children on one's dinner companions. Not that a woman as ruined as she would ever have any companion other than Lord Rutledge.

She had hoped Lord Rutledge would again address her by her Christian name tonight, but he did not. This afternoon's familiarity had oddly pleased her. The longer she thought about it, the more she realized he would never address her so in front of Stevie. Lord Rutledge was, after all, a gentleman. A true gentleman would never set an inappropriate example in front of a child.

As she watched them, she noticed Stevie yawning and saw that he kept rubbing his reddened eyes. Today had been exhausting for him. Too much sun.

Too much excitement. Too much activity. Thanks to Lord Rutledge.

"Darling," she said to Stevie, "you've worn yourself out today. I think you'll have to be early to bed. Peggy can tell you a story until you fall asleep."

He shook his head. "I don't want to go to bed! I want to play soldiers with Uncle James."

"Oh, we'll play soldiers," the earl assured, "but only until eight of the clock. Then you need to go to bed. Your mother's right. You've had a long, tiring day, and you need to get some rest."

After dinner they played soldiers on the carpeted floor of the drawing room. Stevie yawned frequently and continued to rub his eyes. *Poor baby*, Carlotta mused as she sat near the fire sewing a linen shirt she was making for her son. In the weeks he had been in Bath, his mother had been forcefully apprised of how rough Stevie was on his clothing. She was forever mending his breeches or was assisting Peggy in trying to remove foodstuffs from his soiled shirts.

She kept a watch on the mantel's ormolu clock. At eight, she stood up and came to Stevie. "You must go upstairs now, love," she said gently. "Peggy will get you ready for bed."

"Be a good lad," James said, "and I'll have a surprise for you in the morning."

In mid-pout, Stevie's lips stretched into a smile.

Carlotta spread out her arms, and to her delight Stevie plunged into her embrace, his little arms closing around her. Her eyes grew misty. Three weeks ago her son would never have flung himself into her arms.

As she hugged him, she happened to glance at Lord Rutledge, who watched her with a satisfied, cocky smile on his handsome face.

With Stevie gone, Carlotta felt awkward. She was not used to being alone with the earl. Why did he not excuse himself? Normally, when he and Stevie finished their mock battles, Lord Rutledge took his leave. But not tonight.

Should she move to the settee to be closer to him? Sitting in her chair before the fire seemed somewhat sequestered from her guest. She watched him as he put away the soldiers, then came to sit on the settee nearest her.

"Should you like a glass of brandy, my lord?"

He stood up and began to walk toward the far wall of the room. "I'll get my own, thank you. May I bring you a glass?"

"Yes, do." It would at least give her something to do with her hands. She was unaccountably nervous at being left alone with his lordship.

From beneath hooded eyes, she watched as he poured the brandy into snifters, then strolled toward her.

"I beg that you come sit by me, Mrs. Ennis."

Her heart began to race as she stood and walked to the nearby settee. They sat down at the same time, their legs running parallel to one another. She noted that his legs were much longer than hers. She began to quiver on the inside. It had been a long time since she had been this close to a man.

"Stevie tells me you've been taking him to the Pump Room," he began.

Why was the earl asking about the Pump Room? Did he know of her ostracism? Is that why he was questioning her? She nodded self-consciously.

"Did you not tell me the Pump Room held no allure for you?"

Her heart pounded. Was he trying to trace the source of her discomfort at Bath's chief attraction?

Did he think to continue going there now with
Stevie and her? That, she could not allow. She
should die of mortification if the earl witnessed her
being cut, thus learning of her shame. "I detest the
Pump Room, but I was desperate to please Stevie.
Your absence created a tremendous void in our daily
routine. In fact . . ."—she looked into his warm
eyes—"we both missed you dreadfully."

He did not respond, causing her to peer from
her lap to his brooding face. Had she said something that upset him? Or had he become acquainted with her shame? "May I hope you
managed to spare a thought for us during the separation?"

He laughed bitterly.

"What's wrong?" she asked.

"Nothing's wrong."

"Then why are you acting so peculiarly? Why did
you not answer my question?"

He did not answer her for a moment. " 'Tis a sign
of weakness in a man to admit he needs a woman
and child."

The thought of the earl needing her and Stevie
sent waves of contentment over her. "It most certainly is *not,* my lord! A man who protects and serves
a woman and child is utterly heroic."

He did not respond. He sat quietly for a moment.
Then he cleared his throat. "Tell me, why is it that
a beautiful woman like you has never remarried?"

Then he does not know about Gregory, she thought
with relief. It was as if a vise gripped her windpipe.
Finally, she managed: "I've always thought to remarry. It's what I want, but no man has so honored
me by asking for my hand."

He gave her an incredulous look. "I find that difficult to believe."

She shrugged. "I did not even persist in wearing black, as Felicia—the former Mrs. Harrison—did. She wore black for four years for Captain Harrison. But I always meant to remarry."

"Because of your financial difficulties?"

She nodded guiltily. Better he think that than think her a slave to love, especially an illicit love like she lavished on Gregory.

"Then love is not necessarily a prerequisite to matrimony—in your eyes?"

"I know it sounds mercenary, but love is not necessary for marriage. However, I *would* have to admire the man, my lord."

He nabbed her with a pensive stare as his hand closed over hers. "Do you admire me, Mrs. Ennis?"

Her pulse accelerated, and her voice trembled when she answered. "You know I do," she said softly, unable to remove her gaze from his.

"Enough to marry me, Carlotta?"

He was serious! The intensity of his gaze told her he was. Her heart began to race. Surely she was dreaming. Surely the Earl of Rutledge had no desire to link his life to hers. He, of all people, knew how wicked she was. She had to be mistaken. Good fortune never smiled on her. The earl was kind and handsome and wealthy. He was everything she could ever hope for. *Except, of course, he wasn't Gregory Blankenship.*

"What are you saying, my lord?" she finally asked in a quivering voice.

"I want to know if you'll marry me, Carlotta."

She could not find her voice to answer him. It was as if fireworks rocketed within her. Finally, she managed. "I would be honored to do so, my lord."

Ten

James had not meant to offer for Carlotta. Not once had he allowed himself to consciously consider asking for her hand. Not even during those eleven wretched days when every thought of her had tormented him. Not even when she had bestowed her most sincere smile upon him when he returned from Yarmouth Hall. Not even when he had eagerly accepted her dinner invitation that first night back in Bath.

Nevertheless, the moment he found himself alone with her he had blurted out the proposal.

As surprising as was his proposal, her prompt acceptance surprised him even more. Of course, she did not care for him as a woman cares for a man. She had just confessed that her reason for wanting to marry was to gain financial security. He cautioned himself to take her acceptance for what it was, not to read anything more into it than she was willing to concede.

Of course, he *wished* to read more into it. His separation from Carlotta had underscored how deeply he valued her. How deeply he loved her. Though he had come to the conclusion he could not live without her, he had no intention of begging for her hand.

Until he was alone with her, and his words had betrayed what was within his heart.

When she had uttered those words that made him the happiest of men, he fought his immediate urge to gather her into his arms and kiss her senseless. "I . . . desire to take care of you and Stevie for as long as I live."

She nodded, her dark lashes sweeping low. "Because of what happened in The Peninsula."

"Yes. It's my responsibility."

"Then . . . you're not asking that I . . . that I be a true wife to you?"

Yes, yes, God in heaven, yes! He wanted her as his wife more than he had ever wanted anything. But to let her see into his soul was to admit to the long standing of his desire, to admit he had coveted her even when she was another man's wife.

He reached for her hand and covered it with his own. "I would, quite naturally, wish to some day sire an heir, but I shall never force you, Carlotta." He drew in his breath. "I would hope that one day you will willingly come to me."

Carlotta's thoughts swirled in an explosion of emotions. The Earl of Rutledge had offered her his hand in marriage! Since the day she had arrived in Bath so many years ago, Carlotta's chief goal had been to snare a husband. Yet she had never dreamed that husband would be rich and titled. Marrying Lord Rutledge would easily solve all her problems. She would never again have to worry about unpaid debts or be forced to do without. No doubt, she could have every poetry book her heart desired. And she could put the vicious gossips behind her. Who would dare malign the wife of an earl? But the best aspect of becoming Lord Rutledge's wife was that she would never be lonely again. She and the earl and Stevie could become a happy family, something she had never thought she wanted but which now seemed fiercely important.

Never mind that he wasn't Gregory Blankenship. Never mind that she had no love to give him. She *would* do her best to make him a good wife. She looked into his smoldering eyes. "I vow you will never regret your choice, my lord. I shall do everything in my power to make you a good wife."

"My lord? I beg that you call me James."

She nodded. "I'm grateful to have the chance to make you a fine wife, James."

His face came closer to hers. She smelled his sandalwood scent and peered at the dark stubble on his lean cheeks. He came closer, and his lips lightly brushed against hers.

She took a deep breath, then pressed herself into him, her arms closing around his back as he drew her more tightly into his arms, and his lips softly touched hers.

Then the intensity of his kiss deepened. She allowed the seam of her lips to open, but before she felt his tongue, he pulled away.

His breath was harsh. He met her gaze. "Would you object to a speedy wedding, my dear?"

"Not at all."

"Then I shall procure a special license as swiftly as possible."

She smiled. "Stevie will like that. When you were gone, he told me he wanted me to marry you."

His lordship—her betrothed—smiled. "And what did you have to say to that?"

"I can honestly say I had never given the thought any consideration. I've lied to you before, James. You know that. But in this one instance you must believe I never set out to capture you."

He laughed. "It's not likely you'd wish to make a conquest of a man you detested."

"I don't detest you, James."

His finger ran along her aquiline nose. "Not now, perhaps, but you did when I first came to Bath."

She laughed. "I suppose you're right, my lord."

"James."

"James," she whispered. "You do believe I don't hate you any longer?"

"I do. I also know you don't love me."

She refused to lie to him. "But I shall endeavor to please you in every way I can."

Would she have to share his bed? She had heretofore only been bedded by men she loved. And she did not love the Earl of Rutledge.

A pity his life would be wasted on the likes of her. He deserved a woman who would love him as thoroughly as she had loved Gregory.

Yet she loved herself and her son too much to deny the earl. In fact, she would do anything in her power to keep him.

And to keep him from learning about her sordid past and canceling the wedding. "I beg that we marry as soon as possible, my . . . James."

His warm eyes sparkled when he smiled at her words. "We shall, my dear."

With the exception of Gregory, whom she had come to realize had never loved her, men had always fallen at Carlotta's feet. But James Rutledge did not fall at her feet—nor could she ever envision him doing so. First of all, James knew her—and her faults—too well. He could not possibly love her. His proposal was made out of sheer duty, duty to take care of the family of the man whose death he had caused.

Nevertheless, she would see to it the noble lord never regretted his decision to ask for her hand.

The following day she did not see James at all. He had gone to London to get the special license. It was just as well he was gone. She had much to do in preparation for the wedding; yet, despite her pleasant anticipation of becoming Lady Rutledge, Carlotta was plagued with a nagging fear the marriage would never take place. In London, her betrothed could learn that she was Gregory's whore.

While Carlotta apprised Stevie, then Peggy, of the earl's proposal, a gloomy cloud settled over her. She lost her appetite, and her stomach seemed to plummet low enough to tread upon. She withheld her excitement. How could she rejoice at her good fortune when at that very moment his lordship could be preparing to cry off from a grave misalliance? It would only take one chance meeting for him to learn of her great sin.

Her heart pounded, and she wrung her hands while working with Peggy on the gown she would wear for their wedding.

"Oh, madame, just think!" Peggy exclaimed. "Ye'll be Lady Rutledge. I knew ye were a fine lady that first day ye rescued me."

"I implore you not to attach too much significance to Lord Rutledge's offer," Carlotta said. "He can still cry off."

Peggy harrumphed. "He'll not do that, I warrant. I've seen the way he looks at ye."

Carlotta sighed. *If only Peggy were right.* But Carlotta knew better. Lord Rutledge's affection for her was no greater than was hers for him.

Though there was no love, she thought warmly,

there was something between them that in some ways was stronger. With Stevie, they would be a family. A true, caring family. For though Lord Rutledge did not love her, he cared for her.

Somehow, she muddled through the long day. Night came, and she anxiously awaited him.

He did not come.

She did not sleep. *He's found out.* He would never even bother to return to Bath. A peer of the realm was not obliged to cry off with a mere whore.

Oddly, the thought of never seeing James again hurt. It was as painful as losing her chance to become Lady Rutledge.

Throughout the night, she thought of him and of how close they had become. It wasn't love, of course, but it was something she treasured.

And she would miss it. Tears filled her eyes, and she turned into her pillow and sobbed for her lost lord.

The following morning, he came. Though she looked wretched from her lack of sleep, she took pains in dressing before she happily rushed downstairs to greet him.

The couple wed by special license in Bath Cathedral that afternoon. Peggy stood up with Carlotta, and James's valet stood up with him. Stevie, who could barely contain his delight, was the only guest in attendance.

When James slipped an emerald ring on her finger and kissed her at the conclusion of the ceremony, Carlotta drew a deep sigh of relief. They were wed, and no one could ever void the marriage. Though spared from her worst fear, Carlotta was swamped with guilt. She had deprived James of the wife he deserved. For he should have a loving wife. Not only that, it was not fair to saddle him with a fallen woman. Carlotta fleetingly thought of him marrying someone else, someone worthy. Oddly, she grew jealous of the mythical woman. She would have been beautiful. Of course. And quite likely of good birth. Without a doubt, James could have taken his pick of any maiden in the kingdom. Any unspoiled woman.

Carlotta's fingers coiled.

Even though their marriage was secure now, she had no intentions of allowing the earl—her husband, now—to learn of her past. She could never face him were he to know. It was bad enough that he knew what a wicked mother she had been all these years.

And she planned to make up to Stevie for that. She had a great deal of making up to do.

But first, she must get her husband away from Bath, where he was sure to learn that she had been Gregory's mistress.

James had arranged for them to be served their bridal meal at the Sheridan Arms Hotel. With Stevie on her lap, she and James rode in the Rutledge barouche to the hotel.

I must convince him to leave Bath. Carlotta had but that single thought in her troubled mind.

They feasted and toasted each other with bubbling champagne. James faced her, his hand gripping the stem of the glass. "To our happy family."

The thought warmed her. She looked at Stevie's beaming face, then she turned back to her husband, met his smiling gaze, and lifted the glass to her lips.

James had never seen a more beautiful bride than his Carlotta. It was the first time he had seen her wear a color other than a shade of purple. Her gown was snowy white, with lavender ribbons gathered behind her and draping from her train, as well as from her sheer headdress.

When she had come to stand beside him, his hands and knees began to shake like a rumbling volcanic eruption while at the same time he swelled with a heady sense of possession. *She's mine.*

He had never been happier than he was at that moment.

The happiness stayed with him as he sat at the elegant table in the Sheridan Arms dining room, Carlotta at his side.

One day she will truly be mine, he thought.

Eleven

With Stevie between them, the newlyweds walked back to Monmouth Place from the Sheridan Arms.

Stevie looked up at his mother, his eyes squinting in the sun. "Peggy said you and Uncle James have important matters to attend to when we get home, and she and the groom will take me and Bwownie to that park on the other side of the wiver."

"Sydney Gardens," Carlotta said as she and her husband exchanged amused glances.

"Of course you're welcome to stay with us, lad," James said with a wink, "but I daresay it will be as interesting as watching your great-grandmother read the Bible."

Carlotta giggled. How very well her husband understood both her grandmother and her son!

The boy skipped ahead. "I'd wather wide my pony."

"Just as I thought," James said. "Since you'll now be a master to the groom, it's best you learn his name. It's Jeremy."

Oh dear, Carlotta thought. Another name with the Rs her son was unable to pronounce. At first she had been concerned that, at six, Stevie could not speak more plainly, but then she remembered when her brother was a lad he had spoken exactly the same as Stevie. By the time he was ten, though, her brother spoke perfectly.

Carlotta saddened at the thought of him. Like Stephen, her brother had died in The Peninsula. Her sweet brother Andrew. Her heartbeat accelerated at the memory of her double loss: Andrew and Stephen. She remembered, too, how wretched had been her journey home from The Peninsula. She had been so forlorn, and the babe had cried so the entire voyage. She remembered that icy fear that she would bury him, too. Then there had been that gut-wrenching relief when she gave the baby to Gran.

Carlotta glanced down at her son and realized James had replaced her fear of her child with fear *for* him. She vowed to repay James's many kindnesses.

Once they were at the house, Peggy assisted Stevie into riding clothes, and with Jeremy, took the boy to Sydney Gardens.

Carlotta and James sat on the sopha in the drawing room, and she nervously turned to face him.

"My secretary has seen to it that announcements of our nuptials appear in the Bath newspaper as well as in the London *Times*," James said.

Her stomach flipped. How many people reading the announcement would know of her indiscretion? It only took one person to impart the news to her husband. Even if he didn't love her, James would be crushed were he to learn of her past. The dear man deserved better.

I must get him away from Bath.

James took her hand and covered it with his own. "Now that I'm fairly confident Stevie has adjusted well to his new surroundings, it's time we procure a nurse for him. I pray you have no objections to my secretary beginning the search."

Carlotta nodded. "You will now have as much say in my son's affairs as I, for you have chosen to become a father to him."

It was comforting that she would be able to share the grave responsibility of raising a child. Her marriage would liberate Carlotta from the many burdens that had weighed down her fragile shoulders for far too long. There were other reasons, too, that made her thankful to have wed James. She would always have him to share everything with. They were, indeed, compatible and enjoyed many of the same things. He even had an affinity for poetry—not as great as hers, of course—but it was another brick in the cornerstone of their marriage. What they shared might not be love, but in many ways it was far more satisfying.

She looked up at her husband and sighed. "Before I know it, my son will have tutors, then he'll be going off to school, and I'll wonder what became of my little boy."

James squeezed her hand. "Time passes all too quickly."

"Which reminds me," she said, disengaging her hand from his and rising to her feet, "I've got a wedding present for you."

"You shouldn't have . . ."

"It's not anything money can buy," she said. "It's something from the heart."

Coloring over her choice of the word *heart*, Carlotta raced upstairs, then came back down with a piece of vellum in her still-gloved hand. "I've copied a poem for you. A poem that I believe speaks to us," she said softly. She came to him and, with shaking hand, offered him the paper; then she nervously sat beside him as he began to read. She suddenly felt as if she had thrown off all her garments and sat naked before him.

Gather ye rose-buds while ye may;
Old time is still a-flying;
And this same flower that smiles today,
Tomorrow will be dying.

The glorious lamp of heaven, the sun,
The higher he's a-getting,
The sooner will his race be run,
And nearer he's to setting.

That age is best, which is the first,
When youth and blood are warmer;
But being spent, the worse and worst
Times will succeed the former.

—Then be not coy, but use your time,
And while ye may, go marry;
For having lost but once your prime,
You may forever tarry.

To her great surprise, James's eyes moistened as he read. Her heart felt smothered as she pressed her hand to his. *Simpatico.* That's what they were.

He lifted her hand to his lips and sweetly kissed it. "Because we're not in the blush of youth, each day of our marriage *will* be more precious," he said.

She watched him through bleary eyes and nodded. "I shall never regret marrying you, and I pray you'll feel the same." She truly meant the words. She had never been more comfortable with a man. Not with Stephen. Not with Gregory. But with this man whose honor bound him irrevocably to her, she would find some measure of the happiness that had eluded her for as long as she could remember.

He seemed uncomfortable with her heartfelt words and was quick to change the topic of conversation. "Now that you've allowed me to be a part of your life, I suppose we'll have to buy our own home in Bath. You, my dear, have married a very wealthy man. Permit me to allow you to make any selections you like, my lady."

My lady! How strange it sounded to be addressed thus. And how undeserving she was. After the shock of hearing herself addressed as a countess, she remembered her husband's suggestion. *Now is the time for me to act.* She would have to use all the feminine charms she possessed.

She set a gentle hand on her husband's forearm. "Before . . . before we married, I thought living in the country would be to withdraw from living. But now that we're married, I'm longing to make a home for us away from the distractions of a large city like Bath. The prospect of the two of us beginning our married life with only each other's companionship entices me."

"You're saying you want to live at Yarmouth Hall?" His voice was without emotion, his face inscrutable.

She cast her thick eyelashes downward. "If you have no objections, my lord."

"James," he said curtly.

She looked up into his eyes. "James, dearest."

Her words very nearly undid his forced composure. "Nothing could make me happier than taking you and Stevie to Yarmouth Hall."

"It would be like a honeymoon," she said in a tentative voice. "I can think of no better way to get to know you than to see you surrounded by your home and servants—and to keep you all to myself."

She spoke almost as if she feared sharing him with others in Bath society, but they had never mixed with another soul here—something he had always found peculiar. Even today, her wedding day, Carlotta had not wanted a single friend in attendance. Only her faithful, ill-bred maid.

Such lack of friends could be explained by the lengthy illness from which she had only recently recuperated. Felicity, her friend of long standing, was away with her nabob husband. But surely Carlotta had other friends. She was, after all, of good birth. Her position as the widow of Captain Ennis—the son of an earl—alone should have elevated her social standing.

That she had no female friends here, he could almost understand. What woman would wish to be seen with and compared to the lovely violet-eyed widow? Other women, quite naturally, would be jealous of her.

But why no gentlemen callers? Were all the men in Bath blind?

Regardless of the reason for her exclusion from society, James counted himself well blessed to have arrived in Bath at a time when she was only reentering society after her long convalescence.

"You don't have to talk me into it, my love," he said. "If I had my way I'd whisk you away today, but a great many plans will have to be made."

"Such as?"

He loved it when she looked at him cockily like that. "We will have to pack, and I shall have to send to Yarmouth for my coach and four, and I must have the countess's chambers redone for you. And interviewing a nurse will be more easily conducted here in Bath."

She wrinkled her nose. "Not a good excuse among your reasons, dearest. Pray, how far is it to Yarmouth?"

"A full day's ride."

"Then I shall be packed and ready to leave day after tomorrow. I suggest you send for the coach immediately. We can select a nurse from Yarmouth just as well as we can from Bath, and permit me to see to the decor of the countess's chambers after we arrive. All I will require at the present are fresh linens and a room free of dust."

A smile worked its way out from the corner of his mouth. "You've got the makings of a countess."

"Because I'm tyrannical?" she asked, looking up at him with laughing eyes.

He chuckled. "An apt description."

"What a paradox you must find me. First I tell you what a fine wife I'll make, then I proceed to dictate to you as if you were the servant and I the master." She reached out to touch his arm. "Forgive me, dearest."

He could forgive her anything, yet he refused to be her servant. "You, my dear, obviously have strong reasons for wishing to put distance between Bath and yourself."

A flinch of some strong emotion—was it fear?—flashed across her face; then she gathered her composure. "Don't get too confident in your ability to understand me, James. I *do* want to put distance between Bath and me, but that doesn't necessarily mean there's a reason for my dissatisfaction with the city. It's merely time I move on to a new—and better—chapter of my life."

For the next few hours, they each had duties to

perform. James moved to the library, where he drafted letters. The first was to his secretary, instructing him to send the chaise at once and to see that her ladyship's chambers were made ready. The next letter was to his solicitor to inform him of his marriage and his intentions of making provisions in his will for his wife and stepson.

When James expressed his interest in returning to his hotel for some items, his wife protested.

"I'll not have us separated on our wedding day! Wherever thou goest, I goest too, dearest."

He found her behavior decidedly odd. Though he would like to think she had grown utterly attached to his company, he knew his wife better than that. She had a strong reason for not wishing him out of her sight.

Just this morning she had surprised him when she had insisted the wedding take place that very day, when he had thought to marry on the morrow. It was as if she feared losing him if they were separated. But he knew it was not his presence that provoked such strong feelings.

If not that, then what? He prided himself on his ability to read the woman who had become his wife, but he was at a complete loss to explain this new, uncharacteristic behavior.

Instead of going to his hotel, he sent a note to his valet, instructing him to bring some items to Monmouth Place. He and his bride walked to the bank, where he withdrew funds to make settlements on Carlotta's servants who would not be traveling with them to Yarmouth Hall.

As they returned to Monmouth Place, the sun began to sink behind the westward hills. "I'm glad I told Cook to have dinner laid when we returned," Carlotta said. "A pity she'll not be able to go to

Yarmouth Hall with us. I feel wretched dismissing
her and the others so swiftly after engaging them."

James patted her hand. "I'll endeavor to compensate them with generous settlements."

At dinner, they sat beside one another under the
glow of candlelight. Though they had easily fallen
into conversation during the past weeks, now that
they were married, words stuck in her throat. All her
thoughts centered on the one topic she was loath to
discuss: allowing him to take his pleasure from her
body.

When it was not possible to put off the end of the
dinner any further, Carlotta placed her hand over
her husband's. Her voice quivered when she spoke.
"I'm not ready—yet—to be a true wife to you, but I
don't want to be separated from you either, dearest."
She feared he would leave when the time came for
her to go to bed, and what if he should come into
contact tonight with other men—say, at a public
house or a gaming establishment or any of those
other places men frequented? And what if his mention of her brought far more information than she
ever wished him to learn? "Please stay here tonight.
I can sleep on the chaise in my room, and you can
take my bed."

His face fell. And her heart tumbled. *Not yet.* She
would give herself to him. But not yet. She had not
even become accustomed to the idea of being married to him. Indeed, she still reeled from his proposal, still could not believe good fortune had
smiled upon her at last.

She watched him, waiting for his reply. Had she
offended him?

Finally he answered her. "You'll sleep *with* me.
After all, it's our wedding night."

Twelve

After dinner, the newlyweds retired to the drawing room, and Carlotta was only too happy to drink the brandy James offered her. Was it not said that spirits could help still the vapors? Carlotta was most definitely suffering from a severe case of wedding night vapors.

The man she had grown so comfortable with these past several weeks had now taken on a new, threatening persona. Hadn't he said he would not force her? Yet now he insisted on sharing her bed. She knew enough of men and their needs to understand that James Moore, the Earl of Rutledge, was hardly likely to roll over and go to sleep with a living, breathing, not unattractive woman lying next to him. Add to that some measure of affection which he no doubt held for her, and preserving their chaste relationship could prove to be exceedingly difficult.

"Shall we play chess, my love?" he asked as he came to sit next to her on the sopha.

Her gaze dropped to her lap. She suddenly became uncomfortable with him so close to her. She was too startlingly aware of his virility. "I regret to say I don't play games, my lord," she answered ruefully.

He looked at her incredulously. "You don't play games?"

She silently lifted the snifter to her mouth, nodded, then took a drink of the brandy. It burned going down. She could not look her husband in the eye. She was embarrassed that she could not play games.

"I thought you had a brother! Did he not teach you anything?"

She bit her lip. "I always had my head in a book."

"Then I shall have to remedy that, my dear," he said. "When we get to Yarmouth, I shall force you to learn how to play any manner of games."

"Even your infinite patience might be taxed over that task," she said.

"Nonsense! You're an intelligent woman, Carlotta. I have every confidence you'll become adept—if you allow yourself to."

"How reassuring it is to be married to a man who has such confidence in one." She took another sip. Each sip rendered the brandy less offensive. Actually, she was beginning to like it—or the limbering effect it was having on her.

"You do not play whist, either, I suppose?"

She shook her head.

"Surely you play backgammon and cribbage? A child can master those games of chance."

"Then a child has more skill than I possess," she answered, looking up at him with a pout.

To her surprise, he smiled, and his arm slipped around her shoulder. "You're fatigued," he said in a low voice. "Did you not sleep well last night?"

She stifled a yawn. "How well you know me, dearest."

With the back of his hand, he traced her cheekbone. "Then we'll go to bed now. I'll give Peggy a few minutes in which to help you prepare, and I'll understand if you prefer to wear a woolen shift. After all, this won't be a *real* wedding night."

He moved closer, so close she could smell the brandy on his breath. "I said I'd never force you, Carlotta."

"Then I'm relieved you remember your promise, my lord." She scooted to the edge of the sopha, stood up and left the room without sparing a glance at him. Truth be told, it took all her concentration to make a graceful exit. The brandy was rendering her body as pliable as sand.

When Carlotta found Peggy in Stevie's chamber, she was reciting a story to him.

"It's time I help yer mama get ready for bed, lad," Peggy said. "I'll be back in a jiffy."

Carlotta moved to Stevie's bed and sat on its edge, reaching out to stroke the golden hair from his forehead. "Good night, my lamb. I hope it's been a happy day for you."

He answered with a smile. "Now I've got a father like the other lads. Do you think Uncle James will allow me to call him Papa?"

And replace Stephen? she thought with a deep sadness. Then she remembered James telling her how difficult not having a father—like the other lads—had been. *James understands how Stevie feels.* "You'll have to ask him, love," she said as she bent to kiss him.

When she got to her chamber, Peggy had laid out a fine silken shift. "It's rather cold tonight, Peggy. I believe I'll wear the purple I most frequently wear."

"But madame! I mean, my lady! 'Tis yer wedding night! Ye can't wear that purple. It's no better than a horse blanket!"

"I assure you, his lordship won't mind."

Peggy's eyes narrowed. "Oh, I see. Very well, me lady."

What she *saw,* Carlotta realized with a blush, was that the shift would soon be removed.

The maid put up the silk shift, then assisted her mistress into the purple. "Now let's brush out yer hair. His lordship is bound to want to run his fingers through it."

Carlotta sat before the mirror, a smug look on her face, as Peggy removed her hairpins and began to brush out Carlotta's hair.

"I'm so happy ye've married Lord Rutledge. I just hope I can remember to call ye 'me lady.' "

"You will, especially after we get to Yarmouth."

Peggy ran the mother-of-pearl brush through Carlotta's hair, but her glance darted to the looking glass and her mistress's eyes reflected there. "When do we leave?"

"Day after tomorrow," Carlotta said.

"So soon?"

Carlotta nodded.

Peggy cleared her throat. "Does . . . does Jeremy also go to Yarmouth?"

"I believe he will. Just today, Lord Rutledge told Stevie he would now be a master to Jeremy."

Peggy's eyes brightened.

Was Peggy attracted to the groom? Carlotta wondered. The more she thought on it, the more Carlotta realized how similar the two were in age as well as background. And Peggy, with her blond hair and neat little figure, was a taking little thing, to be sure. Jeremy, who was ruggedly handsome in his own right, was bound to return her ardor.

As Peggy set down the brush, Carlotta turned to

her. "I beg that you get my volume of *Kubla Kahn* from the library."

"Ye are going to read on yer wedding night?"

Carlotta smiled. "I am, indeed."

Peggy sighed, her hands fastened to her hips and a scolding look on her face. "Ye forget I cannot read. How will I know which book is that Chinese-sounding name?"

"It's a slim blue leather."

Later, when her husband joined her, Carlotta spoke first. She sat in bed, propped up on a mound of pillows, candles burning at tables on each side of the bed to add to the illumination from the firelight. "Since you have no dressing room," she said, "I won't object if you choose to disrobe in this chamber before coming to bed. I shall close my eyes."

"There's no need," he said teasingly. "I'm not modest."

"But I am," she protested, squeezing her eyes shut.

A moment later, she felt the mattress sink as he climbed on it from the other side of the bed. She turned to gaze at him and was startled to find that he wore no clothing on the upper portion of his body. She did not even want to think what he might—or might not—be wearing under the blankets!

Startling, too, was the unsettling effect his unclad shoulders had on her. It was so terribly intimate. And he was so very handsome. In the glow of the firelight, his skin was golden, with dark hair trailing down his well-formed chest.

As he smiled wickedly at her, she grew even more uncomfortable.

"I perceive you took my advice and dressed for battle," he said.

His levity released hers, and she began to giggle. "I do admire a man with a sense of humor."

He shot her a devilish look. "Enough to kiss me good night?"

"I'm no innocent, Lord Rutledge," she said, meeting his gaze squarely. "I know what damage a sweet kiss can do to a man."

"Then your definition of damage must be different from mine."

Thank goodness, he still spoke with a measure of jest! She shrugged. "I shall give you a chaste kiss," she said as if she were talking to a small child, "then I plan to read poetry to you."

"It is hoped the excitement does not overset me," he said dryly.

She giggled as she leaned into him and quickly brushed her lips across his, then pulled away.

"What? No embrace?" he asked. "And I even plied you with brandy."

"You wicked man." She reached for the book at her bedside table. "Peggy was most puzzled when I asked her to fetch my volume of *Kubla Kahn*."

"Simpleminded chit. You'll have to turn her out," he said with sarcasm, crossing his arms behind his head as he leaned back into the upholstered headboard.

She wanted to reach out and touch him, but such an action could lead to far more intimacy, and she was not ready for the physical side of this marriage. Yet.

"We'll share everything, James," she said softly. "I'll learn to play your games, and you'll grow to love my poems. Long-married people, I am told, blend into one being. That will happen to us—after I become your true wife."

The flippancy drained from his body. Dare he hope his bride meant those words? A wife. A family. That was all he had ever wanted from life. Could Carlotta's cold-as-marble exterior be hiding a woman of warmth and understanding? Only time would tell. He had promised her the rest of his life in which to find out.

"Tell me again what poem we share tonight, my love," he said.

"As you are a man, I thought we'd begin *Kubla Kahn.*"

"So, you're to entertain me?"

Her face scrunched with thought. "I prefer to think I'm assuring the melding of our interests."

He grabbed the book from her and tossed it toward the foot of the bed. Then he began to recite: " 'She walks in beauty, like the night of cloudless climes and starry skies; And all that's best of dark and bright meet in her aspect and her eyes; Thus mellow'd to that tender light which heaven to gaudy day denies.' "

"I'm afraid that's the only stanza I know," he said apologetically.

"I shall always remember you reciting Lord Byron on our first night as man and wife," she said wistfully. "Thank you, James. It was beautiful."

"I have another," he said.

Her brows lifted. "We have more in common than I imagined. Please, go on."

" 'She was a phantom of delight when first she gleam'd upon my sight.' "

Carlotta joined in: " 'A lovely apparition, set to be a moment's ornament.' "

Together, they continued: " 'Her eyes as stars of

twilight fair; like Twilight's, too, her dusk hair; But all things else about her drawn from May-time and the cheerful dawn; a dancing shape, an image gay, to haunt, to startle, and waylay.' "

"I love Wordsworth," Carlotta declared when they finished.

"Though I greatly admire *Kubla Kahn,* it's the ditties about haunting women that I seem to commit to memory," he said, shrugging.

Her lashes dropped. He'd made her uncomfortable. Did she realize he loved those poems of haunting women because they seemed written for her? Had he laid bare his heart too much?

He reached for *Kubla Kahn* and handed it to her. "Here. Lull me to sleep with your voice."

She began to read, but it was not he whom Coleridge's words lulled to sleep. Soon, Carlotta's voice trailed off, and her eyelids dropped. He quietly removed the book from her limp grasp, then got up to blow out her candle.

Before he returned to bed, he also blew out the candle on his side of the bed, then slipped beneath the covers again. In the darkness, he listened to his wife's steady breathing, the breathing of a sleeping person. Though their wedding night had not ended in the manner he would have preferred, he was not displeased. Together, he and Carlotta were laying the foundation of a respectful marriage.

As he lay there in the darkness, drinking in her lavender scent and listening to the soft whimper of her breath, he cursed himself for insisting they share a bed. How could he have been such a bloody fool as to think he could lie beside Carlotta and not want to take her in his arms and love her with all the passion and hunger so long bottled within him?

He ached from his need. If only he could just

touch her . . . He raised up and put his weight on one elbow. Then he began to gently stroke the soft mound of her hips. She did not stir, but he did. He quickly realized what another grave mistake he had made. He could go mad with want of her.

He got up and strode across the carpet to the little bed beside the wall and flung himself onto it, pulling the blankets to cover his breeches—and his exploding need. Need for the woman who had become his wife.

Thirteen

The sun was high in the sky when Carlotta woke with a dull headache the next morning. *It must be the brandy,* she thought, pressing a hand to her throbbing forehead. Then she heard the sound of a man lightly snoring and spun around to see if Lord Rutledge was still beside her, though the sound of his breathing seemed more distant.

Her glance darted to the nearby chaise where he sprawled, sleeping soundly. For the life of her, she could not understand how he slept at all—he appeared so completely uncomfortable. His feet and the lower part of his legs hung off the chaise, which was far too small for him. Thankfully, the breeches he had worn to dinner the night before covered his lower torso. Her glance skimmed his bare upper torso. He had apparently rolled over on the only skimpy blanket he had. Since the fire had now gone cold, she shivered just looking at him.

She tried to remember falling asleep, but she could not. It suddenly occurred to her she must have fallen asleep while she read to him. While she was as close to him as two horses in tandem.

He must have picked up the book and blown out the candles.

When, then, had he decided against sharing her bed? Not that she objected, of course.

She looked at the clock on her mantel. It was well past the time when Peggy normally woke her with a tray of steaming tea and toast. Carlotta smiled impishly. Of course Peggy would be reluctant to come barreling in on the newlyweds.

From her seated position on the bed, Carlotta could see herself in the looking glass. The heavy purple gown looked wretched. And to think she had always prided herself on her striking appearance! The only thing striking about her this morning was how devilishly dreadful she looked. At least she could endeavor to make her hair presentable before waking her husband.

She came down off the bed and quietly seated herself in front of her dressing table and began to brush out her tussled hair. When it was smooth and glossy, she attempted to arrange it attractively, but she was hopeless without Peggy. She merely pushed combs into the sides. *That will just have to do!* She dabbed lavender scent on her neck, then stood up and turned to gaze at her sleeping husband.

As ghastly as she looked, she would now have to wake him. She was concerned over his discomfort.

She moved to the chaise, bent down, and gently nudged him. "James, dearest," she said softly, "please move to the bed where you'll be more comfortable."

His eyes snapped open as he leaped to a seated position. A puzzled look on his face, he looked first at her, then at the chaise, then to the bed some four feet away. Next he spun around to see the clock. "There's no more time for lying about," he said gruffly.

She reached for his shirt that hung on the back of a nearby chair, and she handed it to him.

"Does my bareness offend you?" he asked, a smile sliding across his face.

"Only when the bareness is *below* the waist," she replied primly.

He slipped his arms into the sleeves and began to button the shirt.

"Why did you leave so comfortable a bed for that chaise? You looked so wretchedly uncomfortable there."

He didn't answer for a moment. She watched as he buttoned first one button, then another. Finally, he spoke. "It occurred to me my plan to sleep with you was not a wise one."

She started to ask him why then, having some idea of the feelings that precipitated his action, decided against it. "Oh, dear, I'd forgotten all about your valet. However will you dress without him?"

James sat on the edge of the chaise and reached for his stockings and boots and began to put them on. "I daresay I'll try to make a completely unobtrusive entrance into my hotel, where Mannington awaits to make me suitably presentable."

"I suppose by now all of Bath knows of our nuptials."

He stood up and nodded as he reached for his tailcoat. "Not that I'm a well-known figure in Bath, not like my wife." He shot a searing glance at her.

Her heart drummed. Had he heard of her disparaging past? Had he, surely he'd be more outraged. She watched as he buttoned his coat, then strolled across the room and brushed his lips across her cheeks. "We have much to attend to today. Do you realize by this time tomorrow we'll be on the road to Exmoor?"

"I have much more to do than you. You forget I've lived six years in Bath."

"I've not forgotten. I'll be back to assist you in any way I can."

At dawn the next morning, cold and still sleepy, the three of them climbed into the coach and four. Carlotta spread a rug on one of the seats for Stevie to lie upon. "Go back to sleep, lamb," she whispered to him as he stretched out on the seat. It was the perfect size to accommodate the length of him.

"I've never been to Exmoor before," she whispered to her husband as she sat beside him. "You must tell me about it."

"You will need to make your own judgments about it," he said.

She watched her sleeping son for a moment, then peeked under the velvet curtain as the coach rattled across the River Avon. A moment later, she turned to James. "How long have you lived at Yarmouth?"

His outstretched legs formed a line from one corner of the carriage to the other. "Less than a year. Before that, I had never been there."

"You'd never visited your uncle?"

He laughed. "I'd never even met my uncle. My father, you'll remember, died young, and we had very little contact with his family after his death. My father was a second son. My mother had told me my father's eldest brother, who lived in the West Country, was heir to their uncle's earldom, but it never occurred to us that earldom would fall to me when my father's brother died without a male heir."

How selfish Carlotta had been these past several weeks not to have asked James more about himself. And how peculiar it was to wed a man one knew so little about. "Then you weren't raised in the West Country?" she asked.

He shook his head. "No. My mother's home was in Sussex, and since she had inherited a farm there—and since my father's prospects were slim—he gladly became a country squire of some little prosperity."

"If you had a farm to run, why did you buy colors?"

He shrugged. "My mother had become very independent, having been widowed at so young an age. She ran the farm almost single-handedly."

"Does she still?"

His breath stilled. "She died when I was in India," he said in a voice barely above a whisper.

Ashamed of herself for not even knowing her husband was an orphan, Carlotta offered her sympathy. "You two must have been close—especially since you had no brothers or sisters."

"Except for missing a father, I had a perfect childhood. My mother adored—and spoiled—me."

Carlotta had no doubts that James, who was loyal and noble and sensitive, adored his mother. "Feelings I'm certain you returned."

His eyes sparkled. "Of course."

"It must have been difficult for your mother to have allowed you to become a soldier, to travel all over the world."

"I believe it was difficult for her, though she never admitted it to me. All my life, she said I was destined for . . . this is embarrassing," he said with a chuckle. "She said I was destined for greatness, and greatness could not be achieved by staying in Sussex."

"Then greatness is obtainable in Exmoor?" Carlotta asked in jest.

Another chuckle broke from his throat. "Hardly.

You realize it was my mother who wanted me to become a great man. It was not something I've ever strived for. My needs are far more simple."

Unconsciously, she put a hand on his arm. "What, pray tell, are your needs?"

He drew in his breath and did not answer for a moment. "I want most what I missed as a youth."

A family. She had tread on too personal a ground. It was far too uncomfortable for her. Of course he wanted a loving wife and children and a happy family. And she could never be the loving wife he sought, the wife he deserved.

She grew quiet and once more lifted the curtain to peer at the countryside. The sun had now risen, and farmers were already in the fields. She turned back to James. "You still own the farm in Sussex?"

"I lease it now. I hope to present it to Stevie one day."

Her heart melted. He loved Stevie as if the boy were his own son. Not being James's own flesh, though, Stevie would never be able to inherit Yarmouth. Her stomach tumbled. Perhaps Yarmouth would one day belong to a son of James's. Perhaps a son she would one day bear.

The thought brought no joy. As kind as James was, she did not love him. And the anticipation of intimacy between them held no allure for her. Would she ever be ready to share his bed? Other wives allowed their unloved husbands such liberties. Which meant she was doubly blessed that James had vowed not to take his pleasure from her until she came willingly to him. She wondered how long he would be willing to wait. No man could be saintly forever.

"Is your groom riding the post chaise with Peggy?" she asked to break the awkward silence.

His brows lowered. "Jeremy?"

Carlotta nodded.

"No. He's bringing my horse back. Why do you ask?"

"I believe Peggy has set her cap for him. I hope he's not married."

James laughed. "Sweet heavens, no! He's not much more than a lad. It's only this year that he's taken off and grown like a beanstalk."

"Oh, dear, I hope he's not too young for Peggy."

"She appears youthful," he said.

"Let me see," Carlotta said as she began to count on her fingers. "She was only thirteen when I got her, and that was six years ago." She looked up at her husband. "Which makes her—"

"Nineteen."

"Do you think that's too old for Jeremy?"

"I'd say they're perfectly suited—if a mite too young to be thinking of marriage."

"I was widowed before I was twenty."

He did not answer.

They rode on in silence for several miles before she asked, "You have tenants at Yarmouth?"

He frowned. "Yarmouth is not a typical estate. The land immediately surrounding the estate is farmed, but most of the wealth comes from coal mines located not far from the property."

"Then you've had to educate yourself about mining?" she asked.

"I'm still educating myself. Whether as a farmer, a soldier, or an earl, I don't ask my people to do anything I don't do myself."

"Then you actually have gone down into the mines?"

"Any number of times."

She cringed. "I have a deathly fear of them. They're so dark and dangerous."

"I'm channeling my resources into making my mines safer."

So noble. Like James himself.

"I've had to close down some because of excessive accidents." He stopped. "And lives lost," he said, his brows drawn together.

"Many people of your class would have no care for the lower classes."

His mouth grim, he said, "I couldn't live with myself if I held those opinions."

"Then you must be liberal thinking—not that I'm well informed about *The Rights of Man* and all that."

"Nor am I," he countered. "I only know I must do what I think is right."

Her thoughts fleetingly jumped to James's mother and what a fine job she had done raising him to be so noble a man. How proud she would have been of him.

Then Carlotta's glance flitted to Stevie, curled up opposite her. In repose, his hair moistened to his head, appearing more brown than blond. He slept with his little mouth open. She smiled as she watched him. He really was a beautiful child. Even if he was a mite too thin. Now she had to ensure he was as beautiful on the inside. Thank goodness she would have James to help her raise the lad to become a fine man.

Stevie began to stir, and rubbing his eyes, he sat up and looked at them. "Are we there yet?"

James chuckled. "We've still a long way to go."

"Will it be dark when we arrive?" Stevie asked.

"I hope to get to Yarmouth before dark."

"Tell me again about the stables," Stevie asked, smiling broadly.

"I've no doubt you could recite them to me as well as you can say your nursery rhymes."

"Like 'Pussy Cat, Pussy Cat, Where've You Been?' "

James nodded. "I know very well you can tell me how many horses are in the stable at Yarmouth."

"Eleven." The boy scooted to the window and lifted the curtain to look out. "When we get to our new home, Uncle James," the lad said, "may I call you Papa?"

Carlotta's heart fluttered, and her glance darted nervously to James.

He was silent for a moment, and she feared he would refuse the boy's humble request.

Finally, in a throaty voice, James answered. "I'd be honored. Nothing would give me greater pleasure than being a father to you."

A huge lump formed in Carlotta's throat, and her eyes grew misty.

Their peace and quiet was as gone now as the morning dew, for Stevie spoke incessantly.

At the first break in her son's innumerable questions, Carlotta turned to her husband as he quickly glanced away. He had been watching her, and he must have felt uncomfortable about it.

She turned back to look out the carriage window again. Though gentle hills marked the landscape around Bath, hills were far more pronounced here in the West Country. Carlotta found she could not look away, so mesmerizing was the lonely landscape. A brush of heather covered vast stretches of treeless moors and heath, and smooth-topped hills spread over the landscape like pebbles on sand.

They crossed a river, and she asked James what river it was.

" 'Tis the Parrett—somewhat of a boundary for

the Saxons. You'll learn everything west of the Parrett has retained more of the Celts—including their language—than anywhere else in England."

"The language? Do you mean people in Exmoor will speak Celtic?"

"It's dying out now, but you'll find the speech quite different from what you're used to."

As soon as she thought she was getting accustomed to the West Country terrain, it would change. From broad sweeps of moor to wooded gorges or to lush riven valleys.

She removed her face from the pane long enough to turn and address her husband. "We must be near Exmoor—the geography is so vastly different to what I am accustomed. Why, James, did you not tell me how beautiful it is here? In some ways it reminds me of Portugal."

His vermillion eyes danced as he nodded. "There are similarities. For one, it's warmer here, and certainly hilly and close to the sea. I had hoped you would find it as beautiful as I do."

Soon the carriage rattled over an arched stone bridge covering a narrow, swift river. "We've just crossed the Barle. We're now in Exmoor," James said.

"Now you must tell us what Yarmouth Hall looks like."

He shook his head. "You will have to form your own conclusions on it. I mustn't color your opinion one way or the other."

She had the opportunity to make her own judgment when the coach clattered up Yarmouth's broad avenue at dusk.

As soon as James told her they had reached Yarmouth, she slapped back the curtain and pressed her face to the glass. Sitting high above a sweeping green park, she observed a magnificent four-story brick structure with two shallow wings at either end of the symmetrical building. Its pitched roof was balustraded and dotted with tall, slender chimneys that mimicked the tall, slender mullioned windows.

When they drew closer, she saw that the pedimented entry was on the second floor, with broad steps leading up to the doorway.

Unaccountably, as the coach came to a stop at the front door, her stomach flipped. *I'll be mistress here.* Doubts over her competence besieged her.

James turned to her and drew her hands into his. "Your new home, my lady."

Fourteen

James had forgotten to tell Fordyce to instruct the servants *not* to line up like a daunting regiment to be surveyed by the new countess. The sheer numbers of his vast staff were likely to intimidate his bride. He should know. He had bloody well been intimidated when he had first come to Yarmouth. Still was, actually. Though he'd as lief not let them on to that.

It was not Carlotta he needed to worry about, but her son. Their son now. As they entered the massive entry hall where some forty servants stood at sentry on either side and along the sweep of the staircase, Stevie clung to his mother's skirt and buried his head within its folds.

James nudged up closer to the nervous lad and set a reassuring hand on top of the lad's head. His mother had already claimed the boy's shoulder. " 'Tis all right, Stevie, this is your new home," James whispered.

Still, Stevie would not show his face.

James flicked a glance at the butler and housekeeper, the two whose dress was distinguishable from the other servants' chartreuse livery, and to another man who dressed as a gentleman. "I should like to present you to the new Lady Rutledge." He looked back at Carlotta, who smiled brightly at them. "My dear," James said to her, "Mrs. MacGinnis can conduct you on a tour of the house tomorrow, when you're more rested from the tedious journey."

Carlotta smiled at the housekeeper. "I shall look forward to it. How long have you been in service at Yarmouth, Mrs. MacGinnis?"

James looked at the housekeeper with new eyes. With her silver hair and plump little body, he guessed her to be well past fifty. Mrs. MacGinnis smiled. "I came to my post here two and twenty years ago."

"Then I daresay you know far more about Yarmouth than my husband," Carlotta said with a little laugh.

The housekeeper smiled smugly.

To his secretary, James said, "Mr. Fordyce, permit me to make you acquainted with the new Lady Rutledge."

The well-dressed man stepped forward and took her hand. "Your ladyship," he said as he bowed.

"I forgot to tell you, my dear, Mr. Fordyce is my secretary."

James did not at all approve of the way Carlotta eyed young Fordyce from head to toe before she spoke. "I am pleased to make your acquaintance," she said. "His lordship has mentioned you—and your efficiency—often."

Her words apparently rendered the young secretary speechless. No doubt Fordyce was unused to being addressed by beautiful women, James thought.

Fordyce stepped back.

To the butler, James said, "Adams, allow me to make you known to her ladyship."

The stern, gaunt butler offered his new mistress a stiff bow.

Then James looked down at Stevie and raised his voice. "This lad is Lady Rutledge's son, who will henceforth be treated as my own son. His name is Master Stephen. I'm afraid he's a bit shy," James added.

"Bless his heart," Mrs. MacGinnis said, "he's such a wee one still."

Stevie poked his head out. "I'm not, either. I'm six." Then, like a turtle, his head once again burrowed into his mother's skirts.

To James's delight, the entire staff—including the foreboding Adams—laughed. Which, unfortunately, made Stevie all the more self-conscious.

James felt badly for all the poor servants who were lined up like slaves at auction. He stepped out away from Carlotta and swept his gaze from one side to the other, perusing them. "All of you," he said in a voice louder than that used for normal conversation, "are to be commended on the neatness of your appearance and on the effort you have made to present yourselves to the new Lady Rutledge. Instead of going through tedious introductions, I believe her ladyship will prefer to become acquainted with each of you in the commission of your duties. Be assured I have told Lady Rutledge there is no finer staff in all of England."

His comments were greeted with no fewer than forty smiles.

To his surprise, Carlotta stepped forward to stand by his side, her smiling gaze sweeping from left to right. "I am honored by your welcome, and I look forward to learning each and every one of you by name." Then she bowed her head and slipped her arm through her husband's, her son still clutching her skirts.

James directed his attention at Mrs. MacGinnis and started to speak to her, but she spoke first. "Would milord and milady prefer dinner on a tray in your chambers tonight?"

James shot Carlotta a quizzing glance.

"We can dress and come down," Carlotta said. "I eagerly look forward to my first meal at Yarmouth Hall."

From Mrs. MacGinnis's smile, James could tell she was pleased with her new mistress.

"I trust the rooms are prepared?" James asked the housekeeper.

"Just as you instructed Mr. Fordyce. I didn't realize, though, that the guest chamber was to be used by Lady Rutledge's son. There's no extra bed for the nurse, but I'll have one brought up immediately."

"There is no nurse at present," James said. "Her ladyship's maid is fulfilling those duties until we find a suitable person for the position." He turned to Fordyce. "You've been handling that, I trust?"

Fordyce nodded. "The agency has sent a listing of several prospects. Would her ladyship care to peruse the information tonight?"

"It can wait until tomorrow," James snapped. "Lady Rutledge is fatigued from the journey."

"And," Carlotta said to Fordyce, " 'tis a choice my husband and I shall make together."

Like a true father.

As he and his family mounted the stairway, James swelled with pride. Carlotta fit in as if she were born to nobility. He had done well for himself by selecting her for his countess.

A pity she did not love him.

"Look, Mama," Stevie shrieked excitedly. "The ceiling's golden."

Carlotta slowed and looked up at the molded plaster ceiling. "So it is!"

When they reached the second level, James said, "All of our chambers are on this floor." The first chamber they stopped at was Stevie's. "This was a guest suite during the old earl's day."

"His lordship had no children at all, not even daughters?" Carlotta asked.

James shook his head. "No children at all. In fact, one has to go back nearly one hundred years before children lived at Yarmouth."

"Is there even a nursery?" Carlotta asked.

James strolled into the light blue chamber and spoke over his shoulder. "It's not fit for Stevie. I've instructed Fordyce to proceed with a complete remodel of the nursery, with particular instructions to repair the fireplace, which is currently not working."

"Thank goodness. We can't have Stevie in a cold room," Carlotta said. She glanced around the spotless blue chamber. "This room's blessedly warm."

Now that it was just the three of them, Stevie behaved as his normal self, running and throwing himself on the bed, then standing on it as he began to jump.

"Stephen Andrew Ennis!" Carlotta shouted. "You know you are *not* to jump upon beds. What happens to bad little boys who jump on beds?"

His face fell as he climbed down. "They cwack their heads open."

"Yes, indeed, and if you dare to jump on a bed once again, I shall be forced to spank your bottom."

His green eyes rounded.

James could not imagine Carlotta actually lifting a hand to the child.

"I don't want to sleep in here," the boy said.

"You'll never sleep in here alone, lamb. I promised. And since Peggy's not arrived yet, I daresay you'll have to sleep in your mama's chamber tonight."

A broad smile transformed his pouting face. "Shall we go see your chamber, Mama?"

She looked at James. "Shall we?"

They left Stevie's room, and walked midway down the wide stone hall, brightly lit by dozens of wall sconces.

"The opening into your chambers," James said, sweeping open the door, "is through this study."

They walked into a well-lit room furnished in faded red silks and velvets, a gold Louis XIV escritoire centered on the room's large Oriental carpet.

Carlotta's face was inscrutable when she spoke. "I daresay it was grand in the last century."

"Exactly," James said. "That last Lady Rutledge died in 1799."

Carlotta flung out her arms. "Well, there you have it!"

James moved to the next connecting chamber. The bedchamber. It had once been quite regal and was as large as the entire first floor of Carlotta's Monmouth Place house. The turquoise silk damask on the walls was badly faded from the sun, as were the satin bedcoverings.

Carlotta walked around the lofty chamber, the corners of her lips slightly lifted. Then she turned to him. And he felt unaccountably nervous. He had truly intended to have the rooms redone before she saw them. For some unexplainable reason, it was important to him that she completely approve of Yarmouth and everything in it.

"You know, James," she began, "with fresh paint and new fabrics, these chambers will be quite magnificent." She linked her arm through his. "And I shall have a great deal of fun overseeing the decorating of Stevie's and my rooms."

He could have whooped. "Let me guess. Your room is to be done in purple."

She burst out laughing. "Heavens, no, you silly man."

"But I thought purple was your favorite color."

"Purple *looks* best on me. Because of my eyes. I told you, I wear what looks good on me, not what's in fashion. However, to show myself off to the best advantage, I prefer a room that doesn't compete with me."

"White?" he asked.

She shook her head. "That's a bit too insipid for me."

"What then?"

She thought for a moment. "I believe a light gold."

He nodded. A good backdrop for Carlotta.

She strolled after Stevie, who had passed into the third connecting room, the countess's dressing room. She glanced at it, then at James. "I am very pleased with my chambers. Are yours adjacent?"

His glance shifted to the next door, in the middle of the west wall. "My dressing room adjoins yours, and my chambers are the reverse of yours. Right to left, dressing room, bedchamber, study."

"May I see yours?"

"Follow me, my lady," he said, proffering his arm gallantly.

His dressing room would have been indistinguishable from hers, were it not for the rows of boots and finely tailored gentlemen's clothing.

Beyond that room, they strolled into his bedchamber.

"It's emerald," she squealed as she walked into it.

He spun around to face her. "You don't like emerald?"

"I adore emerald, and I must say, it suits you, James." She studied the room quietly for a moment. "It's a very masculine chamber. Did you select the color yourself?"

He nodded.

"What color did the previous earl have in here?"

James rolled his eyes. "Red."

She burst out laughing. "I cannot imagine you in a scarlet room!"

"Nor can I," he said dryly.

"Can I have a wed woom?" Stevie asked, looking up hopefully at them."

"May I," Carlotta said.

Stevie screwed up his face in a quizzing fashion.

James stooped down to the boy's level. "To speak correctly, you say 'may I', not 'can I'. Your mama's merely correcting you."

Now Stevie spun around to face his mother again. "May I have a wed woom?"

"If you'd like, love. Yarmouth Hall is going to be great fun."

Once more, James felt like whooping.

Later that night, after partaking of an impressive meal with two liveried footmen in attendance, and after James had taught her how to play backgammon in the saloon, and after Carlotta had read

Stevie to sleep in the chaise in her chamber, she climbed on top of the huge full tester bed in her room. She blew out the bedside candle and lay there between sheets which were as stiff as paper. Just the way she liked them. One of her greatest enjoyments in life was having her sheets changed every day, a luxury she had rarely been able to indulge.

She lay in the semidarkness, listening to the crackling fire and Stevie's breathing. A peace like she had not known in years settled over her.

She had never felt more liberated. Most importantly, she no longer feared James would learn about Gregory. She had got him away from Bath!

Even though she did not love him, she looked forward to the new life she would make with him. A life free of financial woes. She would be respected as the Countess of Rutledge. She had a vast army of servants at her disposal and a fabulous ancestral home to call her own. Her own chambers—once they were redecorated—would be magnificent, as magnificent as those in the king's castle, no doubt.

And, after all these years, she had her son at last, never to lose him again.

All of this she owed to Lord Rutledge, the man who had honored her with his name. She drifted off to a contented sleep, her lips lifted into a smile.

Fifteen

When Carlotta came down the stairway the next morning, she came upon a footman in the now-familiar chartreuse livery. "Can you direct me to Lord Rutledge?" she asked.

"His lordship is in the library," he said with nary a sign of emotion.

"Pray, where might that be?"

His eyes darted down the expansive central hallway that ran from the front of the house to the back. "Allow me to show you the way, milady."

She followed him down the broad foyer, gazing up at the massive paintings that covered the walls even into the next story.

At the end of the hallway, the footman opened a tall door into a dark library. Though the room was vast, it had few windows. In their place, tall bookcases ringed the chamber, which was cozy despite its size. A fire blazing in the big marble fireplace and the rich, dark woods suffused the room with warmth.

James, who sat behind his desk, looked up from ledgers he was perusing, his face brightening when he saw her. He promptly stood up and came forward, his hands outstretched. "Good morning, my lady. I thought you'd be touring the house with Mrs. MacGinnis."

Carlotta still had not become accustomed to being addressed as *my lady*. Placing her hands on his chest, she raised up to brush her lips over his. "I believe a more pressing duty this morning is for you and me to look over the information on candidates for Stevie's nurse."

"I daresay that is more pressing," he said. He went back to his desk. "Here is the information Fordyce received from the agency on all the candidates." With several sheets of paper in his hand, he came to sit on the sopha beside her.

After yesterday's long ride, she should have become accustomed to sitting near to the man who was now her husband, but she still felt uncomfortable when they were so close.

The thing of it was, the man was far too virile. She had not been cognizant of his masculinity when he had first come to Bath—most likely because he was *too* nice, too apologetic, too disinterested in her as a woman. But now . . . now she had come to realize how manly he was. Not just in the physical way—which he most definitely was—but also in the way he commanded respect, in the way he showed so keen an understanding of human nature—including her own selfishness—and in the way he counseled with such wisdom.

Because he was so masculine, she knew she would be unable to deny him physical intimacy indefinitely, intimacy she wanted no part of. As they sat there, their thighs parallel to each other's, she became vitally aware of their closeness.

He leaned back and crossed his legs, boot to thigh, and watched the nearby fire for a moment before he spoke. "Stevie's almost too old for a nurse, but he needs someone to watch after him. As mistress of Yarmouth, you'll have many duties and cannot have a child constantly underfoot."

"What are you proposing?"

"The lady we engage should have qualities of both a nurse and a governess. It's time the lad learned how to read and do sums. His intelligence is most keen. You would appreciate the grasp of military strategy he's displayed. I shouldn't want to hold him back."

"I thought perhaps it was just I who perceived how bright a lad he is," she said with a smile.

He nodded. "He's as bright as a newly minted guinea—were guineas still being minted."

"Before looking at these papers," James said, "I propose we first draw up a list of qualities we seek."

"An excellent suggestion."

He went to the desk for paper and pen, which he promptly handed to his wife. "Penmanship is not my strong suit."

Carlotta folded up the vellum to several thicknesses and made ready to write. "First, I think, should be age. Stevie was most attached to his second nurse—who came to him when she was only eighteen. The next one was grandmotherly, and he did not favor her nearly as well."

James's eyes danced. "So the lad undoubtedly likes them young and pretty."

Carlotta suppressed a smile. "Sara—the second nurse—was, now that I think on it, quite pretty." She began to write.

"I beg that you don't put *pretty* down on paper. I was only jesting. Such a quality is really not relevant."

She gazed up at him through her thick lashes. "Then a fine appearance is not something you seek in a woman?" As soon as the words were out of her mouth, Carlotta regretted them. Now she was behaving as the old Carlotta always had. The flirtatious Carlotta. The Carlotta who was confident in her own beauty. The Carlotta she wished to bury in Bath.

He laughed. "Would that it were so," he said ruefully, his heated gaze sweeping over her from the tip of her ebony head to the toes of her satin slippers.

Her insides began to tremble as she wrote down "Age: under five and twenty." Then she looked back at him. "What next, my lord?"

"James," he snapped. "You're to call me James."

Her lashes dropped. "Yes, James," she said softly.

He lifted her chin with a flick of his hand. "It's as if you're trying to distance yourself from the fact that you're my wife."

She shook her head. "Never that. I'm very happy you have made me your wife. You're . . . you're only the second man I've known in the six years since Stephen died whom I would wish for a husband." She saw that he stiffened at her words. *I should have lied and told him he was the first.*

His eyes flashed angrily. "Who was the other man?"

If she did not know better, she would wager James was jealous! She shook her head. "No one important. No one who returned my feelings." She picked up the plume again. "What next?"

James was silent a moment. "Someone who has demonstrated her amiability with young children."

Carlotta nodded as she wrote.

"And this person should be proficient at reading and writing and working with sums."

While she was writing, a knock sounded on the

library door; then Mrs. MacGinnis entered the room.

"My lord," she began, "Mr. Fordyce tells me you are in the process of selecting a nurse for the young master." She came to stand before them, a nervousness in her countenance, her hands twisting together.

James lifted a brow. "We are."

"If I might be so bold," Mrs. MacGinnis said, "I wish to recommend my niece for the position."

"Your niece has experience being a nurse?" he asked.

The housekeeper shook her head. "Not actually, but she would be wonderful. You see, she loves children. She was responsible for her young brother and showed remarkable patience and maturity in her care of him and in the execution of her duties."

James leaned back, hooking his thumbs together, his gaze fixed on the housekeeper. "Tell me about her, if you please."

She sighed. "Her mother—my sister—is housekeeper to Sir Eldridge in Middlesex."

He nodded.

"My niece Margaret was the third of four children. She had two elder sisters who are now married. Her prospects of attracting a husband of her own, unfortunately, are limited due to her plumpness."

"She is fat?" Carlotta asked.

Mrs. MacGinnis shook her head. "I wouldn't say *fat*. It's just that she's a bit too round."

The girl must bear a resemblance to her aunt, Carlotta thought. "How old is she?" Carlotta asked.

"She's nineteen and has a strong desire to secure a post as a nurse or governess."

James's brows shot up. "A governess? Then she is educated?"

Mrs. MacGinnis nodded. "Oh, yes, milord. And you should see her penmanship! 'Tis like a work of art."

"She's in Middlesex now?"

She nodded.

"Thank you, Mrs. MacGinnis," James said in a dismissive voice. "My wife and I shall give serious consideration to engaging your niece."

Once the door was closed behind the housekeeper, James's and Carlotta's eyes locked.

"What think you?" he asked.

"She sounds perfect!"

"I agree. Should you like to engage her, sight unseen?"

"You've spoken so highly of her aunt, the girl obviously comes from good stock."

"And the fact that she's educated should move her to the top of our list."

Carlotta nodded. "Go ahead, dearest. Engage the girl."

"Very well."

Carlotta's tour of the house was delayed for half an hour as the housekeeper drafted and posted a letter to her niece. While Carlotta waited, she went to fetch Stevie from Peggy.

"Perhaps now that I'm relieving you of Stevie," Carlotta said to her maid, "you'll have time to unpack your own things. I know you didn't arrive until quite late last night."

"I'll unpack and press yer things as well, milady."

Carlotta nodded and gave her hand to Stevie.

"Come, lamb, we shall go take a tour of our new house."

As they descended the stairs, Stevie said, "Yarmouth doesn't seem like a house, Mama. It seems like a palace. It's so big!"

"That it is. I pray we don't get lost."

But once she saw the house, Carlotta realized its perfect symmetry should keep her from getting lost. Thank goodness, she thought, there weren't haphazard additions jutting out at all angles, as there were in many old houses belonging to the nobility.

During the tour and the seemingly endless procession of bedchambers, Stevie asked Mrs. MacGinnis how many bedchambers there were.

"Three and forty," the housekeeper replied with a pride equal to that of an owner.

"But I thought the old earl had no children," Stevie said.

"You must understand, lamb," Carlotta said, "earls are very important people who have many guests who come stay with them."

"King George the First himself came to Yarmouth in 1719," the housekeeper boasted. "He liked to hunt in the nearby wood."

Stevie's eyes rounded. "Think you our king will come here?"

"Our king's very sick—and besides, Lord Rutledge is not acquainted with him," Carlotta said. She stopped to examine a portrait of a wigged-and-powdered gentleman.

"That was the old earl," Mrs. MacGinnis said.

Carlotta studied the portrait carefully but decided he bore no resemblance to her husband.

"Were there children here when the other king came?" Stevie asked Mrs. MacGinnis.

"Indeed. The third earl had fourteen children."

"I wish my mama—and papa—had fourteen children."

Carlotta set a hand to his shoulder, silently pleased at the ease with which Stevie had accepted James as his father. "I daresay you'll find children here to be your friends."

Mrs. MacGinnis nodded. "This place is going to come alive now. It has been far too dreary for far too many years. Very few of the bedchambers have even been used since I came here." She began to mount the stairs to the top floor. "When I first came, the old countess was alive, and she was happiest when all the rooms were filled. Then the poor lady took a fever and died suddenly." Mrs. MacGinnis shook her head sadly. "The old earl was never the same after she died."

Carlotta paused in front of a window near the stairwell and gazed first at the parterre garden to the rear of the house; then the magnificence of the land north of the estate arrested her attention. Patches of farmland in varying shades of green gave way further north to smooth hills lush with vegetation.

"I should think," Carlotta said to the housekeeper, "the lack of residents here, though, has surely made your position easier."

Mrs. MacGinnis shrugged. "I would prefer to be worked ragged. I take great pleasure in setting a full table and in having the guest rooms bursting with people. Perhaps his lordship, now that he is married, will bring life back to Yarmouth."

"Perhaps," Carlotta said, though she did not wish to open up Yarmouth and jeopardize her secure position as the wife James valued. Were others to converge on the house, James would be certain to learn about Gregory.

Mrs. MacGinnis led the way to the top floor.

"Has my husband made many changes since coming here?" Carlotta asked.

"Most of us believe he's saved Yarmouth."

Carlotta's brows drew together. "How?"

"As I said, the old earl lost interest in everything, including Yarmouth, after the countess died. He reduced the staff because he did not wish to keep three-and-forty chambers cleaned and dusted for guests who would never come, never be invited. He allowed the house to begin to fall to ruin."

Carlotta glanced around her. "It seems well maintained to me."

"That's because the new Lord Rutledge has worked tirelessly to restore the house to what it should be. He's put most of his fortune back into it—and into the mines." Mrs. MacGinnis chuckled. "When we heard the new Lord Rutledge was a young bachelor, many of us expected he would drain the estates to feed his lavish ways in town."

Carlotta burst into laughter. "So you expected him to be the absentee earl! That is too funny. To know my husband is to know of his acute sense of duty."

The housekeeper nodded her agreement. "Nearly every person here in Exmoor owes his livelihood to Lord Rutledge, and all of them think he likely hung the stars in the sky."

So it's not just I who owe him so much. "Pray tell, why is he so highly regarded?"

"Even though the old earl did not choose to spend money, he was obsessed with making it. The mines were unsafe, but he refused to put money into making them safer and would not hear of shutting down the unsafe ones."

Stevie looked up at her. "Did anyone die in the mines?"

"Aye, lad," Mrs. MacGinnis said, nodding mournfully. "There have been three tragedies in recent years. A total of one and twenty lives lost."

Carlotta winced. "You're saying these are losses that could have been prevented?"

Mrs. MacGinnis shrugged. "That's what I've been told. As soon as your husband learned the details, he called all the miners together and told them he would do whatever it took to make the mines safe. He told them one life lost was one too many. They cheered him mightily."

Carlotta was filled with pride. "He told me he's had to close some of the mines that were unsafe."

"At a great financial loss to himself, I am told." Mrs. MacGinnis stopped, took a key from her pocket, and opened a chamber door. "This is one of the maid's rooms—actually, it's not occupied at present because Kate, the one who formerly lived here, married and took a post in Minehead."

Stevie ran into the room and glanced all around. "It's not nearly as big as my chamber."

"But it's a comfortable-looking room," Carlotta defended.

"Aye," Mrs. MacGinnis said, exiting the room, waiting with key in hand to relock it. "All the rooms on this floor are occupied by the staff."

They started back down the stairs.

"Where is Mr. Fordyce's study?" Carlotta asked.

"Forgive me, my lady, for neglecting to show it you. When you see it, you'll understand how easy it would be to forget it. Mr. Fordyce's office is almost like a secret room off the library. Come, I'll take you there now."

They walked down to the first floor and into the

library. Carlotta's glance flicked to her husband's desk, but he was no longer there or anywhere in the room. Mrs. MacGinnis slid her hand along a shelf of Latin books, and then a twelve-foot-tall section of the shelves swung inward into Mr. Fordyce's brightly lit study.

He was sitting at his desk by the window when he looked up and saw them. "Good day, my lady," he said as he stood up. "To what do I owe this pleasure?"

"I thought to get acquainted with you." Carlotta glanced at Mrs. MacGinnis. "Please take Stevie to my maid, if you will, Mrs. MacGinnis. He'll be needing to get some sunshine."

When Mrs. MacGinnis went to leave the room, she began to close off its entry.

"That's not necessary, Mrs. MacGinnis," Carlotta said. "You can leave it open." Carlotta must endeavor to keep any kind of scandal from further tarnishing her name.

Alone with Mr. Fordyce, Carlotta said, "So this is where you work." She strolled about the chamber, then came to stand in front of him. "May I sit down?"

"Please do." He waited until she sat before he did likewise.

The exceedingly fair secretary looked to be slightly younger than James, yet a seriousness about him—and the fact that he wore spectacles—made him seem older. Although his clothing and his voice were that of a gentleman, his unstylishly slicked hair was completely at odds with a man of fashion.

"How long have you been at Yarmouth, Mr. Fordyce?"

"I was with the old earl for a year, and I've now been nearly another year with the new earl."

"And my husband is an agreeable employer?" She was puzzled over the way James had snapped at him the night before.

"Most agreeable."

"Would you describe him as a difficult taskmaster?"

He pursed his lips. "He demands much of me, but he tempers his demands with consideration. It would not be difficult for me to understand what an outstanding officer he was when he served in India."

Since James had come to Yarmouth straight from India, Carlotta realized that Mr. Fordyce must not be acquainted with the fact that James had also served in Spain, Portugal, and at Waterloo. She was unaccountably proud of him, and had to fight the urge to enlighten the secretary on her husband's military accomplishments.

"Tell me, how does one go about becoming a secretary?" she asked.

He gave a shy laugh. "One doesn't set about to become a secretary. In my case, when I left Cambridge—after an undistinguished two years there—a friend recommended me to the previous Earl Rutledge, who at the time was seeking a new secretary."

"And the position suits you?"

He thought for a moment before replying. "My own capabilities, it would seem, are perfectly suited to this position. It's rather simpatico, actually."

Simpatico. The very word she had used to describe how well suited James was to her.

Smiling, she stood up. "I've taken enough of your time. I wish to get to know you, as his lordship tells me I will have the liberty of using your services when needed."

He hastened to his feet. "Services it will be my pleasure to give."

"Oh, there you are," James's voice thundered from behind her.

Carlotta spun around to face her husband, who directed an angry gaze at her.

Sixteen

James's angry gaze upset Carlotta. This brooding man bore little resemblance to the man whose kindnesses had won her favor and secured her hand in marriage. Meeting his flashing eyes with only bare civility, she brushed past him and spoke icily. "You wanted me, my lord?" Knowing how greatly he disliked her addressing him as *my lord,* she had thrown the title in to spite him.

A sudden, painful grip on her arm stopped her in mid-stride. She spun around to see his hand coiled around her arm and the fury in his eyes. He closed the hidden doorway behind him, then spoke to her in a guttural voice. "You are never to address me as *my lord,* Carlotta."

The corners of her mouth lifted with false mirth. "But you're acting so very lordly, dearest."

He released her arm and began to move further into the library. "I'm out of charity with you, if you must know."

She stopped abruptly and shot him a scorching gaze. "Pray, what could I have possibly done to draw your wrath?" she asked, her voice quivering. "I honestly have no idea."

He indicated a seat on the sopha nearest the fire. She narrowed her gaze and flung herself down into the silk cushions. James was treating her as if she were a servant.

"I've been looking all over for you," he said. "You could have shown the courtesy of allowing me to know your direction."

Her eyes blazed with anger. "You had only to ask Mrs. MacGinnis. She knew very well where I was." She glared at him and spoke coolly. "Furthermore, it was not my understanding that I was to inform you of my every move. Am I to be treated only as your chattel?"

He winced and ran a hand through his sandy hair. "Forgive me," he said in a gentle voice, coming to sit beside her and take her hand.

Unaccountably, her stomach fluttered when he did so, undoubtedly due to the combination of so gentle a voice and the warmth of his big hand. "You must confess, James, since we have arrived at Yarmouth, you've been a veritable bear."

He nodded remorsefully. "While you, on the other hand, my love, have behaved in such a manner as to make me swell with pride."

She looked up at him with hopeful eyes. "I have?"

"You will make a fine countess, Carlotta."

She agonized over her own unworthiness, yet beamed at his compliment. "I meant it when I told your staff last night I would learn each and every one of their names. I started with Mr. Fordyce, but I perceive you do not care for him."

James shook his head. "But I do! He's extremely competent."

"If awfully shy."

"The shyness is merely a barrier he erects with women. Fordyce has had little intercourse with the fairer sex."

"Then he is more congenial with you?"

"Not at first, but we get on well together now."

"It's my ardent wish that your ill humor with him doesn't send him running to a new employer."

"I've been that bad?"

"You have been a positive ogre. I pray Stevie never sees that side of you. The child is far too young and sensitive to understand the shifting moods of a step-father."

His eyes went cold. "I beg that you not refer to me as Stevie's stepfather. It's my greatest wish that the Yarmouth staff come to think of him as my own son—though I vow I shall never let the boy forget the fine man who was his real father."

She squeezed his hand. "Being treated as your own child, I believe, is what will make Stevie happiest, too."

"Speaking of Stevie, I thought you and I could walk with him to the stables he's so keen to see."

"It's a fine day to explore your lands."

"Our lands," he said.

"Oh dear, I don't know if I shall ever become accustomed to all of this."

"A year ago I felt the same." He glanced at the window. "You've been out today?" he asked.

"No, but I gazed out at the wonderful parterre garden and saw how brightly the sun is shining. I shall be pleased to accompany you and Stevie. He's already outdoors because it's his mother's belief that sunshine is good for children—provided the air is free from chilling winds, that is."

"I agree with you. I was an exceedingly healthy lad and was rarely indoors."

Her glance swept over him, over his lightly bronzed face and well-muscled body. He looked to enjoy extraordinarily good health. "You still spend a great deal of time outdoors?"

He laughed. "Nothing when compared to the hours I was outdoors as a child, but if the sun's out, I'm out. I don't like it when Ebony does not get exercised."

"I take it Ebony is your mount."

He nodded. "You'll see him today. Do you ride?"

"I do, but not well. My grandmother could never afford to keep a stable. Stephen presented me with a horse when we lived in Portugal and insisted I become proficient at handling her. Keeping a mount in Portugal, as you know, was less expensive than in England."

"Everything was less expensive in Portugal! And in India."

"You had a batman?"

"He's with me still. Mannington, my valet, is my former batman."

"It seems I learn something new about you every day."

He grinned. "Enough of me. The sun is wasting. Shall we go find Stevie?"

If James had swelled with pride over his bride the night before, then today his pride was increasing tenfold as he and the wife and son he had chosen walked over the land that had come to mean so much to him. Though he had not been born to Yarmouth, it had become as vital to him as breathing. He had walked every inch of the estates, had inspected every dark crevice in the mines, had learned every servant and employee by name.

It was hard to believe he had not spent his entire life here. During the past year he had rectified that by becoming an astute student of the Rutledge family. He had learned the first earl's title had been bestowed upon him by Queen Elizabeth, and the second earl had been the first to reap riches from the mines located between the Hall and the Bristol Channel. He had discovered his great-grandfather was the earl who had fathered fourteen children.

As he and his new family covered the velvet-like expanse of green parkland, he found himself wondering if his children would ever succeed to the earldom, or—he wondered morosely—would his title pass to one of the Moore cousins he had never met?

"Is Bwownie here yet, Papa?" Stevie asked.

Papa. It was the first time the lad had addressed him thus. Nothing purchased with mere money could have meant so much to James. "Not yet, but today I shall allow you to ride on my mount with me."

Stevie's little steps covered only half the distance of James's. "What's your mount's name?" the boy asked.

"Ebony."

"Do you know what Ebony means, Stevie?" Carlotta asked.

He shook his head, his fair hair flying from side to side.

"It's another name for black."

"Then Papa and I are simpatico, too," the boy said.

"Why?" she asked.

"Because I named my pony for the color bwown, and he named his for black."

"I declare, we are simpatico," James said, "but how did such a small boy learn such a big word?"

"I learned it back in Bath. Mama said you and she were simpatico, and I asked her what that meant."

His heart soaring, James tossed a glance at his

wife, who looked up at him nervously. To his complete surprise, color hiked up her smooth cheeks, something he had never before witnessed in his confident wife.

"I daresay that's what I said when I learned you have more than a passing interest in poetry," she explained.

He smiled smugly. He had a new favorite word.

"James?" Carlotta interrupted his thoughts. "I declare, there's a saltiness in the air."

"That, my dear, is because we're not far from the sea."

"Can we see the sea?" Stevie asked.

"May we," Carlotta corrected with a playful smile.

At the stable, James and Stevie went from one stall to another, with James telling the boy each horse's name, but when the boy asked for the horses' ages, James had to defer to the undergroom, Jeremy, who was already beginning to saddle Ebony.

While James and Stevie examined each and every horse, Carlotta began a conversation with Jeremy.

Though James continued to stroke a flank or help Stevie feed a carrot to one horse after another, James grew angry as he listened to his wife laughing with the handsome young groom. His thoughts flashed back to Portugal and how well Carlotta had mixed with the bachelor soldiers there. Though he had never known of any impropriety connected with her, he had always thought her an outrageous flirt and wondered how her husband could have tolerated such brazen behavior.

Sweet heavens! What had he himself been thinking to have taken this woman for his bride? When he had found her in Bath, she had seemed nothing more than a demure widow. But just last night she admitted to a previous attachment to a man she had *not* married! Surely he had not allowed a lightskirt to become the new Countess Rutledge!

A blue funk settled over him.

Once Jeremy had Ebony and a gentle filly saddled, James hoisted Stevie on Ebony, then with Jeremy giving him a leg up, James joined the lad on top of the mount.

Later, as Carlotta and her husband were cantering seaward, she asked, "And what is my horse's name?"

"Merry May," he said. "She was born the May before I arrived."

"You're so knowledgeable about Yarmouth, it seems as if you've always been here," she said.

He smiled. "As it seems to me. I'm content here."

"I believe I shall be, too," she said wistfully.

It was difficult to stay angry with her. She had a facility for saying what he wished to hear.

Though he had intended to ride as far as the sea, his wife had other ideas.

"Oh, James, I have so been hungering to stroll through the parterre garden with you."

He began to rein in his horse in the direction of the hall. "I can't have my wife hungering," he said teasingly.

She did not deign to look at him after his suggestive comment.

Soon, they were tethering their horses near the garden.

"I want to ride Ebony," Stevie protested, a pout on his unhappy face.

James reached down and ruffled the boy's hair. "We will soon enough, son. A man has to learn that to promote harmony in his household, he must allow the women to have their way."

With a smile, Carlotta directed a look of mock

outrage at her husband. "You make it sound as if I'm a veritable shrew!"

Smiling devilishly, James came to offer her his arm.

They began to stroll among the parterre garden's many crisscross paths. "I assume the parterre garden was here when you inherited," she said.

He chuckled. "It was here, but it had become overgrown with weeds. It seems my uncle never replaced the elder gardener when he died, leaving one man in charge of all the gardening on the estate."

"With all the improvements you've made at Yarmouth and at the mines, it's a wonder you have any money at all left."

His brows lowered. "How have you come into possession of such information?"

"Most of it comes from Mrs. MacGinnis, who claims you hung the moon."

"I daresay she's delusional." He patted his wife's hand. "Never fear, my love, my estates—our estates now—can afford the expenditures I've made."

She stopped to pick a red tulip. "The older I become, the fewer my needs are. Jewels and ball gowns have ceased to hold allure for me. Give me a garden, poetry, a child . . . an agreeable husband and the peace obtainable only in the country and I shall be happy."

"Then the woman I knew in The Peninsula has ceased to exist," he said somberly.

She gazed at him and spoke in a faraway voice. "So she has."

"Somehow, my love, I cannot picture you with shovel and hoe in a garden."

A little laugh broke from her. " 'Tis because I have not been in possession of either since my eighteenth year, but I assure you before that if I did not have my head in a poetry book, I had shovel in hand and was puttering in my grandmama's garden—which was not nearly so beautiful as yours."

"Then you plan to garden here at Yarmouth?"

"With the greatest satisfaction!" Her glance skimmed across the landscape from east to west. "Tell me, what is the name of the gardener who takes care of all this?" She waved her arms over the geometrical plots of various colors.

He paused a moment. "Richards. Does he not do a fine job?"

"Oh, he does. I'm eager to know what flowers he will set out when spring comes."

"You are at liberty to visit the greenhouse and see them for yourself."

"I believe I'm in heaven," she said with a smile.

They walked along every path in the garden, with Carlotta occasionally stooping to remove a fledgling weed or to pick flowers for a bouquet she planned to make. James's thoughts wandered to the days he had walked these paths alone, and he had longed to share it all with another being whose life would be irrevocably linked to his own. He lifted that woman's hand and kissed it.

"Tomorrow, my love, I shall take you to the mines," he said.

Her brows dipped. "Will I have to go in them?"

He studied her face. It was creased with emotion. At last he realized it was fear. "I'll never make you do anything that's unpleasant to you, Carlotta."

Seventeen

"Then the mines are between Yarmouth and the sea?" Carlotta asked her husband the next day as they rode their mounts side by side across the farmland surrounding Yarmouth Hall.

His eyes alighted on her, and he nodded. In her deep purple velvet riding habit, she was a feast for his—or any man's—eyes. Perhaps taking Carlotta to the mines was not such a good plan. After all, the miners would have to return home to their plain wives tonight after beholding the extraordinary beauty of Lady Rutledge.

James had thought by bringing her to the mines he could demonstrate his family's personal interest in the colliers. It never occurred to him he would appear to be flaunting his good fortune.

Soon the farmland where his sheep prospered was behind them, and they were surrounded by a steep, densely wooded area of uneven land. "This looks as I pictured Sherwood Forest when I was a child," she said.

"Actually, much of this was a royal hunting preserve dating back to Henry the Eighth."

"How could the crown ever give this up? It's so beautiful here."

"My feelings exactly. It pleases me that you feel the same as I," he said.

"Only a blind person could fail to honor such natural glory."

Natural glory. It was easy to imagine his wife a poetess. "Do you write poetry?" he asked.

She shook her head, her blue-black tresses catching on the wind. "I'm much too discerning in my poetic taste to please myself."

"Then you've tried your hand?"

She laughed. "Very crude efforts, I'm afraid."

"Have you attempted any of those crude efforts since I've become acquainted with you?"

"Twice, actually," she replied after a moment. "Once after watching my angelic son sleep, the other the night you offered for me."

Carlotta had written a poem about him! He felt the same as he had after a schoolboy fight when the wind had been knocked from him. The exultation which filled him quickly gave way to curiosity. "If I might be so bold as to ask," he finally ventured, "what emotions did my proposal inspire in you, and," he added in jest, "I pray *fear* is not among them."

"I could never fear you, James," she said in a gentle voice. "You've been far too good to me—except when you're in one of your ill humors as you were yesterday morning."

"Forgive me," he said. She had not precisely answered his question. He had thought to repeat his query but decided against it. She obviously still did not feel comfortable enough to discuss her emotions with him. Nor did he with her, for that matter.

"I must tell you, James, I had the most difficult time understanding Jeremy yesterday. It's as if he's speaking in a foreign tongue. I don't think I'd ever really spoken to him before."

James chuckled. "You've now had a conversation with a born-and-bred Exmoor *man of the hills,* as they like to call themselves. In time, you should come to understand their dialect."

"In Yorkshire I always prided myself on being able to understand many of the local dialects, but I declare this West County talk is something altogether different."

"You had more Viking influences in the north. Here, the people remained Celts."

She could feel her breathing change as the altitude climbed. "In what ways are these men of the hills different from other men?"

"It's said that men of the hills are forced to live a more rugged life. Like the Scots, the men in these parts fancy themselves almost invincible with their might. Were they to be called to bear arms, no doubt they would distinguish themselves."

"The miners are hill men, too?"

He nodded. "To a man, they're a rugged lot."

" 'Tis a rugged job," she said with a shiver.

"How is it you know the perils of mining so well?"

"There are mines in Yorkshire. And mining disasters. I must have been at a most impressionable age during one particular disaster, where a shaft caved in, burying several men alive. It has always struck me as the most brutal death possible."

"Exactly what I did *not* wish to hear on a day when I plan to go down into the mines," he said in an attempt at levity.

"I do not understand why, if you're prosperous, you insist on taking so active an interest in the mines. There are mines on Lord Worth's estates in Yorkshire, and he has a most agreeable arrangement with a mining company that works the mine in exchange for a percentage of the ore's value. To my knowledge, Lord Worth's never stepped foot in the mines and is in no way responsible for them."

James rode ahead and lifted low-lying branches to ease her passage through this particular gully. "I take it you don't approve of my role in the mines."

She shrugged. "I have no control over what happened or what you did before I married you."

"But, nevertheless, you disapprove of my interest in the mines."

"Do you not have a man who manages them for you?"

"I do."

"Then I don't see why you jeopardize yourself."

"It's the way I am, Carlotta. It was the same when I was in the military. If my men are at risk, then I, too, must be at risk."

"I don't approve."

He shot her a mischievous smile. "One would think you actually cared for me. You realize I've made arrangements that will leave you a very rich woman if something should happen to me."

She winced. "Money—even great amounts of it—cannot replace people, and I should prefer to have my husband than his money."

"May I ask why?" His heart soaring, he watched her classic profile as she directed her gaze at the path before her.

"I don't know how to put it. Before I knew you my life was cold and gray and hopeless, and since you've come into it there's warmth and purpose and someone to share everything with and . . . a future I look forward to." She gazed up at him, her great eyes shimmering. "These are not things obtainable with money."

Sweet heavens! She might not love him, but what she felt for him was in many ways as special. He wanted to yank her from her mount and kiss her passionately. Instead, he rode on in silence, a thick lump in his throat.

Some little while later she broke the silence. "I hope you don't mind that I didn't wish to bring Stevie today. I did not want to color his opinions about the mines with my own fears."

"I trust he's far happier with Peggy and Jeremy."

"And Brownie," she added. "One would think that animal was a long-time member of the family, he adores it so." Her glance darted off to a heath just below them where several ponies ran wild. "Speaking of Brownie, I declare that pony over there must be his twin!"

His glance followed hers. "That's an Exmoor pony. They're completely wild here—and unique to Exmoor."

"Then I take it, Brownie's an Exmoor pony?"

"He is, but was raised at Yarmouth from a foal."

"Now I shall worry the animal will wish to return to the wild—with my son on his back!"

"It's not a matter of returning. He's never been in the wild and wouldn't know how to forage. He's had life much too easy ever to want to join his kin."

They rode toward a swift stream. "We'll follow the stream to the mine," he told her.

For the next ten minutes they followed the water, breathing in the pungent smells of the forest. Then Carlotta eyed the churning of a huge wooden wheel that was nearly as tall as Yarmouth.

"Is that where the mine is?" she asked.

"Just beyond. The wheel provides our power for pumping."

Soon they came upon the main mine, where a

dozen or so black-faced males were coming and going.

"Who lives in that house?" Carlotta asked, pointing to a nearby white cottage.

"The mine's captain."

"And his name is . . . ?"

"Hastings. He's been here for fifteen years."

They dismounted, and James took her hand. She felt unaccountably nervous. First, she feared she would not be able to understand a word the men said. It was important to her husband, she knew, that she be at ease with the colliers and them with her. She was also afraid one of them might touch her, and she did not welcome the prospect of being streaked with black coal dust.

These men must be hungry indeed, she thought, to choose a life working in the coal mines.

A tall, huskily built man who was less grimy than the others came striding toward them after they tethered their horses. He bowed to them.

Carlotta found his appearance most peculiar. Clear green eyes stared at her from his black face. Her eyes traveled to his hands, which were also black. His curly golden hair belied the fact that before his mining days he must have been fair skinned. His clothing, of good quality, was less black than that of the colliers she saw nearby.

"Ah, Hastings, allow me to make you known to the new Lady Rutledge," James said.

So this was the man who ran the mine, she thought. The captain.

"Forgive me for not taking your hand, my lady, but my reasons for such abstinence should be abundantly clear."

This man did not speak like one from Exmoor. "I am delighted to make your acquaintance, Mr. Hastings. That the mines are in your capable hands is most reassuring to my husband."

Now he addressed her husband. " 'Tis good to have you back, my lord. The men were beginning to fear you were never returning."

"Exmoor's now my home," James said. "I'll not be leaving it."

Hastings turned his attention to the new Lady Rutledge. "Permit me to give you an orientation to the facility," he said, turning back in the direction from which he had come.

She passed wagons heaped with coal coming and going from the mine shaft, and all the men who handled them were black from head to foot. She wondered if they ever bathed or if the coal had embedded itself so deeply into their skin that it rendered cleaning impossible.

At first she thought some of the men quite small, especially since James had been telling her about the ruggedness of men of the hills. She thought she would not wish these fellows to be protecting her in the event of a war.

Then one turned around. And she saw that it was a lad who could not have seen more than ten summers. Thinking of her own little Stevie, she was filled with outrage, but she would defer speaking of it because of her desire to please James—James who deserved some display of loyalty from her.

Her husband began to introduce her to the colliers, and as she had feared, she could not understand a word they said. She merely bestowed an enormous smile upon them and nodded as if she knew quite well what they were saying.

It nearly broke her heart to count a total of five

lads working here above ground, and she prayed none were down in the pits. No sooner had she thought these thoughts, when a tiny lad not much larger than Stevie emerged from the mine, completely black from head to toe.

Her smile vanished.

James called that lad by name. "Willy, I beg that you go back in and tell the miners I wish them to take a break and come meet the new Lady Rutledge. I daresay, she's not receptive to the idea of going under."

The lad, apparently understanding every word her genteel husband spoke, smiled and disappeared back into the mine.

Within minutes another twenty or so colliers filed out of the mine, and Carlotta found herself smiling widely and nodding at a sea of black faces. Once the introductions were complete, James dismissed the men to return to their duties; then James began a discussion with one of them, and she was unable to understand a word they said. James was using technical language, and the collier spoke with an indistinguishable West County tongue.

She turned to Hastings. "How many men have you working here?"

"Thirty, plus me."

"Is it one of those situations where if their father and grandfather were colliers, then the sons have no choice but to follow?"

His face clouded. "Aye, that it is."

"But you, Mr. Hastings, had a choice."

"Engineering's in my blood. The captainship followed."

"You're married?"

He gave a bitter laugh. "I came here with a bride, fifteen years ago. She soon discovered she wanted no part of mining life, and ran off with a horse trader."

Carlotta's brows lowered. "I'm sorry." Sorry she had summoned so personal a response. He elicited much sympathy for the personal sacrifices he had made for the mines, yet she also empathized with the wife who had run off. As beautiful as Exmoor was, Carlotta abhorred the mines. And, after thinking on it, she thought she would also abhor being intimate with a coal-covered man.

James finished his conversation and turned back to her. "Forgive me, love, but I'll have to go down in the mines. I promise I shan't be long." He tossed a glance at Hastings. "Be a good man and offer my wife a cup of tea."

Her heart in her throat, she watched as James descended into the mine. She did not at all wish to think of her husband being down in the pits.

"Follow me, if you please, my lady," Hastings said, moving toward his two-story cottage.

There, he instructed his cook to put on the tea, and he offered Carlotta a wooden chair. "You won't get dirty in this chair," he said. "I avoid it so I'll have a clean chair when visitors come." Glancing around his tidy cottage, he added, "You'll have to pardon that it looks so filthy here. We learn to live with the soot."

The man spoke the truth. Despite the fact that everything was orderly, the walls were gray with the soot, as were the curtains and the pieces of upholstered furniture. Yes, she could well understand how a gently bred woman could run away from such a life.

"Then you have visitors here?"

He laughed. "Occasionally."

From her chair near the hearth, she glanced

around the cottage with its thick stone walls. "Your home is cozy," she told him.

Despite the coziness, she could not put a stop to the trembling inside her. She feared for James.

Mr. Hastings looked her in the eye. "You're just like Alice—my wife. You hate the mines."

"Then it shows?"

"I know the signs. Hopefully the miners don't. Their wives apparently accept it."

"As I must. Though I'd as lief not."

"Don't worry. Thanks to your husband, the mines are most likely the safest in England."

"I wish I could take comfort in your words." She watched the door, hoping James would hurry and come.

As she sat there she was struck by the contrast between Mr. Fordyce and Mr. Hastings. Both men had only just met her, but one seemed ill at ease in her company while the other established an easy camaraderie. Perhaps it was the difference in their ages. Mr. Fordyce had most likely not reached his twenty-fifth year, and Mr. Hastings was likely forty.

She looked up when Mr. Hasting's middle-aged cook, an apron tied round her waist, brought their tea tray and set it on a table in front of the sopha where Mr. Hastings sat. Carlotta came to pour the tea into two ironstone cups. "I think what disturbs me most—next to having my husband hundreds of feet below the ground—is the age of some of the lads I saw here today." She handed his cup and saucer to him. "Why must you employ them?"

"What else would they do?"

"What did you do when you were ten or eleven?" He set down his cup. "I was in school."

"As were my husband and my brother."

"But there are no schools for the lads of their class, and their size can be most helpful in mining."

"They're only children! Besides the dangers, they are too young to be responsible for life-or-death procedures. You allow your safety to be held in one of their small hands?"

"They're well trained."

Her cup clattered into the saucer. "But they're children."

The door opened and James stepped into the room. "What children are we talking about?" he asked, his eyes settling on her.

She gazed at her husband with narrowed eyes. Now he, too, was covered with soot. "The mere lads whom you allow to work in the mines."

"We'll discuss this when we're alone," he snapped. "Are you ready to return to Yarmouth?"

She set down her cup. "I am."

On the way back to Yarmouth, she broached the subject of her dissatisfaction that boys were employed in the mines.

He glared angrily at her. "I beg you never express your opinions in front of the colliers."

She stiffened. "I would not because I know it would displease my husband."

"Perhaps I shan't have you come here ever again."

She jerked up her head haughtily. "Then you plan to tell me where I can and cannot go?"

He muttered an oath. "Woman, you are trying my patience."

"Forgive me," she said without sincerity. "If my words displease you, I shan't speak to you the rest of the way home."

And she didn't.

Eighteen

Though he was vexed with his wife, at dinner that night James attempted to put his anger behind him. He would put from his mind Carlotta's stubborn silence that afternoon and treat her as if they had chatted contentedly all the way back to Yarmouth. His plan worked. Once Carlotta realized James was not going to dredge up the afternoon's disagreement, she readily returned his amiable banter throughout the remainder of the dinner.

"I see that you have been successful in removing the coal from your skin," she remarked while spooning potatoes onto her plate.

"A bath is all that was needed."

"Yet I perceive the colliers certainly do not bathe every day."

He shrugged. "They're used to the soot, and I daresay their families are, too."

Carlotta grimaced. "Then I'm thankful my husband is of a different ilk, for I could never get used to the horrid blackness. Did you see how grimy Mr. Hastings's house was? I declare, everywhere you looked was either black or gray. It's so dreary."

James smiled at hearing himself addressed as her husband. A short time earlier, though, he had been unable to smile. When she had glided into the dining room, the sight of her and the lavender scent of her had nearly overpowered him. Her graceful movement and the intensity of her beauty caused a profound physical reaction in him. He had thought that by now he would have become immune to her, but she still wielded an almost magical power over him.

Even now, as she cut the mutton on the plate before her, he watched her hungrily. Soft candlelight from one of the overhead chandeliers cast a circle of light where she sat. Her glossy hair was swept back from her pensive face, and her lashes swooped down as she concentrated on her cutting. His eyes trailed over her flawless, milky skin from her brow down to her romanesque nose, to her slender neck, to the plunging bodice of her orchid silk gown.

"I beg that we avoid discussion of the mines tonight," he said. Eventually, he knew, they would have to discuss their differing views on the subject, but not tonight. Not after this afternoon's estrangement. Tonight he only wanted peace.

Next, he directed his attention to Stevie, whom they had agreed could continue sharing their dinner until his nurse arrived. James had warned Carlotta that Stevie would likely be uncomfortable in another new setting and should be permitted to dine with them during his first week at Yarmouth.

"To make up to you for not taking you to the mines today," James said to the boy, "tomorrow you'll have my full attention. Should you like to go angling?"

Stevie's eyes grew large, as did the smile which seemed almost too big for his small face. "I should love it above all things!"

James tossed a glance at Carlotta. "I don't suppose angling appeals to you, my love?"

She shook her head. "About as much as sitting

and watching my grandmother read the Bible," she said with a wink and a giggle. "Tomorrow should be a day just for the males. I'm certain you'll have a much better time without me. I have a profound aversion to worms." She paused. "Besides, there are so many new poetry books here that I'm longing to read. I shall just curl up before the fire in your library and read the live-long day."

" 'Tis not *my* library, but ours," James countered.

"I confess it's not with ease that I can call all of this mine. To do so would make me seem a usurper."

James laughed. "But how could you usurp anyone since I've neither been married nor engaged, and the last Yarmouth countess died two decades ago?"

She shrugged. "If I'm not a usurper, then I fear I seem mercenary. Don't forget, just a few months ago I was living in rented lodgings in a not-too-genteel rooming house."

He reached out to set his hand on hers. "You're not mercenary."

Stevie, his brow wrinkled with concentration, glanced at James. "Papa?"

James's heart quickened. "Yes, son?"

"Do you have a fishing pole for me?"

"I do. You will have your very own."

"I wish it were already tomorrow," the boy said.

" 'Twill be soon enough, lamb," Carlotta said in a gentle voice.

James had swelled with pride when the boy had called him Papa, then again when he saw what tenderness Stevie elicited from Carlotta. For a flash of a second, James wondered if Carlotta would be equally as gentle with a child of theirs. His heart grew light, his chest tightened, and a lump formed in his throat for love of the child that might never be.

Since he had brought Carlotta to Yarmouth as his

wife, James's seesaw emotions were in a constant state of turmoil. As he watched Carlotta, burgeoning desire once more swept through him. How long would he have to wait to possess her? Fear gripped him. Would his thirst for her ever be slaked? He could go mad with his want of her. He doubted he could wait much longer.

Since she had confessed that her affections had been engaged somewhat recently, jealousy had consumed James. Hatred toward this unknown man surged within him. Who was the man? How could he have been unable to return Carlotta's ardor? James wished him to hell.

When dinner was finished, Carlotta turned to James. "I shall just run along upstairs to tuck Stevie in with a bedtime story."

"I'll go with you," James said.

The three of them ascended the stairs, talking and laughing and making plans for the morrow. After Stevie dressed for bed, it was James whom Stevie wanted to tell him a story.

James and Carlotta sat side by side on the edge of the boy's bed while James told the lad a tale of the good farmer who slayed one of the wicked Doone bandits. Though Carlotta had once protested that stories of violence and death were not *bedtime* stories, Stevie could never seem to get enough of them—and, she had to admit, with no ill effects to her son.

After each of them kissed the lad on the cheek, James and Carlotta went back downstairs to the saloon, where the servants had set up a card table in front of the fire.

"Should you like some brandy?" James asked her.

She nodded as she sat at the table.

Moments later the two faced one another, and

James began to instruct her how to play cribbage. She caught on quickly, and to his surprise, she was not just playing to please him. She actually wanted to win. Which was an excellent start.

As the play grew more intense and the brandy bottle less full, Carlotta mellowed before his eyes.

"You, my dear," he said, "are possessed of an excellent, quick mind. I look forward to many years of looking across the game table at my lovely bride."

Her finger twirling her hair, she smiled across the table at him. "Has anyone ever called you Jim or Jimmy?"

He shook his head. "My mother thought James a more commanding name, more fitting for my future importance," he added with a wink.

"I should have liked your mother," she said. "You realize you are an important man?"

He laughed. "The Lord of Exmoor."

"I wasn't thinking of the way others here perceive you, though they most certainly find you a very important personage. I was thinking of how important you've become to Stevie and me."

"As have you and Stevie to me," he answered, hoping his voice held the steadiness the rest of him presently lacked.

She blushed as she advanced her peg.

"Should you wish to call me Jim or Jimmy?" he asked.

She looked at him with her great violet eyes. "Sometimes, when the brandy has rendered me warm and pliable, I wish to call you Jimmy, but I don't think the name suits you nearly as well as James."

Warm and pliable. It was difficult to keep his mind on cribbage when he thought of his wife as *warm and pliable.*

* * *

What a fool he must think her! The mental picture of herself, thick-tongued from the brandy, addressing Lord Rutledge as *Jimmy* was utterly ridiculous.

It was important to her that he find her not only intelligent but also a worthy opponent for the games he enjoyed every night. She must concentrate on her play so her skill could compel him to forget her foolish behavior.

Playing the nightly games with her husband was small repayment for all he had done for her and Stevie. She pictured James as he had looked when he had told Stevie the manly story at bedtime. He gave every indication he enjoyed relating the story as much as Stevie enjoyed listening to it.

And tomorrow, she thought with satisfaction, her *men* would spend the day together fishing.

Because of Stevie, James had come into her life and filled it. The earl was completely devoted to the boy. She doubted he could care more for the lad had he been his own son.

Thinking of the earl having a son of his own—or not having a son of his own—saddened her. He deserved a son and heir. And as a man, he surely desired the intimacy which could produce that child, though she thought he had seemed content with their nonphysical relationship.

Or had he? There had been instances when she had caught him looking at her hungrily. At least, that was how she had perceived it. A man, after all, did not have to be in love with a woman to desire to make love to her. It was the nature of men. And the Earl of Rutledge was most certainly a man.

His looks of naked desire puzzled her. Were she

one to wager, she would have wagered James married her because of his affection for her son—as well as his guilt over what had happened to Stephen. Never because he wanted her. Surely, he couldn't even like her. He knew her many faults better than anyone else on earth.

Since she had first met James, she had been struck by his seeming immunity to her physical attributes. For anyone else to think such conceited thoughts about her own appearance would be sheer arrogance. For Carlotta, it was like commenting on the weather. Compliments on her beauty had always been as commonplace as observations on the day's sunshine.

She drew a card and matched it with another in her hand. James, she lamented, deserved her unwavering physical affection. Why could she not be attracted him?

It wasn't actually that she was not attracted to him. She was. Not only was he the finest man she knew, he was also possessed of a high level of intelligence and a handsome appearance.

She thought the reason she had been unaffected by James's many charms could be laid at the door of Gregory Blankenship. After Gregory, she had been injured so deeply and her pain was so all-encompassing, she had lost the ability to feel. To feel was to be exposed to hurt.

When she thought of Gregory now, however, her stomach no longer vaulted. In fact, during the past few weeks, she had come to realize she could finally think of Gregory without experiencing a single stab of pain. She had finally accepted that Gregory was in love with his wife. And she, Carlotta, was no longer in love with Gregory Blankenship. If only she could fall in love with James.

She stifled a yawn.

"At the end of this hand," James said in a gentle voice, "we shall have to call it a night. You're tired."

"So I am," she said through another yawn, as her hand covered her gaping mouth.

When they finished the hand, they agreed to continue the game the following night. She and James mounted the stairs together, his hand resting possessively at her waist.

At her door he paused, and she lifted her face to his for a kiss.

Nineteen

The feel of her soft lips brushing against his was wildly intoxicating. Even better—or at least as good—was the knowledge that she had initiated the kiss. He drew her into his arms and she, too, slipped her arms around him. He thought he would explode with need when her lips parted and the kiss deepened.

Moments later, though, she released her arms and drew away, stepping back into the door to her chamber. His soaring heart sank. For a moment he had allowed himself to believe she wanted him in her bed. Now he realized it was only an illusion conjured by his own starvation.

His lips a straight line, he nodded to her as if the passionate kiss had never occurred. "Good night, my dear."

He started toward his own chamber as she called to him, "Good night, James." He fought the urge to return to her and gather her into his embrace. But he had to preserve his pride, as fragile as it was, though his maddening wife made it difficult.

As he lay in bed that night he questioned his own sanity in allowing himself to be so closely exposed to Carlotta day after wretched day. Every hour he was in her presence was another hour of torture.

His constant companionship, he realized with a deep, wrenching grief, had not had the effect he had hoped for. He had thought their continued proximity would result in his wife growing to love him.

Perhaps if he were not always in her pocket . . . That gave him an idea. Perhaps he should begin to distance himself. If his presence became scarce, she might come to crave his company. He remembered how delighted she had been to see him after his long absence from Bath.

As difficult as it would be to deny himself the pleasure of being with her, he vowed to stay away as much as he could.

Before he fell asleep, he came up with a framework that would henceforth guide him in his dealings with Carlotta.

That first day her husband had taken Stevie fishing, Carlotta had enjoyed being alone. Since it was somewhat gray, she basked in a comforting warmth sitting before the fire rereading Shakespeare's sonnets.

Little did she know that day was only the first of many from which James would exclude her. The day after that he spent with his steward, after that with his secretary, after that at the mines; then, he started all over with Stevie again. James decided Stevie was experienced enough in the saddle to learn the finer points of riding, and he set about teaching them to his stepson.

Carlotta sent to Bath for painters and linen drapers and busied herself making decisions on the redecoration of her chambers and Stevie's.

When Stevie's nurse came, Carlotta felt herself

even less needed, for her son and Miss Kenworth
quickly slipped into a comfortable familiarity.

Miss Kenworth had a cheerful countenance and
quick mind to go with her acute sense of humor.
Added to all these attributes was her keen understanding of and interest in what young boys liked
best. If Stevie wished to play soldiers, she was down
on the floor joining him. Were the lad desirous of
playing hide-and-seek in the woods, she would attempt to conceal her roundness behind a stout tree.
If imprisoning a family of frogs was what pleased
Stevie, Miss Kenworth would endeavor to hunt them
with her charge. In short, whatever Stevie wanted,
Miss Kenworth aspired to allow him.

Carlotta no longer worried that her son lacked
for playmates, for in Miss Kenworth he had the
greatest playmate of all: one who always did exactly
what he wished to do.

Before Miss Kenworth had been six weeks at Yarmouth, Stevie was reading eagerly. He was also
learning to do his sums because James felt com-
pelled to impart such knowledge on a daily basis.
Both of her son's teachers praised Stevie's keen in-
tellect. Not that she saw her husband with any fre-
quency. On most nights he took dinner with her,
and on some nights they played games after dinner.
But never again did her husband give her another
passionate good-night kiss.

She supposed he did not desire her, after all. He
had only married her because of Stevie.

One night at dinner, he asked her if she would
like to entertain guests.

His question startled her. "Who, pray tell, would
we entertain?" she asked, looking up at her stern-
faced husband.

He shrugged. "The gentry from hereabouts?"

Her brows shot up. "I was unaware there was gentry hereabouts. I thought, perhaps, we were hours from anywhere, save that mine of yours."

"Then you've been too much isolated."

Her hand coiled around the stem of her glass. "Honestly, James, I've not felt isolated. I love it here at Yarmouth, even though I have only you and Stevie for companionship—and despite your not being a particularly close companion as of late."

He chuckled. "What of other women? I thought women required other women."

Her heated glance flicked to him. "You know I'm not like other women."

"Then what of the admiration of men, my dear? In Portugal, you always seemed to thrive on men's adulation."

She could not deny his claim. Sadly, he spoke the truth. Even though she had never acted upon any of the flirtations, she had—at that time—required them. With crippling guilt, she had later come to regret her flirtatious manner. Stephen had deserved a wife who was far more devoted to him than she had ever been.

"As one grows older," she said, "one regrets the things one does in one's youth."

James gave out a little laugh. "Quoth the graybeard of five and twenty."

After the sweetmeats were laid, he revisited the subject. "Why do not you and Fordyce work together on a guest list for a dinner party to be held at Yarmouth?"

Her stomach dropped. She had no desire to entertain, to have her own home invaded by someone who might know of her past and use that information to estrange her husband from her. Or to estrange him more than he already was. But James asked for so very little, if this was important to him . . . "I am perfectly happy not entertaining, but if it would please you, I will get together with Mr. Fordyce tomorrow," she said.

"I have all the social intercourse I need. It's you I'm concerned about." Though his tone was light, something in his manner convinced her his worry was genuine.

She held her head high and bestowed a smile upon her husband. "You need have no worries on my account. I'm blissfully happy, especially now that spring has arrived."

He picked up his fork and spoke casually. "I notice that you've taken to wearing a bonnet when you work in the garden."

"I was unaware you noticed me at all," she chastised.

"When I'm doing something else, I occasionally spare a glance at the lady of the manor with a bonnet on her head. At first I did not believe that was my Carlotta because my Carlotta does not wear bonnets."

My Carlotta. Oddly, his words pleased her. "I am in the sun so much, I've had to begin wearing a broad-brimmed hat to keep my face from getting too dark. Your flattering comments on my lovely skin have not gone unnoticed. I should not wish to disappoint you. You married a not unattractive woman, and I shall endeavor to stay that way."

The countless hours she had spent in the garden had kept her busy and continued to give her a sense of purpose, especially since neither her husband nor her son seemed to need her any longer.

When dinner was over, he said, "I beg that you'll excuse me tonight. I must go to the library. There are many papers that require my attention."

She tried to conceal her disappointment when she spoke. "I'll be reading in my study—if you should finish sooner than expected and wish to play a game."

He stood up and came to pat the top of her head. "Don't wait up for me, my dear. I expect to be quite late."

Perhaps she should have agreed to entertain. She was growing hungrier and hungrier for another adult to talk to. Someone besides Mrs. MacGinnis, who would inquire about how her ladyship liked the turbot prepared or ask Carlotta if the draperies should be removed and cleaned.

As Carlotta trudged up the stairs for another lonely night of reading, she realized she had come to rely on James, and she missed him rather painfully.

If she could not have her husband to talk to, perhaps she could strike up a friendship with Mr. Fordyce. The following afternoon—while James was spending the day at the mines—she went to the secretary's office.

When he looked up from his desk, his spectacles slipped midway down his nose. He jumped to his feet, one hand pushing his spectacles back to their proper place. "Good afternoon, my lady, how may I assist you?"

"It's been rather a long time since I've spoken with you, and I thought perhaps we could have a little visit. Should you like to come see my garden?"

His glance darted to the pile of work on his desk, then back to his employer's wife. "I would be honored, my lady."

As they walked along the narrow lanes of the parterre garden, Carlotta pointed out the various flowers she had planted, while praising the gardener who was responsible for overseeing the greenhouse.

Before they had strolled very far, she asked, "Pray, is my husband always as busy as he's been of late?"

"Being the Earl of Rutledge carries with it enormous responsibilities. Your husband has taken his responsibilities far more seriously than his predecessor. Though the present Lord Rutledge trusts all of us who work for him, he insists on keeping abreast of everything we do. His intelligence is so keen, he has even taught me some time-saving shortcuts in my own work."

She was proud of James, yet at the same time jealous that his secretary saw more of her husband than she did. "You keep my husband's ledgers?"

He nodded.

"I've worried the mines might be in financial trouble. Is that why he spends so much time there?"

"The mines turn a tidy profit," Fordyce said. "If Lord Rutledge spends a great deal of time there, I believe it's because he has great empathy for the lot of the colliers. I knew a fellow at Cambridge who was a great deal like your husband. He was a Benthamite."

Did Mr. Fordyce expect her to know what a Benthamite was? She had never heard of it, yet she was afraid to admit her ignorance. Finally, a possible definition flashed through her brain. "A follower of Jeremy Bentham?"

"Yes. Have you read him?"

"Goodness, no. I only read poetry. Have you read Mr. Bentham?"

"Yes. He promulgates the utilitarian theory."

"I'm afraid I've never heard of it, Mr. Fordyce."

"It's the philosophy that everything should be

done for the greatest good of the greatest number of people."

Such a philosophy sounded rather like Christianity to her. She raised her brows. "Are you a Benthamite, Mr. Fordyce?"

He laughed. "I don't think of myself as anything in particular. However, I find much merit in the utilitarians, and whether your husband realizes he is one or not, I believe him to be. He's definitely not old guard. He's most liberal thinking."

"Then perhaps you can persuade him to become a Whig in Parliament," Carlotta suggested.

He slowed and turned to face her, his blue eyes flashing, a smile lifting his narrow face. "The thing of it is, I really believe Lord Rutledge is apolitical. I'm not even sure he's ever read Jeremy Bentham. It's my belief that your husband is inherently good. He has an acute sense of right and wrong."

It was nothing Carlotta did not already know about her husband. She could think of more than a dozen instances in which James had been unflinchingly unselfish. It was his lot always to do what made another person happy, his lot to empathize with others' suffering. "I know that to be true."

Neither she nor the secretary spoke for a moment. She was glad she and Mr. Fordyce had taken this walk. Speaking in such an environment—and speaking of someone other than himself—had relaxed the timid secretary.

"I know my husband has no wish to enter politics. He's perfectly happy doing what he's doing here in Exmoor. However, I cannot stop thinking about his lordship's late mother. She always believed her son would grow up to be a great man. What she did not realize was that he could be a great man without leaving a mark on civilization."

"You should be a philosopher, not a poetess, my lady."

She laughed. "I'm really not a poetess. Would that I were. I'm merely addicted to poetry."

"It seems to me your setting and position should put you in the perfect situation to write poetry."

She thought on this for a moment. What he said was true. She was surrounded by beauty, and the abundance of servants enabled her to have the time to pursue anything she wanted. It was just that she had never been fanatically attached to the idea of *writing* poetry. She was fanatically attached to reading it. Why should she try to pen a thought when those more talented than she had already done so with far more eloquence?

"I feel things deeply, as a poet does," she said, "but under normal conditions I'm never drawn to writing down my feelings. When I do, my efforts are most inferior to the poets I so admire."

While she was strolling through the garden with Fordyce, James rode up on Ebony. He scowled when he saw her laughing.

Dismounting, he directed a harsh glance at her. "Should you not be dressing for dinner, my dear?"

"It's not dark yet," she countered, glancing up at the late afternoon skies.

"I have some things I need to discuss with you, Fordyce," James snapped.

As the two men walked away, Carlotta stooped and, with trembling hand, removed a weed.

When Carlotta saw that her husband would share the dinner table with her, she was pleased. There had been too many nights as of late when he had taken a tray in his library. But her pleasure was short lived. He sulked throughout dinner and barely uttered a word.

After dinner he expressed an interest in continuing her chess lessons, which he did—while drinking several glasses of brandy.

Though his skill showed no signs of weakening as the game progressed, his tongue became looser. "Tell me about this man who did not return your affections, Carlotta," he demanded.

She began to tremble. Had he learned of Gregory? Is that why he was treating her with such thinly cloaked anger? "There's nothing to tell. He chose to marry another. End of story."

"But *not,* I take it, the end of your affections."

"No, it wasn't. I hurt for a long time afterward."

He pinned her with a malicious stare. "Even now?"

She looked into his fiery eyes. "Not now. I'm over him."

"Then what other man is there, Carlotta? Is it Fordyce? For I know the lovely Carlotta must always have a man."

She whirled at him and spat out her denial. "I have no man."

He laughed bitterly. "Especially not your husband."

Her heart drummed. She had known this day would come. After all, James was a man. A man could only go so long without a woman. "Then . . . *that* bothers you?"

He pounded the chessboard with his fist. "Damn it all to hell, yes, it bothers me! Think you I am not a man?"

Her voice softened. "I could never forget that you're a man, James."

He stared at her with glassy eyes. "Do you hate all men, or is it just me?"

"I don't hate you."

"You just hate the thought of my bedding you, Wife."

"If . . . if you wish me to be the dutiful wife, I shall be." She began to tremble and her voice shook when she spoke. "Should you like to come to my bedchamber now?"

Twenty

She had known her husband would not turn down her offer. For weeks now she had read the signs. As fine a man as he was, James needed her as a man needs a woman. Since he was not the kind of man who would seek sexual release under the skirts of whores, she knew he had been without a woman for far too long. She knew enough of men to know such abstinence could cause them to be short-tempered, prone to heavy drinking, and in physical as well as emotional pain.

For weeks, James had been displaying the signs. She had seen the naked desire in his eyes and had been oddly exhilarated by it.

She had also known he would never beg for her sexual favors. But he wanted them keenly. Even if he did not love her, he needed her. And he had every right under God's and man's law to take his pleasure from her body. And she owed him so much.

It was time. Time to give herself to the man who had rescued her from bleakness.

As soon as she had offered herself, his bitterness swept away, to be replaced with a seductive smile as he left his seat and moved to her, his smoldering eyes never leaving her.

His arms settled around her as she lifted her face to his for a lingering kiss; her lips parted for the intimacy she was enjoying as much as he. He fell to his knees beside her at the card table, kissing a trail of butterfly kisses down her neck. Her breathing—like his—accelerated as if she had been running.

When he lowered the bodice of her gown and closed his mouth around her taut nipple, she sucked in her breath, but did not want to do anything which might cause him to stop what he was doing. She was senseless with physical pleasure. Through her fogged brain, she was conscious that she was not responding to him as a lady should. She wanted to be more distant, more respectable, but her own need, she realized with shock, was as great as her husband's.

It was as if she could not get enough of him. Her hands hungrily moved over his shoulders, down his arms, under his shirt—then down lower and lower. She cupped her hand over his bulging need and let out a little cry.

"Come, my love," he whispered throatily, "let us go upstairs."

Unable to take her eyes from him, she nodded as if she had been drugged and gave him her hand.

Together, they mounted the stairs, James's arm settled around her. She thought he would leave her at her chamber to prepare for . . . for this delayed wedding night, but he did not. He followed her into her chamber, which was lit by firelight and a single taper beside her bed.

She turned around to face him. "Should you wish me to dress in a night rail I've saved for this night?"

He shook his head, his eyes hungrily sweeping over her eager body. "What I'd like, Carlotta, is to watch you undress."

She had never undressed in front of a man before. Not in front of Stephen, whose sexual relations with her had always been conducted in the dark. Not for Gregory, either, who preferred coming to her bed after her clothes had been removed.

Yet the thought of undressing in front of James strangely intoxicated her. Most likely because of her own acute arousal. Then she thought of the bulge she had felt beneath her hand and she became even more excited. More anxious—if possible—to feel her husband inside her.

She moved to him seductively and hooked her arms around his neck. "I shall need your assistance."

He crushed her to him and savagely kissed her as his hands roamed over her flesh. Then she felt a rush of cold air on her breasts as he lowered the top of her gown. Next, she heard the sound of her gown tearing and watched helplessly as it dropped to the floor.

His eyes swept over the length of her, and his breath became even more ragged as he gathered her into his arms and carried her to the bed. He was too impatient to remove the silken counterpane, but laid her on it. With Carlotta on her back, James hastened to remove his own clothing. Since the candle still burned, she greedily watched as he removed first his shirt, then his breeches. When they fell to the floor, she gasped, her eyes feasting on his sinewy body, golden in the flickering candlelight.

His eyes riveted to hers, he mounted the bed and placed one knee between his wife's thighs as his hands reached down to cup her breasts.

She found herself raising her hips in order to feel the brush of him at the juncture of her thighs. With each of her thrusts, James's breath grew more ragged.

Soon he lowered himself into her, and both of them began to cry out with pleasure, more frantically with each maddening thrust.

She would never have believed she could be so hungry for this mating, but it was as if she had been starving, and James was her feast.

When she felt his warm seed within her she shuddered beneath him, each quiver matched by the man who plunged into her until he collapsed over her, groaning with pleasure.

He soon removed his weight from her, turning to face her. She looked at him, her hands gently stroking his body. The body that had given her such mindless pleasure.

His arms encircled her as he planted moist kisses over her eyes, her nose, her lips.

Burying her head into his chest, she sighed contentedly. Then she waited for the sweet words of love she craved to hear.

Finally, he ran a gentle finger along her nose and spoke. "Thank you, dear wife. You've made me the happiest man in the kingdom tonight." He stopped and tenderly kissed her cheek. "This has been . . . far better than ever I hoped for."

They weren't words of love, but she would take her consolation in them. At least, she had made him happy. Also, she drew a strange satisfaction in knowing how strongly he desired her.

Her husband soon drifted into a sated sleep, his big hands splayed across her hips, their bodies pressed flesh to flesh.

She continued to lie within the circle of his embrace, her own hands softly tracing over his supple muscles. She wanted to be ashamed of her own heated eagerness to take him inside her, but she could not. She had enjoyed it too much. More than that, what had occurred between them felt so right, so utterly satisfying. It was as if she had been born to give pleasure to this man.

When she awoke the next morning, James was no longer in her bed. She whispered his name, thinking he might be in the adjoining dressing room, but she heard no answer.

Clutching the sheet around her, she got up and snatched her dress from the floor before she remembered it had been torn from her. Her cheeks hot, she went to the linen press and removed a virginal sprigged muslin dress and proceeded to dress herself. Once she was dressed, she flung open the door of her dressing room, and moved from it to her husband's adjoining dressing room, hoping to find him, but he was not there.

She opened the door to his bedchamber. He was not there, either. Her glance fell on his bed—on the rumpled covers—and her heart sank. He had come back to his own bed during the night! He had not wanted to spend the night in her arms.

Gravely disappointed, she returned to her bedchamber and collapsed in front of her dressing table. Now that she was truly James's wife, she had wanted to feel as if they were married in every way. She had wanted to wake in the morning with him beside her. She had wanted to cheerfully discuss each other's plans for the day. She would have taken great pleasure in watching him dress.

She had been foolish enough to believe that now that she had shared her bed with him, their old camaraderie would return and he would no longer put such distance between them. His secretary, his steward, the mine captain—even her own son—saw

more of her husband than she did. She longed for
him to spare time for the woman he had married.

She lifted her bottle of lavender water, fully in-
tending to hurl it into her looking glass as Peggy
came striding into the room, a cocky expression on
her face. "Don't ye go breaking no more mirrors,
my lady."

Carlotta set the scent down and waited for her
maid to dress her hair.

Nothing in his entire life had ever been as painful
as leaving Carlotta's bed at dawn. He had wanted
to make love to her again and again. But such be-
sottment did not fit into his plan to win his wife's
love. His scheme to earn her affection by his absence must already be working. Not only had his
beloved Carlotta consented to share her bed with
him, she had given herself to him with a hunger as
greedy as his own.

As he rode Ebony over the moors, he became
aroused at each memory of the magical blending
between Carlotta and him the night before. He had
wanted her for so long and had imagined how fulfilling making love to her could be, but he had not
been prepared for how much more powerful the
living, breathing, seductive Carlotta could be than
the woman of his dreams.

He had hoped she could tolerate his passion for
her. He had not thought her own passion could ever
equal his own.

That night he came to her bed again. They had
played just one hand of cribbage. He had been un-

able to play any more because of his overwhelming lust for her.

He had begun to put up the pins, watching her hungrily as he did so. "Shall we go to bed, my love?" he asked in a throaty voice.

Her long lashes lifted and she nodded seductively.

As they had done the night before, they mounted the stairs, his arm resting possessively at her waist. He followed her to the dimly lit bedchamber, where she turned to face him, her gaze intense.

He moved to her and crushed her against him, their lips meeting and melding breathlessly. Her hands stroked his body as eagerly as his stroked hers. He deftly unfastened her dress and brushed it to the carpeted floor. He reverently cupped her breast and bent to take it in his mouth as she whimpered. He was soon carried away with her rhythm as she ground into his thigh.

His hand reached down to stroke the pelt between her thighs and she moaned with pleasure as he slipped a finger into her moist crevice. Slowly, she backed into the bed and sat on its edge, her thighs parted to better receive his manipulations. She reached down to remove first one stocking, then the other, never removing her eyes from his as his finger plunged deeper and swifter.

Then she slipped her hand beneath his breeches and began to stroke his engorged shaft until he thought he would go mad. He threw off his pants and lunged for the bed and his precious Carlotta, and he frantically buried himself within her.

When his release came, he shuddered convulsively over her, and with maddening exultation listened as she whimpered beneath him, each of her shudders perfectly matching his own.

Once his heartbeat returned to normal, he slid

off his beloved wife, careful not to disengage himself from her down low. Then he passionately kissed her. He wanted to tell her how much he loved her, but that was not part of his plan.

He wanted to grow sturdy again within her, but that, too, had no part in his plan. Instead, he stroked her hair away from her moist forehead and held her close until she fell into a deep slumber.

Then he left her and went to his own chambers, feeling totally bereft.

He knew Carlotta did not love him, yet. But she was growing to crave him as he had long craved her. He would have to take consolation in that debilitating pleasure.

Twenty-one

Carlotta was leading a small army of footmen bearing baskets when she nearly collided with Fordyce, who was attempting to post a handful of letters.

"I beg your pardon, my lady," he said to Carlotta, his glance flicking to all the baskets. "Is there a function for which I have not been informed?"

Carlotta's eyes danced. "Not even my husband has been informed. I'm going to surprise him at the mines by bringing the colliers a hearty respite."

"The footmen are assisting you?"

"Only on this end." She lowered her voice. "His lordship, I am sure, would not wish to flaunt his wealth or servants in front of the colliers."

Mr. Fordyce nodded. "Say! If you're going to the mines, I beg that you get his lordship's signature on a document for me. I'll just run back and fetch it."

At the heavily laden carriage, Carlotta had to laugh when she saw Stevie lifting a basket that was nearly as tall as he.

"See how strong I am, Mama," he boasted.

She and Miss Kenworth exchanged amused glances.

"Here's the document," said Fordyce, who had just come from the house.

Carlotta took it, glanced at Stevie's nurse, then back at Fordyce. "You are acquainted with Miss Kenworth, are you not, Mr. Fordyce?" she asked.

He nodded shyly to Miss Kenworth. "She was kind enough to invite me to dine with her last week."

"If you have spent an hour in Miss Kenworth's company, then I daresay she knows enough of you to name your childhood friends. Miss Kenworth has a facility for making fast friends."

"I must protest, my lady," Miss Kenworth said. "You give me attributes I do not possess. I know no more of Mr. Fordyce than I did when I was at Middlesex. Methinks he finds dinner conversation obtrusive."

"I beg your forgiveness, Miss Kenworth, if I gave that impression," Fordyce said.

Eying the remorseful Mr. Fordyce and the suddenly bashful Miss Kenworth, Carlotta soon realized that the secretary's timidness lay beneath the misunderstanding. And even if Miss Kenworth was no beauty, she was a female, and Carlotta had reason to believe Mr. Fordyce was extremely reticent with members of the opposite sex.

"Miss Kenworth, if you desire conversation with Mr. Fordyce, you have only to speak of the new philosophers—like Mr. Bentham—or government, and his tongue will loosen."

"Our curate back in Middlesex was a keen proponent of Jeremy Bentham," Miss Kenworth said, looking up at Fordyce, then clamping her mouth closed.

Carlotta could not remember Miss Kenworth ever stopping at just one sentence. She glanced from her to the young secretary and came to the conclusion that both of them were exceedingly shy in each other's company. And that just would not do!

Carlotta slipped her arm through Fordyce's. "Mr. Fordyce, I beg that you accompany us to the mines today. It's a lovely day to be out of doors."

"His lordship doesn't pay me to trek through the countryside, my lady," he replied.

She patted his arm. "Don't worry. I shall take full blame. I promise you, my husband will not object to your coming."

She could see that the man was torn. "Besides," she added, "I have need of you this afternoon, and James said I was to have access to you whenever I wanted. So there you have it!"

"Very well," he said.

They watched as the last of the baskets were tied on top of the carriage; then Stevie bounded into the coach. Fordyce assisted Carlotta in, and she sat beside her son. Next in was Miss Kenworth, then Fordyce last.

"When shall we be there, Mama?" Stevie asked.

"In about an hour, love. The drive by way of coach is nearly twice as long as it is by horseback because the coach is restricted to the more out-of-the-way roads."

"In preparation for his first visit to the mines, Master Stephen has learned to spell some new words. Spell the words for your mother, dear," Miss Kenworth said.

"Coal. *C-o-a-l,*" Stevie said. "I thought it was spelled *c-o-l-e,* but Miss Kenworth taught me the proper way to spell it."

Fordyce looked at Miss Kenworth with admiration. "But I thought you were the boy's nurse. I did not know you were a governess."

"Fortunately for me, I can be both," she answered.

"I perceive that Miss Kenworth enjoys the outdoors," Carlotta said. "Therefore, after the lessons, she and Stevie indulge in the pursuits that make a lad happy."

"We found an injured baby sparrow last week," Stevie said excitedly, "and Miss Kenworth and I are nursing it back to good health."

"Where do you keep it?" Fordyce asked.

"Presently, in Master Stephen's room."

"Should you like to come and see him, Mr. Fordyce?" Stevie asked.

"I believe I would."

"I've been unable to impart to Master Stephen that birds may not wish to be covered with blankets," Miss Kenworth said with a laugh.

"I know he likes it," Stevie said stubbornly. "I got a little piece of wool from Mrs. MacGinnis that is the perfect size for a sparrow blanket."

Miss Kenworth shrugged. "The sparrow's gender is another matter over which Master Stephen and I are not in accord," Miss Kenworth said with dramatic flair. "I say the bird is a she, and he insists it's a he." She looked up at Fordyce with no hint of a blush. "Pray, Mr. Fordyce, can you tell if a bird is a male or female?"

He sputtered out a cough, shaking his head. "Perhaps there's a book in his lordship's library which might enlighten you . . . on the subject."

"An excellent suggestion," Miss Kenworth said.

As the carriage trudged up a hill, Carlotta had the opportunity to observe her son's nurse. A pity the first thing one noticed about her was her plumpness. It wasn't that she was fat. She really wasn't. It was just that she had no waist whatsoever and was not blessed with height; therefore, she seemed the same circumference from top to bottom as she was from side to side.

More the pity was the fact that her coloring was quite lovely with a peaches-and-cream complexion and hair and eyes that were quite dark. She would have been considered quite pretty, if it weren't for her cursed frame.

Carlotta thought Miss Kenworth contrasted well with Mr. Fordyce's fairness and slimness. She also thought there could be no more that five years between their ages.

"Mr. Fordyce?" Stevie asked.

"Yes?"

"Did you know that Miss Kenworth can play cricket?"

The secretary ran an appreciative glance over the nurse, who began to blush. "I did not."

"You must come play with us one day," Stevie said. "You *do* know how to play cricket, do you not?"

A smile crossed his face. "Aye, I do. When I was a lad not much older than you, I played cricket at grammar school. Then again at Cambridge." He directed a glance at Miss Kenworth. "Pray, how is it you know how to play?"

"My mother was housekeeper to Sir Eldridge, who sired four sons. They were always begging that I join them."

"Because she's good," Stevie said. "There's nothing of the girl about her," the boy added.

Carlotta saw that a deeper scarlet hiked up the nurse's cheeks. "That's not really the case, lamb," Carlotta said. "Miss Kenworth just happens to indulge you with things a lad enjoys."

"No," Stevie protested, "she told me she was a tomboy. Always."

Carlotta shrugged. "She's also a very fine lady."

"Tell me," Fordyce said to Miss Kenworth, "were you well acquainted with the curate at Middlesex?"

"I was. Before he brought his bride to our village."

"Then you and he had discussed Benthamism?"

She nodded, then the two began to discuss utilitarianism until they arrived at the mines.

James was in the pits when Willy scurried down. "Lord Rutledge! Lady Rutledge is here, and she's brought victuals for everyone."

But Carlotta hated the mines! Brushing off his hands and muttering under his breath, James hunkered down and moved through the blackness toward the direction of Willy's voice. Turning at an elbow in the shaft, he then followed the light—and Willy— from the pit.

Above ground, he squinted against the sun's brightness and looked around until he saw his wife. Carlotta was directing the unloading from the carriage of a dozen baskets and two folding tables. She and Miss Kenworth supervised the unpacking of the baskets and spread out the feast. There was smoked venison, giblet pie, apples, puddings, ham, and a basketful of pastries. Another basket held plates and utensils.

Clearing his throat of the coal dust, James walked up to his wife, then immediately broke into a fit of coughing.

A look of concern swept over her face. "Fresh air is what you need, not that wretched air down in the pits," she chastised.

He ignored her comment. "What, pray tell, is the

special occasion?" he asked his wife, his gaze shifting to the tables heaped with food.

"When I came to Yarmouth, I vowed I would learn all your employees by name. This, I think, will be a good start," she said. She walked up to him and set her hand on his. "And please don't be angry with Mr. Fordyce. I forced him to join us. He and Miss Kenworth had a most pleasant journey. They have, I think, much in common."

James would have been jealous of Carlotta spending time with any man, and since Fordyce was the only other gentleman available, the unfortunate secretary bore the brunt of James's vehement jealousy. James wished to believe Carlotta had brought the secretary today merely to advance his friendship with Miss Kenworth, but James's illogical jealousy gripped him too tightly.

In the middle of James's scowl, Carlotta raised up on her toes and kissed his black cheek. His thoughts leaped back to the night before and how receptive she had been to his lovemaking. It was all he could do not to drag her to the carriage and have his way with her right there.

Instead, he stiffened, then removed a handkerchief from his pocket and rubbed the coal soot from her lips. "I thought you detested the black," he whispered.

"It looks as if I'm going to have to get used to it if I'm married to you." She took his hand. "Come, dearest, allow me to prepare a plate for you."

She piled his plate high with food, and he had to admit it was most welcome. A man could work up a hearty appetite down in the mines. He sat on a large stone to eat—and to watch his wife personally greet each miner with extended hand. When they would balk at getting her dirty, she scoffed.

"Please," she would say time after time, "it will wash off."

James thought she had never looked more beautiful than she did, standing there in a simple cotton lavender dress, her hands black and her eyes warm. As she brushed a stray lock of raven hair from her brow, a streak of black left its mark on her milky skin. She was without a doubt the loveliest creature he had ever seen.

When he finished, he came to stand beside her. "How is it you're better at understanding the collier's speech?"

"Peggy and I are learning the dialect from Jeremy."

"Ah . . . tell me, are Peggy and Jeremy . . . ?"

She shrugged. "Not yet. I learned from the upper groom that a local girl snared Jeremy's affections before he met Peggy. I suppose we'll just have to wait to see which one Jeremy will finally choose."

"The poor local girl doesn't have a prayer if my wife has anything to say about it."

"Would that I could cast spells," she lamented, her eyes narrowed in jest.

He broke out laughing.

Carlotta turned to address the nurse. "Please, Miss Kenworth, prepare a plate for Mr. Fordyce and yourself now. All the miners have been served."

James saw that Carlotta watched Miss Kenworth and Fordyce walk some little distance away and sit down to eat with each other. He also noticed that no matter what Carlotta was doing, she never had Stevie far from her vision. No doubt, she feared he would wander into the pits she had so strong an aversion to.

He was proud that even though the lad's nurse was present, Carlotta refused to be complacent about her child's safety. She had become a fine mother, at last.

A tightness clamped his chest as he thought of her mothering a child of their own. A child that quite possibly could already have been conceived. He could shout his happiness from the top of the hills.

He listened as an affable collier—Douglas Covington—told Carlotta about his wife and children.

"Enjoy these days while ye can," Douglas told Carlotta, "for once those babes begin to come, ye'll have no time for anything. I should know. Me blessed wife just presented me with our ninth child, and me poor wife never has an idle moment."

"It sounds to me your wife *is* blessed," Carlotta said. "Is the new babe a boy or girl?"

Douglas's teeth looked exceptionally white against his black skin when he smiled. "Ah! Another fine lad."

"I shall have to go see the babe," Carlotta said.

James had never been more proud in his life.

Twenty-two

The following day Carlotta and Stevie rode over the moors to the cottage of Douglas Covington's family. The white house sat some little distance up on the heath above a brook. Next to the house lay a small vegetable garden, and a cow grazed just off in the distance.

Carlotta grew unaccountably nervous as she dismounted, took her son's hand, and walked up a muddy lane to the house. It was a good thing the door was painted a dark brown to better hide the sooty handprints, she thought as she knocked on it.

A woman near Carlotta's own age, with rosy cheeks and dull, unkept brown hair, answered the door.

"Mrs. Covington?" Carlotta asked.

"Ah, my lady, please to come in."

So Carlotta's visit was not unannounced. Still clutching Stevie's hand, Carlotta stepped into the parlor that had obviously been tidied in preparation for her visit.

A newborn babe lay in a handmade wooden cradle near the hearth.

"May I see the babe?" Carlotta asked.

A smile came over the woman's face. "Me Douglas said as ye were keen to see the babe, but I'll tell ye, he's a runt. Smallest babe I've ever had. Me and Dooglas have been a tad worried about him."

Carlotta moved to the cradle and bent over it, cooing to the sleeping babe. She glanced up at Mrs. Covington. "May I pick him up?"

"Please do. He never cries when he's being coddled. Ye can sit in that chair near the fire, if ye like."

Carlotta lifted the little bundle who seemed to weigh no more than her pillow. In fact, she remembered wistfully, the babe was the same size Stevie was when they had sailed from Portugal back to England. Stevie had been small, too. She wistfully remembered that Stephen had been worried over the small size of their infant son.

Carlotta held the infant to her breast, and a warmth rushed over her. A pity she had been so afraid of her own son on that long-ago sailing. But in her heavy bereavement and weak physical state so close on the heels of her confinement, she understood now how difficult her nineteenth year had been. She prayed that all her miseries were behind her.

Stevie, biting his nail, edged up to her and poked his face near the babe's. "What's his name?" Stevie asked.

Carlotta looked toward the mother.

"Daniel."

"He's so little," Stevie remarked, unable to take his eyes from the infant.

"You were this tiny once," Carlotta said. Then she looked at Mrs. Covington. "You've nothing to worry about. Little Daniel seems perfectly healthy. I daresay your other children were just exceptionally large babes."

"Ah, that they were."

"Stevie," Carlotta said, "give Mrs. Covington the present we brought for the babe."

With pride, Stevie presented the woman with knitted booties and mittens.

Mrs. Covington's hazel eyes brightened. " 'Tis the first new thing the babe's received. Poor tot, has to wear his brothers' and sisters' hand-me-downs."

"How many brothers does he have?" Stevie asked, his glance flitting to several children scattered throughout the gray room. Carlotta's gaze swept over the assembled children, and she was surprised they were all blond. She had been unable to determine the color of their father's soot-covered hair the day before.

"We've got seven boys and two girls," Mrs. Covington said.

Stevie's eyes rounded. "Seven brothers! I wish I had seven brothers."

"Allow me to present me lads to ye," Mrs. Covington said, taking hold of Stevie's hand and turning toward her brood.

An amused grin on her face, Carlotta watched the children and could not determine who was the shyest, Stevie or the Covington children.

" 'Tis a pretty day to be out of doors," Mrs. Covington said. "Why do you not take Master Stevie and show him our newborn lamb?"

A thin little girl who appeared to be twice Stevie's age came and took his hand. "Should ye like to see the baby lamb?" she asked as if she were speaking to a toddler.

His eyes wide, Stevie nodded happily.

The room suddenly cleared, except for the two women and the babe.

"Please sit near me so we can talk," Carlotta said to her hostess.

Mrs. Covington pulled a wooden chair up next to Carlotta.

"You are blessed to have so many children," Carlotta said. "And all of them in such fine health."

The woman grew solemn. "We lost our last babe, a little girl, and it liked to have killed me Dooglas."

"Nothing could be more painful than losing a child," Carlotta said softly. "I'm very sorry for you both."

"I had to be strong for Dooglas and the other children. I think me greatest fear was that I'd lose the others next. I had nightmares, not about my little lost Mary but about her brothers and sisters following her to the grave. It was a most difficult time. Then I learned I was increasing with Daniel, and it seemed to help Dooglas and me both. Ye met me Dooglas, did ye not?" The woman's tired face brightened.

"Indeed I did. He's very proud of his family."

Mrs. Covington smiled. "He's a fine man. As fine a husband and father as ever there was. I've loved him all me life. There was never anyone else for me."

"How old were you when you pledged yourself to Mr. Covington?"

She thought for a moment before she answered. "I was fourteen. He was sixteen. We married three years later. Me Dooglas wanted to build the cottage before we got married."

Carlotta glanced around the room. "Your husband began to build this when he was but sixteen years of age?" Her own brother—and her husband—had been mere schoolboys when they were sixteen.

Mrs. Covington nodded proudly. "Of course, he had five brothers of his own to help."

"How old was your husband when he began to work in the mines?"

"Eleven."

Carlotta's eyes narrowed. "And your eldest child now is . . . ?"

"That'd be Sally. She's the one what took yer boy's hand. She's eleven."

"You'd be willing to let your boys go down into the mines when they're still lads?"

Mrs. Covington shrugged. "What else is there for them? I wish they didn't have to. I wish me Dooglas didn't have to. If anything ever happened to him . . ." Mrs. Covington's eyes moistened.

James would be furious with Carlotta if she went poisoning people's minds against children working in the mines. It was a matter upon which she and her husband were not in accord. At the present, she would not say anything to Mrs. Covington because she meant to work with James, not against him. But she must sway her husband. There had to be something else in Exmoor for young boys to do. She would discuss the matter with James.

Mrs. Covington brushed away a tear. "If I'd had more notice of yer visit, I'd have procured some tea to serve ye, me lady. Could I offer ye a glass of fresh milk?"

Carlotta shook her head. "Thank you, no." Carlotta had decided to come here the very day after speaking to Mr. Covington to prevent them from rushing out and buying costly tea. Carlotta well remembered going without her tea many a time because its price was too dear and her money too scarce.

She glanced down at the warm bundle she held. Little Daniel slept contentedly. She had forgotten babies' little fingers were not much bigger around than a piece of yarn.

"You and Lord Rutledge will be a-startin' a family soon now."

Carlotta's stomach fluttered as she remembered James so thoroughly making love to her the night before. She had not recently given thought to bearing James's babe. Now that she did, something deep and fulfilling stirred within her. "It's my fondest wish," Carlotta said. And she truly meant it.

While Carlotta and Mrs. Covington talked, Carlotta perused the parlor, where a large metal bathing tub was placed a few feet away from the fire. With Douglas Covington covered with black soot, Carlotta was certain the tub was a necessity. A pity it was not used every day. And a pity the room was so dreary, with the color of graphite everywhere.

The babe, his little eyes still slitted shut, began to make feeble sputtering noises.

"He'll be a-wantin' to eat," his mother said, reaching for him.

Carlotta stood up and handed him to Mrs. Covington, then said her farewells so the mother could nurse in private.

Outside, Stevie was reluctant to leave. "Can my new friends come play with me someday?" he asked his mother.

"Anytime they like," Carlotta said cheerfully. Directing her attention at the tallest of the boys, she said, "Do you know where Yarmouth Hall is?"

"Aye," the boy said.

"Please come," Carlotta said. Then she and Stevie untethered their mounts and left.

"And what did you do today, my dear?" James asked his wife over the dinner table that night.

"Stevie and I went to the Covington's cottage."

James's eyes rounded. "Douglas Covington's?"

Carlotta nodded as she spooned peas onto her plate.

"What for?"

"I wanted to take a gift to their new babe. He's ever so precious." She held her hands parallel, a little over a foot apart. "He's only this long and does nothing but sleep." Her voice softened, and a wistful look came over her face when she spoke of the babe.

James's chest tightened as he imagined how she would be with a babe of their own, and he was suffused with a deep contentment. During these past several days he had surged with pride over his beloved Carlotta. Not only had she been a passionate lover, but she had also warmed to her duties as the Countess of Rutledge. He could not have selected a finer bride.

A pity she did not love him. Since she had so thoroughly given herself to him, he had fought both his urge to proclaim his love and his powerful need to spend more time with her. He had to remind himself his plan would not be successful until Carlotta voiced her love for him. Then he could allow himself the pleasure of wrapping her in his love. But not until her love was secured.

Even if Carlotta still did not love him, James had never been happier. She had done such an astounding turnaround; he felt her love creeping closer every day. Before the long days of summer arrived he expected to own her heart.

"And what gift did you bring the babe?" he asked.

"Mittens and booties I knitted myself."

"But surely you only found out about the babe yesterday."

She nodded. "But before that I had decided I would begin knitting baby items for new children of your employees as they come into the world. I began the ones I gave to Daniel Covington the day before yesterday."

He set his hand on hers. "Thank you for being so fine a countess."

She rolled her eyes. "You forget I have a daunting example to follow in the earl who happens to be my husband."

So she admired him. They were getting close. Very close. "And how did you find the Covingtons' cottage?" he asked, his eyes twinkling.

"Quite filthy looking—from the coal. I really don't know how those people can stand it. They keep a bathing tub in their front parlor."

He chuckled. "And how did Stevie find the Covington children?"

"He had a wonderful time playing outdoors with them. I declare, I was afraid he would not understand their speech, but apparently he had no difficulty."

"He's with Jeremy every day. I daresay he's becoming accustomed to it."

"He wants the Covington children to come to Yarmouth," she said.

"I hope they do. Their father's a fine man."

"That's what Mrs. Covington told me. After all this time and all the squalor, she's still quite madly in love with him." She took a sip of wine. "Did you know that Douglas Covington began working in the mines when he was but eleven years old?"

"Many of the colliers do."

Her brows lowered with concern, Carlotta met his gaze. "It's wrong, James. They're still but children."

"I know very well your views on the subject, and quite frankly, I agree with you. But I've only been here a year, and I don't mean to make enemies by eliminating a practice that's gone on for generations. Many of the lads who work the mines have no fathers, and their mothers depend on the income they bring home."

"Surely they can do something else besides work in those dangerous pits!"

He stroked her arm and spoke in a low voice. "I'm doing everything I can to make the pits safe."

"James?"

He set down his wineglass, lifting a brow.

"Even if the lads weren't working in mines, I should not be satisfied. I abhor the idea of eleven-year-olds having to earn a living. They're still children!"

"I know, but they're ignorant. It's not as if they could go to school like those of our class."

Carlotta set down her fork. "They're ignorant because they've never been given the opportunity to learn to read and write. Literature and the reading of history open up a whole world, a world they'll never know. All they'll ever know is living off the land, either above the ground or below it. It's really quite sad."

He frowned. "I read an essay in the *Edinburgh Review* that actually proposed universal education to be paid for by the government.

"As favorable as I would feel to such a plan, I cannot see how it could ever work. There are children in sparsely populated areas where it would not be economically feasible to initiate such a program, and the costs to initiate compulsory education anywhere would have to be so staggering as to make it completely unfeasible."

"I daresay it could work in London, but as you said, the cost would be prohibitively staggering."

"A pity."

The footmen cleared the plates and bowls from the table, then removed the cloth in order to serve sweetmeats.

"You know, James, why could we not start a school just for the children of Exmoor? You've told me many times you're very rich."

"As much as I would like to, my dear, I assure you the people of Exmoor would be vehemently opposed to such a maneuver. Their children are a great deal of help to them raising sheep and milking cows and churning butter and any number of jobs. The men in these parts consider themselves well blessed to have a large family to help with the farming chores."

"Does it not occur to them how much more work a woman has for each additional child?"

He gave her a somber look. "You object to large families?"

"I would love to have a large family, but I have a small army of servants. I was thinking of women like Mrs. Covington, who has no servant to help her."

Carlotta would love a large family! Her words had made him happy indeed. Even more satisfying was the change that had occurred in her in the last few months. He doubted the Carlotta he had met at Mrs. McKay's lodgings would ever have wanted a large family. She had not even wanted the one child she had borne.

That night he went to Carlotta's room again, and it was all he could do during their heated, thoroughly satisfying lovemaking not to tell her how completely he loved her.

Twenty-three

Each morning when Carlotta awoke she hoped to find her husband beside her, but each morning he would be gone, and with disappointment she would realize he had left her during the night. It was as if he did not wish to be truly married to her, that she satisfied him only on a physical level.

She had been trying to make him a fine wife, not just to win his affection—though she sorely wanted that—but because she wanted to do what was right. After all, her husband's own actions served as a model to emulate. He was the finest man she had ever known. Only by performing acts of kindness and by striving to be a finer person could she ever hope to be worthy to call herself his wife.

More with each passing day, her heart would race when she thought of her husband. When she was not with him, she longed for his presence. He and Stevie had truly become the light of her life.

She slipped her night shift back on when she heard Peggy's step in the hallway outside her chamber door. Of all the servants at Yarmouth, Peggy's footfall had the most distinctive, dragging sound.

Carlotta's chamber door eased open, and Peggy carried in a tray of tea and toast.

"Please put it upon the dressing table. I don't feel

like lingering here this morning," Carlotta said, springing from the bed. "I shall need you to fashion my hair."

Carlotta sat in front of the looking glass, nibbling on her toast while Peggy styled her hair.

"Oh, my lady, Stevie can hardly contain his happiness this morning!"

Carlotta watched her maid's reflection in the mirror. "Why, pray tell?"

"That sparrow he's been tending is flying all about his bedchamber."

Carlotta broke into a smile. "Hurry with my hair, if you please. I must go see the bird."

"It's quite a sight. Miss Kenworth, as ye know, ain't much bigger than Master Stevie, and she's been a-tryin' to reach the bird, who goes straight up to the tall ceiling. Then Miss Kenworth takes to hoppin' on the beds, and still she's not nearly tall enough. Master Stevie begged her to go fetch Mr. Fordyce, seeing as how the gentleman had expressed a desire to see the bird."

"Then I take it my husband is not here to be of assistance?" Carlotta swallowed the lump in her throat.

"He's gone for the day, me lady."

Soon Carlotta's hair was put up, and Peggy assisted her into a lavender morning dress before Carlotta fled down the hall to her son's chamber.

Her entry coincided with that of Mr. Fordyce, who swept open Stevie's door for her.

"Oh, please close the door," a most agitated Miss Kenworth screamed.

Carlotta broke into laughter when she spied Miss Kenworth's round body leaping into the air, her dark hair swirling high over her shoulders, her skirts lifting to show her very short, very stocky legs, and all the while she cursed the winsome bird which flitted above her. "Come down from that ceiling, you aggravating, ungrateful, feathery fiend!" To make matters even more comical, Miss Kenworth's leaps brought her only inches closer to the bird than she had been with her feet flat on the bed.

Ever the gentleman, Mr. Fordyce refused to join Carlotta in laughter. He strode straight to the bed and offered Miss Kenworth his hand. "Allow me," the secretary said with a commanding air.

Miss Kenworth took his hand and came down from the bed, gathering her dignity about her.

Instead of taking Miss Kenworth's place, Mr. Fordyce turned to Stevie and spoke calmly. "I see, Master Stephen, that your ministrations on behalf of the ailing sparrow have been successful."

"Does *ministrations* mean *doctoring?*" Stevie asked, shooting a glance at his mother.

She nodded.

"Then my ministrations have worked," Stevie answered.

Mr. Fordyce came to stand by Stevie, placing his hand on the boy's shoulder. "Tell me, when you brought the bird to your chamber, what was it you hoped to accomplish?"

"I wanted him to get well so he would be able to fly again."

Mr. Fordyce nodded. "And you have been successful. Birds were made to fly." He paused. "Do you think God gave birds wings so they could fly around your chamber and bump their heads on your ceiling?"

Stevie's face fell as he shook his head.

Mr. Fordyce spoke with gentleness. "I'm certain that when the bird was sick, he was happy to be in your chamber, but now that he can fly again . . . where do *you* think the sparrow wants to be?"

Stevie spoke in a voice barely above a whisper. "He wants to go back to his friends and his trees and the sky."

Mr. Fordyce nodded. "And what do you think you can do to assist him?"

Stevie's eyes widened. "I can open the window!" His glance darted to Miss Kenworth, who nodded her approval before bestowing an adoring glance on Mr. Fordyce.

Stevie ran to the window and drew open the draperies, then opened the casement.

The bird did not leave immediately. Its first concern appeared to be keeping distance between himself—or herself—and the overpoweringly large humans. As fresh air filled the chamber, though, the bird must have recognized the smell and feel of the outdoor air and soon followed it out of Stevie's room.

Stevie's lower lip stuck out. "I'm going to miss Wobert."

"Robert, as you must perceive," Miss Kenworth said to Mr. Fordyce, "is what Master Stephen calls the little girl sparrow."

"It's not a girl!" Stevie argued.

Miss Kenworth put hands to her ample hips. "I ask you, Mr. Fordyce, did that sparrow not fly like a graceful female?"

Carlotta smiled as she watched Fordyce, who did not desire to side with Stevie or his nurse, even though the nurse was acting in jest, a fact that seemed to escape the stuffy Mr. Fordyce.

Mr. Fordyce cleared his throat. "I daresay a bird's gender is not determined by its grace of flight."

"Let's go to Papa's library and find that book you

were talking about, Mr. Fordyce," Stevie said. "That book that explains how to tell boy birds from girl birds."

Mr. Fordyce looked perplexed. "That's not precisely what I said. What I said was that his lordship *may* have a book that deals with . . . that particular aspect of animal anatomy."

Stevie advanced toward the secretary. "Come and help Miss Kenworth look."

Mr. Fordyce looked from Stevie to Carlotta. "I-I don't know . . ."

"Oh, do, Mr. Fordyce," Miss Kenworth said. "I should not wish to be accused of coloring the evidence to support my own claim."

"Well, if you think I could be of assistance . . ."

"I insist," Carlotta said. "Lord Rutledge shan't object." Carlotta's motives had nothing to do with evening the playing field for Stevie and his nurse and everything to do with foisting the timid Mr. Fordyce on the gregarious Miss Kenworth. For Carlotta had decided their differences, when combined, would be their strengths. They should complement each other well. A smug smile settled on her face as the three of them went downstairs to the library.

Carlotta especially glowed at the way Stevie had referred to the library as *papa's*. The name had fallen quite naturally from his lips.

An hour later, Stevie came barrelling into Carlotta's study. "Mama! Mama! Papa's come to take me fishing!"

She looked up from her desk, where she was penning a letter to her grandmother, and her heart melted. Her son had come to love fishing with his papa above all things. Even more than riding Brownie. James's devotion to Stevie—and Stevie's to James—caused her heart to overflow with happiness.

Stevie came up to her desk. "But I'm worried about Miss Kenworth. She'll be lonely without me. I invited her to come with us—for, you know, she is a tomboy and enjoys fishing like fellows do."

"I am persuaded Miss Kenworth will manage quite nicely without you, darling. She most likely has letters to write to her family."

He shook his head. "She wrote them this morning when I was practicing my penmanship."

"Then perhaps she can sew," Carlotta suggested.

He wrinkled his nose. "Miss Kenworth said she doesn't like sewing. She doesn't like things that you do, Mama, because she's a tomboy."

Carlotta smiled.

"Can you not demand that Mr. Fordyce spend the afternoon with Miss Kenworth so she won't get lonely for me?" Stevie implored. "She told me she's very fond of Mr. Fordyce."

Miss Kenworth did not have to tell Carlotta, who could see that Miss Kenworth held Mr. Fordyce in great affection. "I suppose I could," Carlotta conceded.

Carlotta put her quill down and followed her son from the room. She found Mr. Fordyce and Miss Kenworth still in the library. "Miss Kenworth, you may have the afternoon off since Stevie and his father will spend the remainder of the day fishing."

Then Carlotta turned to Fordyce. "I beg that you, too, Mr. Fordyce, take the afternoon off to provide amusement for Miss Kenworth. I fear my son frets that Miss Kenworth will be bereft without him."

Miss Kenworth whipped around to face Carlotta.

"Pray, I can find a great many things to do without forcing Mr. Fordyce from his many important duties in order to entertain me," she said.

"That's what I told my son, but he won't be happy until he knows Mr. Fordyce will assure that you have a pleasant afternoon," Carlotta said. "Besides, Mr. Fordyce also deserves an afternoon off. He works much too hard, and so I shall tell my husband." Carlotta glanced at the secretary. "I pray that you will now go off and find something amusing to do with Miss Kenworth." Being so despotic did not come naturally to Carlotta and made her feel wretchedly uncomfortable.

In what Carlotta thought a rather gallant gesture, Mr. Fordyce offered Miss Kenworth his arm, and the two of them strolled from the library.

"By the way," Carlotta said after them, "did you learn how to tell a male bird from a female bird?"

Miss Kenworth whirled around to face Carlotta. "Not yet." Then she spun back around, a look of joy on her face.

Just knowing that James was at Yarmouth sent waves of deep contentment—and excitement—over Carlotta. Of course, he would be leaving any moment to go angling with Stevie. A pity she could not fish.

She gave her letter to a footman to post, then an idea struck her. A wonderful idea, it seemed to her. Why could she not go angling, too? Never mind that angling had never appealed to her before. Today it held a most alluring attractiveness. Being with James—and her precious son, too—now seemed of paramount importance. And she wouldn't actually have to fish. Watching them and enjoying this spring day would be enough amusement for her.

She must find her husband before he took off. She went first to his library and was rewarded with a glimpse of him sitting behind his desk. As she peered at him, her stomach did an odd flip. In recent days the sight of James had provoked a number of unusual physical responses in her, none of which was unpleasant.

He looked up at her. "Hello, my dear."

She covered the distance between them and came up to kiss his forehead as he sat looking over a stack of papers.

"I have decided I shall accompany you and Stevie on the angling expedition."

He gave her a quizzing glance. "You want to fish?"

"I didn't say that," she protested with mock offense. "I merely wish to accompany you. I find it a pretty day to be outdoors."

"We shall be delighted, and if you should like instruction on fishing, I would be happy to oblige."

She shook her head. "I shall be quite content, I assure you, with my volume of poetry I plan to read while you fish."

"Of course," he said, amusement in his voice.

The three of them were soon off, the River Barle their destination. The terrain between Yarmouth and the point of the Barle where the fish were said to be plentiful was difficult to traverse. There were only the skimpiest of paths through the lush brush of the rugged hills. It seemed to Carlotta they kept going upward and never down.

"Are we in a forest?" she asked.

He nodded. "This is known as the Bagworthy Wood."

Finally they came to the summit of the hill, and caught a glimpse of the twisting Barle shimmering below; then they zigzagged down the forested hill through a maze of ash trees and pines.

Now that spring had arrived, the verdant hills were full of birds and red deer and even a wild Exmoor pony here and there. Wherever they went they heard gurgling water and the chirping and cackling of curlews and snipe and woodland birds.

It was such unspoiled land, except for the site of the mine, she thought grimly. How she detested the place! Yet she would not voice her hatred for the mines to anyone because she was James's wife, and she would never work at cross purposes against him.

Carlotta and James rode side by side behind Stevie.

"I should think a man of action such as yourself would be bored by fishing," Carlotta said. "I understand that most of the time spent angling involves waiting."

He chuckled. "You are correct. I've never been able to understand the lure angling has for men. I only know its pull is strong. I've always felt it. So does our son."

Her heart fluttered. This was the first time he had dared to call Stephen's son his own. Though she should be affronted, she was not. Instead, she was filled with pleasure. And pride. It made her happy to feel so united with James. To feel the three of them were a real family.

Her thoughts flitted to the likelihood that she would someday bear James's children, and she was suddenly consumed with a hunger—a ravishing need—to do so. Nothing could bring her greater pleasure. Well, actually, there was one other thing . . . Her heart accelerated when she thought of it. Above everything she would wish to receive James's love. It was now very important to her that this man who knew her so intimately should be able to overlook her many faults and find room in his heart for her.

Her breath grew ragged as she thought of what a tender, passionate lover her husband was. She knew she pleased him on a physical level. Now, if only he could be pleased with her on another, even more important, level.

Soon they were at the banks of the swiftly flowing Barle and they dismounted. She watched as they unpacked their gear and headed to a rocky clearing on the riverbank to claim a spot. Once they had baited and cast and were settled in, she went in search of the perfect place to sit and watch them. She wished to be in the sun because the shade was too cool. Only a pair of beeches had rooted far enough away from the evergreen canopy to bask in a puddle of sun. She went to the closest one, but the soil around it was soggy. The beech just above it was dry. She sat down and used the tree as a backrest while she watched her husband and son.

Without being didactic, James imparted pointers to Stevie with calm and patience while managing to praise the boy for his skill in casting and his ability not to grow impatient when the fish did not bite immediately.

She listened as they chatted to one another about past excursions and swapped fish stories. When they fell into a lull, she opened the pages of her book and began to read. She had selected this particular volume for its tales of spring, but it was the verses about love that captured her attention.

A stanza from young Shelley spoke to her:

When I arose and saw the dawn
*   I sigh'd for thee;*
when light rode high and the dew was gone,
And noon laid heavy on flower and tree,
And the weary Day turned to his rest,
Lingering like an unloved guest,
*   I sigh'd for thee.*

Her heartbeat accelerated when she thought of James putting his arms about her—and when she remembered the bliss his lovemaking always brought her. She looked up at him, and her heart drummed even more rapidly. The very sight of his handsome face, of his long, sinewy limbs stretched out along the river bank, the sound of his gentle voice when he spoke to *their* son. All these things combined to sweep her away with a maddening rush of emotion.

And she suddenly realized she had fallen madly, irrevocably in love with her husband.

Twenty-four

Her husband had gone to the mines. Carlotta jerked a weed from the parterre garden. She hated it when he went down into the wretched pits. Even more so now that she realized how desperately she loved him, how much she needed him. To lose him was unthinkable, the pain unbearable.

Just knowing he was at the mines put her in a foul temper. She heard the sound of laughter and pushed up the brim of her sunbonnet to see Peggy strolling across the park land with Jeremy, both of them laughing frequently. A smile lifted Carlotta's lips. Young love.

Carlotta returned to her weeding. Her mind—as it so often did lately—focused on her own lover. Her memory lingered over their magical blending the night before. Every blending with her husband was magical, even more so because James appealed to her on every level: the physical, the intellectual, and the spiritual. In all three ways, he touched her, making her strong where she had been weak, giving light where there had been only darkness. Every minute in his presence was intoxicating, fulfilling. She had never felt so complete.

Only one thing was lacking to prevent her perfect happiness. James did not love her. She had come

so very close to telling him how dearly she loved
him last night, but her errant pride would not allow
her to. How foolish she would have seemed to
blather on about her love for him when she meant
no more to him than a compliant body to warm his
bed and assuage his manly needs.

She could not allow herself to proclaim her love
until he did so. But that day might never come. How
could she, of all people, ever hope to earn James's
love, especially when he knew her faults only too
well? Except the greatest of her faults.

Was there anything more she could do to try to
secure his love? There was nothing she *wouldn't* do.
But as she thought on it, she came to realize she
was already doing everything in her power. She had
become a loving mother. She welcomed her husband into her bed every night. She wished to bear
James a son and heir and as many other children
as the Lord would bless them with. She meant to
be a good mistress to all his employees. She would
not undermine any of her husband's pursuits, no
matter how vehemently she objected to them. She
was eager to learn the games which so excessively
pleased her husband. She took pains with her appearance and denied herself extra servings of food
to keep from getting fat so he could remain proud
of her appearance, even if he was not proud of her.

She could not think of another thing she could
do to try to secure her husband's love but vowed to
continue working at it and to seek new avenues of
earning his affection.

For now she would have to take consolation in
the fact she must be doing something right. James
had not absented himself from her bed one single
night.

It pleased her that he took pleasure in her body.

Even though she was alone there in the parterre garden, her mind and body filled with the feel of James, and color rose in her cheeks as she remembered how greedily she hungered after her husband and his body that brought her such pleasure. If only she could be more reserved—and less like the courtesan she once had been. Though even with Gregory—whom she had loved recklessly—she had never been so abandoned, so uninhibited, as she was with her husband. James's very touch was a potent aphrodisiac to her. Nay, even the sound of his voice sent her heart racing.

Throughout the afternoon, she busied herself in the garden. She removed the spent growth from the rhododendrons. She planted sweet alyssum. She enriched the soil. And she savored the feel of the sun.

As she worked in the garden, four Covington brothers came strolling up toward Yarmouth. Seeing them and recognizing them off in the distance, Carlotta got up and met them in the park.

"Have you come to play with my son?" she asked.

"Aye," the eldest replied, his glance darting from her to the huge, four-storied manor house.

"Follow me, if you will," she said. "Should you like to see the house?"

The boy, dressed in clean homespun, shrugged. "We might be too dirty."

"Nonsense! Come in," she said, striding to the tall doorway and entering. She instructed the footman to find Master Stevie and inform him he had callers. Then Carlotta gave the boys a quick tour of the rooms directly off the entry hallway.

By the time she was finished, Stevie had come downstairs and happily greeted his new friends, all of whom were bigger than he.

"It's a lovely day to be outdoors," Carlotta said

to the lads. "Stevie, why do you not take your friends to see the mews?"

"We've got eleven horses—and one pony," Stevie said proudly as he turned to exit the house, the four taller boys following him.

Carlotta looked up to see Miss Kenworth standing behind Stevie.

"Should you like me to go with them?" Miss Kenworth asked.

"I daresay that won't be necessary. The Covington lads seem mature enough."

"Praise the good Lord, Master Stephen's so much more well behaved than my brother was," Miss Kenworth said, pressing her hands to her hips. "Imagine, if you will, a son coming on the heels of four sisters! To say that my mother—and the rest of us, for that matter—spoiled my little brother is an understatement. I daresay David thought there was nothing he could not get away with, and I daresay there was nothing he wouldn't try to get away with! Not at all like Master Stevie, who's sweet through and through."

Carlotta beamed. Stevie's goodness must have come from his father. "I wish I could take credit for my son's admirable traits, if indeed he does possess them, but alas, I cannot. As you must know, my son spent his formative years with my grandmother, who is the woman who also raised me as a mother would have."

Carlotta cleared her throat, then told Miss Kenworth something she had never told anyone before, not even James. "You see, my first husband's death left me almost penniless. I thought Stevie would be better off with my grandmother, whose own funds were rather limited. I had decided I would snare a husband in order to regain my son and be able to raise him as the grandson of an earl ought to be raised.

"What I never imagined was that it would be six long years before I received a proposal of marriage. And, I assure you, I never imagined that proposal would come from an earl—or from a man whom I would come to love so dearly." Carlotta's face colored. "Oh, dear, I'm blabbering my dreary life to you, telling you far more than you ever wanted to know, I daresay."

"Not at all, my lady. I love fairy book romances like yours and the earl's."

Fairy book romance? It was all Carlotta could do not to burst into laughter.

"I must say, I've never seen a man more in love than the earl appears to be with you."

Carlotta's stomach fluttered. Perhaps the poor girl needed Mr. Fordyce's spectacles! "I should like to think there's truth in what you say," Carlotta said, pulling off her gardening gloves. "Tell me, did you and Mr. Fordyce enjoy your walk the other day?"

Now it was Miss Kenworth who blushed. "I can't speak for Mr. Fordyce, but for myself it was most enjoyable. Mr. Fordyce is a decidedly interesting, intelligent man."

"I certainly appreciated the way he handled Stevie with the sparrow."

"He made me feel like a raving imbecile," Miss Kenworth said. "Why I never gave a thought to freeing the bird, I do not know!"

"Sometimes it just takes another person's perspective to see what should be as plain as the noses on our faces."

"Aye, that it does."

Carlotta glanced at the window. " 'Tis another lovely day. Why do you and Mr. Fordyce not take another walk? I daresay Stevie will be busy with his new friends until dinner."

"I couldn't impose on Mr. Fordyce. He has very important work to attend."

Carlotta sighed. "I suppose I'll have to once again order him to take time to smell the roses." She began to walk toward the library. "Come along. I think it is very good that you have another young person who speaks in the same tongue as you, so to say."

Miss Kenworth laughed. "To be sure. I've not yet learned to understand this Somerset dialect."

"In these parts, I daresay their speech is closer to a Devonshire dialect."

"Coming from Middlesex, I know neither."

Carlotta pressed open the swirling bookcase and came presently into Mr. Fordyce's office.

He stood to greet the ladies.

"My dear Mr. Fordyce, can you not guess why we're here?" Carlotta asked him.

His eyes flashed for a second, then he was mute, shaking his head.

" 'Tis another beautiful spring day, and my son has left Miss Kenworth in order to play with some neighboring lads. I desire that you amuse dear Miss Kenworth."

He glanced from Carlotta to Miss Kenworth. "I should not wish to disappoint you, my lady."

When Carlotta came down to dinner that night, James was not at the table. Her heart sank with disappointment. Since they had started sharing a bed, her husband had only been absent from their dinner table one night. She liked to think he was beginning to enjoy being in her company as much as she enjoyed being in his.

"Has my husband taken a tray in the library to-night?" she asked one of the footmen.

"No, my lady."

"Do you know what time he came home?"

The second footman shrugged. "To my knowledge, his lordship has not returned."

Carlotta's eyes rounded. *Not returned?* Why, it had been dark for over an hour! Surely James would not think of riding home over this rough terrain in the dark! Now she was going to be excessively worried about him. As if his insistence on going to the mines had not already caused her enough grief!

She was angry enough to scream like a banshee at him whenever he did return. Besides her worry, Carlotta hated eating alone. It quite made her lose her appetite.

The other footman moved closer and handed her the salver of buttered lobster, and she filled her plate from it and the smaller dishes which were close at hand. With each bite she took, her worry over James mounted.

She looked up at the nearest footman. "Would you instruct Adams to let me know when his lord-ship arrives home?"

Nodding, he scurried from the room.

Carlotta attempted to empty her plate but found she had lost her appetite. With every tick of the clock, her worry over James increased. Throughout the day her stomach had knotted when she had thought of him being down in those wretched mines, and now that he had not come home . . . where was he? Had he, perhaps, been injured in a fall from his horse? Why, in heaven's name, had he been foolish enough to try riding these hills at night? Her chest tightened. What if he was not riding home? What if there had been an accident at the mines?

Her fingers gripped her wineglass. Perhaps she should send out a search party. It wasn't at all like James to be gone this late. He was far too intelligent not to know the dangers of Exmoor—and the Bagworthy Woods—at night.

She looked at the clock on the mantel. Half past six. If he had not returned by seven, she would send out all the servants of Yarmouth to seek their master.

The very thought of James being hurt sent waves of fear rushing over her. She began to tremble and her heart drummed in a deep, frightening rhythm.

She pushed her plate away and rose from the table.

"Her ladyship does not wish the second course served?" the footman asked.

She shook her head. "I'm not hungry." Then she swept from the room. She went first to the foot of the stairs near the front door and met the gaze of the footman who stood there.

He shook his head solemnly. "Lord Rutledge has not returned."

Biting her lip, she nodded and strode down the marble hallway to James's library. She left the door open so she would hear James when he came home. Then she began to pace from one end of the Turkish carpet to the other. Every few minutes she would stop to read titles on row after row of gold-lettered book spines. Then she would commence pacing again, her heart racing madly, her hands trembling, her fears growing.

She glanced at the clock above the library's fireplace. Twenty more minutes until the hour. Then she would not hesitate to order everyone at Yarmouth to go out searching for their master.

As she paced, her eyes filled with tears, but she would not allow them to slip from her eyes. James wouldn't like that. And, she thought with a gush of emotion, James was, after all, her master.

The hands on the clock moved so slowly, Carlotta began to wonder if the clock were broken. As soon as she would decide to monitor it, the long hand would swing to another minute. *Soon it will be seven of the clock.*

By the time it was two minutes to seven, Carlotta lost all patience. She fled the room and began to gather up the servants. "I'm much concerned about Lord Rutledge," she told them once all of them were assembled in the central hall. "He should have been home by now, and I'm afraid he's come to harm. It isn't like him to stay from home so late. I desire that you pair up and head in the direction of the mines to seek Lord Rutledge."

As Carlotta spoke, a heavy knock thundered at the front door. The footman whose task it was to answer the front door started in its direction, but she swept past him and threw open the door.

She thought her heart would explode when she saw the black-faced miner standing before her. He inclined his head, then began to address her. "I'm sorry for bein' so late, but his lordship wouldn't allow us to come through these parts by horse at night . . ."

His lordship! At least James was alive!

". . . Seeing as he's down in the pit, he didn't know when it became dark, and he feared ye'd be worried when he hadn't arrived home by dinner . . ."

She wanted to yell at the man to get on with it! Why wasn't her husband home?

"There's been an accident at the mine," he finally said.

"James!" she shrieked. It was like a knife tearing into her heart. "What's happened to my husband?"

"Lord Rutledge is unharmed. There's been a cave-in, and two miners have been trapped. His lordship's been down there working to free them."

"How long ago was the accident?"

The miner's eyes flickered with fear. "Just as we was gathering up our things to go home."

Carlotta stiffened. Cut off from ventilation, the stranded pair of miners would surely be dead now. Yet James refused to give up. All she could think of was that she had to get James out of there.

"I beg that you take me back with you," she said.

Twenty-five

Before Carlotta raced upstairs to fetch her pelisse, cloak, and gloves and to change into sturdy boots, she sent Adams to request that Mr. Fordyce accompany her to the mine. During every step up the stairs, then while lacing her boots and grabbing the cloak, her heart drummed with worry over James.

As soon as her boots were tied, she flew down the stairs, where Mr. Fordyce, surrounded by more than a dozen liveried footmen, awaited.

"All the men wish to be of assistance at the mines," Mr. Fordyce said.

Carlotta glanced at the black-faced miner, who stood in his shirtsleeves just inside the doorway. He nodded. "Aye, all the extra hands would be appreciated."

"Then hurry and fetch coats!" Carlotta snapped. "It's cold in these hills at night, and we don't need any of you coming down with lung fever."

Next, she directed her attention to the miner. "Pray, how long did it take you to reach Yarmouth?"

He shrugged. "I was movin' at a right steady clip. I'd say it took me half of an hour."

Carlotta was horribly impatient to take off to the mines. "What's your name?"

"Matthew."

"Come, Matthew. Let us be off. The others will catch up."

The three of them left Yarmouth Hall on swift feet. As soon as they had cleared the hall, a gust of wind caught Carlotta's hair, blowing it across her face. She pushed it aside to restore her vision, not that one could see particularly well in the darkness. She looked up into the black sky to confirm there was no moon tonight.

The wind continued to rip and howl from the north, cutting into her. She gathered her cloak around her and pulled its hood over her head, but was otherwise oblivious to her discomfort. Her every thought centered on James and the unthinkable danger that surrounded him. *I've got to persuade him to get out of there!*

She could not remember ever being so scared in her entire life. She couldn't lose James. Not now. Now that she had discovered how dearly she loved him. Not after all these years of struggle and loneliness. Now that her dreams had come true. All but one, but even that she would gladly forgo to have her husband alive and healthy.

Both men who walked with her were solicitous of her comfort and safety, but she was determined not to hold them back. Even if her legs were shorter and her constitution more delicate, she vowed to keep up with them.

Soon she heard the deep voices of the throng of footmen who had chosen to come to the miners' aid, and she decided to make it a competition of her own not to allow them to pass her. No matter how cold or how fatigued she would become, she would not let down.

The moors at night were eerie and full of creature noises. Carlotta was thankful—though still not entirely comfortable—that she was surrounded by men.

Soon they cleared the moors and were mounting a heath that turned into a forest. If she had found the moors eerie, her walking through a forest at night was fraught with fear. Nocturnal creatures with their glowing eyes had always frightened her, and though they did their best to flee from her now, she was still keenly aware of their presence. She was also frightened of what she would see past each tree trunk. Added to her imagined fears was the real threat of stumbling over thick, aboveground roots or any of the heaps of irregular organic matter that lined the floor of the forest. But her greatest fear of all was fear for her husband.

"Take my hand, my lady," Fordyce said to her, holding out his hand.

She took it gratefully. Each step, now, felt more secure. If only she could feel secure about James's safety. She continued on through the wood, and though her face stung from the cold and her leg muscles burned from the unaccustomed strain, she refused to allow herself to slow down.

After half an hour, they cleared the woods, and the miner told them they were almost there.

Within minutes, she heard the churning of the huge wheel beside the stream, and she started to run toward the mine.

As she came up, the captain, his grim face almost unrecognizable with the black, was emerging from the mine. "Lady Rutledge!" He ran a quizzing glance over her.

She did not at all like the solemn look on the man's face. "My husband? Is he all right?"

He nodded. "Since he's the biggest, strongest

man here, he won't give up. He's trying to single-handedly dig out the two men who were shut off."

Her brows lowered with concern, and she spoke softly. "Any luck?"

He sadly shook his head.

"It seems to me if there's already been one cave-in, things have got to be unstable," Carlotta said, her voice trembling with fear. "Can't you get him out of there?"

"There's not a man among us who wants to leave our men down there without hope."

Her eyes moistened. "Surely you can't possibly hold out any hope? How long now have those men been without air?"

He shrugged, and she saw the pain on his face. "We can't give up hope."

She began to wring her gloved hands. *I must get James out of there!* How selfish she must seem when two other men—men who also had wives who loved them—were surely dead now. She met the captain's somber gaze. "Tell me, Mr. Hastings, do you honestly hold out hope for the two men?"

He glanced away and slowly shook his head.

"Then why not recover their bodies by daylight tomorrow? Why continue to jeopardize my husband—and others' husbands—tonight?"

"It's not my decision to make, Lady Rutledge. I take all my orders from Lord Rutledge, and he's the one who will not give up."

She had been so worried about James she had failed to notice that entire families of women and children had assembled around the mine. A glance at them made Carlotta feel wretchedly guilty.

Then she heard a familiar woman's voice and looked to see Mrs. MacGinnis and a bevy of maids and cooks from Yarmouth Hall coming up, laden with baskets and looking exhausted. Thank goodness her housekeeper had thought to bring provisions. Carlotta herself had been too upset to think rationally.

"Servants from Yarmouth have brought food—and, I hope, drink—for your men and their families," Carlotta said to the captain.

She turned toward the mine shaft. "Now, if you will, please take me down into the pit."

For the last hour, James had known his frantic digging and reinforcing, digging and reinforcing would not save his men. By now, they were long dead. He not only felt their loss keenly, but his heart bled for their families. Loving wives and much-loved children. He swallowed hard; then with his hands coiled tightly around the handle, he heaved the pick into the cold stone.

He was to blame for these men's deaths. He had cockily thought his improvements had rendered his mine completely safe. He had given his men false confidence. He should have closed down the rickety mine when he came here last year. He'd been reluctant to do so and deprive the men of their livelihood. Now he had deprived them of their lives.

He heard the cable being lowered and held up his lantern to see who was approaching. At first all he saw was purple velvet. Then he smelled lavender. Carlotta's scent. His heart began to race.

It could not be his wife. She was deathly afraid of the mines. She would never allow herself to be lowered down here. And, truth be told, he did not want her here. Especially not after what had happened here today.

He held his lantern higher and squinted into the

darkness. By God, it was Carlotta! An inexplicable fear tore through him. "What are you doing here?" he demanded.

"I've come to beg that you come out."

His Carlotta, who had vowed never to enter a mine, had lowered herself into this one for the sole reason of persuading him to leave. He was deeply moved by her concern for him. As she came to stand beside him, he went to stroke her beautiful face with his black hand, then stopped. He had never been more proud in his life.

Nor had he ever been more in love.

"I can't," he said. "I've got to try and get these men out."

"James," she said in a gentle voice, moving closer to him and setting a gentle hand on his arm, "you know there's no hope. Mr. Hastings even admitted as much to me. Please, will you not come back tomorrow when it will be safer and you can be more refreshed?"

Though he could only barely see her face now, he knew she was crying. Was his beloved sobbing because she was so terrified down here? Or was she gripped with fear for him? Either way, she obviously had come to care deeply for him. For the first time in hours, his heart felt almost light.

"Stevie and I need you. I . . . we couldn't bear it if anything happened to you." She reached up and set a lily-white hand at each side of his black face. "Please, my love, come up. Mrs. MacGinnis has brought food."

He set down the lantern and drew her into his arms. Never mind that his blackness would rub off on her dress. His desire to kiss her was more powerful than was his fear of a cave-in. He greedily lowered his lips to hers for a swirling, open, hungry kiss.

Though she was receptive at first, she soon drew back. "Please, love, let's go up."

Her need for him, indeed her deep affection for him, moved him to a place where he felt there was nothing he could not do. He felt as if he could single-handedly raise the roof of the entire mine. But he had to get his beloved wife out of here. And he knew the only way she would leave was with him.

"I'll follow you," he said curtly. He knew when he came up, the others would lose all hope. Even more difficult than facing the hopeless miners, though, would be facing the dead men's families.

With his arm about his wife's waist, they came out of the shaft and into the dark night. He saw by now that grim-faced family members had gathered around. His thoughts flashed to Waterloo and his men who were slain there. Men whose families he had to notify. Only writing a letter, as painful as it had been, was easier than coming face-to-face with a bereaving widow and fatherless children.

Hastings came up and set a hand on his shoulders—his mute attempt to express the comfort he was unable to convey with words.

"We've done all we can," James finally said. "I've decided not to risk any more loss of life. The men need to go home to their families tonight," he told Hastings. He cleared his throat. "And I need to console the two families."

"I'll go with you," Hastings said.

James nodded.

Carlotta stepped forward. "I'm going, too."

He was curiously torn between conflicting emotions of utter grief over the loss of life and elation over his wife's courage and devotion.

He nodded and moved closer to the assembled families. "There's nothing more we can do tonight," James began.

A woman's low, mournful wail cut into his speech and sent his stomach plummeting. It was too dark to see faces, but he knew at least one of the widows was here.

"We'll gather back here tomorrow morning and try to bring the bodies up."

Silence fell over the group. Even the children were stone silent.

He couldn't tell them now what was in his heart. That he would have to close the mine. It was too much for them to take in the span of one day.

He stepped back and whispered to Hastings. "The widows are here?"

"I'm told that Linderman's family is here. I don't know about Covington's."

Another woman shrieked, and James turned to see that it was his own wife.

"Douglas Covington?" she asked hopelessly.

He nodded.

"His poor wife . . ." Tears began to glisten on Carlotta's face.

He moved to her and closed an arm around her waist.

"I must go to Mrs. Covington," Carlotta said, sniffing and brushing tears from her wet cheeks.

"We'll go together."

First, James and all the miners' families gathered around Mrs. Linderman, who clutched a handkerchief to her swollen eyes as she softly sobbed. "My Harry. Why my Harry?"

James dropped to one knee before her and spoke softly. "I know, Mrs. Linderman, there's nothing I can say that will bring your husband back. I want you to know how highly I thought of him, what a dedicated worker he was—"

"For all the good it did him!" she wailed.

James nodded. "Please know that your family will never be in need. I will see that you never want for anything."

She broke into a sob. "Thank you, my lord." Then she began to wail, and several women gathered around her.

James got to his feet and turned back to his wife, holding out his hand. "We'll go now to the Covingtons'."

Hastings accompanied them on the ten-minute walk to the Covington cottage, but before they reached it, they came face-to-face with the entire Covington clan walking two abreast across the moors.

As soon as Mrs. Covington saw Lord and Lady Rutledge, she stiffened, and James knew that she knew.

"My Dooglas is dead," she said morosely.

Carlotta and her husband came to a stop, and Carlotta nodded. "How did you know?"

There was an emptiness in the widow's voice when she answered. "One of the lads what was at the mine came here to tell us our Dooglas was trapped down under. I never even thought about harm coming to him tonight since he said he'd be home late because of helping Mr. Hastings with some extra duties after work." Mrs. Covington broke into anguished cries.

Carlotta settled a gentle hand on the woman's shoulder. "Let's go back to your cottage. It will be warm there."

It was the longest walk Carlotta had ever taken. The two Covington daughters cried hysterically, and even the lads were unable to hide their tears. James offered to hold the babe, who was being held by the eldest girl, and Hastings lifted up a little boy who could not have been more than two years of age.

At the cottage, Carlotta settled the widow onto her dreary sopha, and the woman's children gathered around her.

"Mrs. Covington," Carlotta said, "I cannot tell you how terribly sorry I am for you."

James stepped forward. "Douglas Covington was one of the finest men I've ever known."

Mrs. Covington nodded. "He was the finest man, the best hoosband, and the greatest father there ever was."

"Indeed he was," Carlotta whispered, clasping the widow's hand. Carlotta could still picture the pride that came over the man when he spoke so affectionately of his family. With a stab of pain, she remembered, too, the words his wife had so recently uttered. *I don't know what I'd do if something ever happened to me Dooglas.*

How well Carlotta understood the emotions tearing at the woman right now. Until just minutes before, Carlotta had been crippled with the same fear—fear that she would be deprived of her own beloved husband.

"You are blessed that your Douglas left you such wonderful children," Carlotta said in a feeble effort at consolation. "As time passes, your fine sons will help to fill the emptiness and will serve to remind you of your husband."

Instead of their desired effect, Carlotta's words caused fresh waves of tears to burst forth from Mrs. Covington.

A knock sounded at the door. Hastings opened it, and a half-dozen miners' wives rushed into the room and threw their arms around the grieving widow.

Carlotta had thought to stay with Mrs. Covington this first night, but after the other wives came, she realized the widow would be more comfortable with these women of her own class.

Before they left, James told Mrs. Covington he would make provisions for her to assure that neither she nor her children would ever be in need.

Outside, Carlotta and James separated from Hastings, and slowly began the lonely trip home.

Twenty-six

The moors took on a macabre aura that moonless night as Carlotta and her brooding husband trod over the tussocks on their journey home to Yarmouth Hall. The only sound heard in the eerie silence was the fall of their footsteps. Blackness blanketed everything, including Carlotta's somber thoughts. She could not rid her mind of the gruesome vision of Douglas Covington's black body buried beneath the cold stone mine.

"I know you have to be completely exhausted," she said at length. "You left the house early this morning."

He sighed. "That I am."

Carlotta's thoughts settled on Douglas Covington's poor widow. It had just been a matter of days since she had told Carlotta how dear her husband was to her, how highly she regarded him. Carlotta remembered how the woman's face had brightened when she spoke of him. No more wistful smiles for the poor widow now, Carlotta thought morosely.

Her heart went out, too, to the unfortunate lads who would miss having a father to teach them about becoming a man. Her thoughts flitted to Stevie and how fortunate he was to have James.

Her heart sped up. How fortunate she was, too.

By the time Carlotta and James arrived at Yarmouth, Mrs. MacGinnis and her staff had already returned.

"Mrs. MacGinnis," Carlotta called to the housekeeper, "I must thank you for having the presence of mind to bring food to the miners. Your thoughtfulness was much appreciated."

James stepped forward and spoke to the woman. "You are much appreciated."

Mrs. MacGinnis smiled shyly.

Carlotta came closer and spoke with command tempered with sweetness. "I should like you to have Cook prepare feasts to take to the homes of the dead miners tomorrow. Would it also be possible to arrange to bring refreshments to the mines in the afternoon?" Carlotta glanced at her husband, wordlessly seeking his approval.

He nodded as Mrs. MacGinnis said, "We should be happy to help in any way we can."

"Now, if you please," Carlotta said, as she began to follow her weary husband up the stairs, "have hot water brought to my husband's chamber."

While waiting for James's tub to fill, Carlotta knelt at his feet and assisted him in removing his muddied boots.

"Never mind me," he said. "I daresay Mannington can manage with me. You'll need to remove the soot and mud from your own self."

She met his gaze and spoke throatily. "I wish to send Mannington away."

Now he understood. As exhausted as he was, he understood and his body feebly responded to the velvet tone of her seductive voice.

Mannington stepped from the dressing room with clean clothing for his master.

"I shan't need you anymore tonight, Mannington," James said, his eyes never leaving Carlotta's.

"Very good, sir," the valet answered flatly as he set the clothing on James's bed, then turned on his heel and departed.

With the firelight as a backdrop, James watched the footmen pour the last kettles of water into the tub, then leave the bedchamber.

Watching her husband with smoldering eyes, Carlotta reached for his buttons. James drew in his breath. She began to unfasten them, one by one. When she was finished, she laid her hand over the hair that matted on his chest. "So white there compared to here," she whispered as her hand reached to stroke his blackened face.

His breathing grew more harsh, his mind and heart shaken to their depths by her gentleness—and his ever-swelling love for her.

Slowly, she removed the shirt from him. "Shall we stand?" she whispered.

James answered her without words, pulling her up with him. Her hands slipped to the bare skin beneath his breeches, and she gave them a tug. "I shall require your assistance in removing these, my darling."

My darling. Good God in heaven! He was beginning to believe his wife had, indeed, fallen in love with him. He jerked off his breeches and watched as her eyes flitted to the center of his body, then back to his face.

"Get in the tub, love, and I shall wash you," she said in a husky whisper.

He obliged her.

She dropped to her knees and stirred her hands

in the water, then lathered the soap in them. "Scoot down, love, and I'll start with your hair."

He slipped completely beneath the water, then allowed just his head to come above the water line.

Carlotta began to lather his wet hair, then moved her gentle hands to his face, avoiding his eyes. "There!" she said when she finished. "You may rinse yourself now."

He plunged once more below the water. When he came up, his wife was holding out a towel. He grabbed it and dried his eyes, then his hair, then tossed it back to Carlotta.

Next, she began to wash his shoulders and his chest. Each gentle swirl of her magical hands sent his heart racing. With the firelight playing on her face, he smiled at the black smudges there.

He thought of the rush of emotions that had filled him when he had pulled her against him as they stood in the dark mine shaft. She had not cared that he dirtied her dress. As, indeed, she seemed not to care now that she was most likely dirtier than she had ever been in her entire life.

He loved her all the more for it. She had put him above herself. She loved him! He could storm from the room and shout his love for her from the rooftop!

"We shall need to trade places, my love," he said. "Next, it shall be my turn to wash you."

A smile slid across her face, and her eyes danced.

He stood up, his feet planted in the metal tub.

She offered her hand. "Come, allow me to dry you before the fire, love."

As she dried him, he began to unfasten her dress, despite being nearly debilitated by her seductive actions. Finally, she let the toweling drop and stood before his naked body as he finished removing her

dress; then he picked her up and carried her to the
bathing tub and set her in the water so gently the
water seemed to part to receive her ivory body.

With erotic pleasure, he slowly wiped the black
smudges from her delicate face. She slipped further
into the tub, and her ebony tresses became sub-
merged.

Next, his soapy hands moved to her breasts with
lingering circular motions.

She gave him an imploring look with those great
violet eyes of hers.

"Is it time, love?" he asked, his voice heavy with
his need.

She nodded.

He stood and lifted her from the tub, the toweling
gathered in his hands. In front of the firelight, he
tenderly patted her dry, then swooped her up into
his arms again, swathed her in the toweling, and
carried her to his bed, where he laid her on the
emerald velvet counterpane.

By now he thought he would surely explode with
his own need.

Her hand reached to cup him where his need
was greatest, and he flicked it away. "I can't wait,
sweetheart."

He put one knee on the bed, then the other between her knees as the first knee came to settle on
the other side of her.

She whimpered as her hands came up to stroke
his inner thighs.

He could wait no longer. He drove himself into
his wife's warm sheath with a ravaging, throbbing
hunger. She, too, ground herself into him. It was as
if he could not plunge deep enough to fill her. She
frantically pounded up into him until at last she

shuddered uncontrollably beneath him and cried out his name.

Long after her exhausted husband had gone to sleep, Carlotta lay in the circle of his embrace. Despite the tragedy that had occurred this day and the grief they all had endured, she was the most fortunate woman alive. First, because her beloved husband had been spared. Second, because James, in the heat of their lovemaking, had said, "God, but I love you, Carlotta!"

Knowing little pride where her husband was concerned, Carlotta had answered, "And I love you, dearest, with all my heart."

Though their lovemaking had always been passionate, tonight's was the most exhilarating yet. She had never felt more content. More complete. She felt as if she could burst with her limitless love for this man she had married.

Making the night even more special was the knowledge that this was the first time she had lain in her husband's bed. Now she was truly his countess. Her heart swelled when she wondered if the next Earl of Rutledge could have been conceived in this very bed.

Tonight would be the first time they would stay together all through the night. She wondered if they would make love again in the morning.

When morning came, she felt James stirring beside her and her lids lifted to discover him, his head propped on his hands, looking happily down into her face. She reached out to stroke his muscled arm and grew excited to remember neither of them wore any clothing whatsoever.

"Your touch may get me started again, love," he warned.

"A pity," she said playfully, continuing to stroke him.

He dove at her, and in minutes, they were spent and panting beneath the covers.

Allowing only enough time for his breath to return to normal, James bolted up. "As much as I should cherish spending the entire day in bed with you, love, I have grave duties to attend to today."

He got up and strode to his dressing room.

She watched his supple muscles, admiring the well-formed body of the man she loved; then she got up and followed him so that she, too, could get dressed. "I'll help you with your boots if you will do my buttons," she said with a smile. "How is it that both Peggy and Mannington knew to stay away this morning?"

"No doubt it's a sixth sense servants seem to be born with."

They went down to breakfast together. He would have to put his pleasurable thoughts behind him now for he had grim duties to perform today.

Throughout most of the breakfast they were quiet. He was amazed at how well Carlotta had come to sense his moods. Even last night, her gentleness, her loving, was the only emotion he could have stood. She had known how deeply he was hurting, and she had known how to balm him.

"What are you going to do about the mines?" she asked.

Good Lord, she had learned how to read his thoughts!

Their eyes met and held in confirmation of the melding of their minds.

He shrugged. "What will the men do if I decide to close the mine?"

She closed her small hand over his much bigger one. "You'll think of something."

He nodded grimly, then stood.

"I'm going with you," she said, getting to her feet.

He knew he had to allow her this. As much as he did not want her to come, she was truly his other half now. No longer could he exclude her.

Despite Carlotta's pleas that her husband not go into the pits, he did. She had known he would. And as long as he was under, she refused to leave.

It had been late afternoon before they were able to open up the caved-in shaft and pull out the asphyxiated bodies of Douglas Covington and Matthew Linderman. Carlotta turned her head when they brought the bodies up. She wished she could have turned the heads of the women and children who had gathered around throughout the day. Especially the children.

Once she was assured her husband would not go back into the mines, she left for the Covington cottage, James insisting that young Willy accompany her.

Several women were still gathered around the grieving widow, who sat in the same place on her sopha where she had sat the night before. Only today she held her infant—Douglas's infant, too—to her breast. She looked up at Carlotta with hollow eyes, red-rimmed from crying.

"Thank ye, me lady, for sending the victuals to

me children," Mrs. Covington said. "I daresay there's enough to last a month."

"I know how difficult it will be for you to cook, with your grief being so great," Carlotta said.

Tears sprang to Mrs. Covington's eyes, and she nodded.

"I've come to see if there's anything else I can do for you," Carlotta said.

"I want me Dooglas's body here."

Carlotta's heart tripped. "They're bringing it now."

Mrs. Covington buried her face in her hands and began to weep.

Carlotta stayed until a half-dozen miners, accompanied by her own husband, brought in Douglas Covington's body. The other wives promptly got up to clean the dead man and prepare his body. Carlotta wished to keep the children from beholding so grim a business. She leaped to her feet and announced, "Children, please join me outside." Her glance swept to each and every one of the blond youths.

They dared not disobey the Countess of Rutledge. Eight children filed from the house. Outside, she gathered them around her. "I thought it fitting that we come outside where we're closest to the Almighty. I wish to offer a prayer for your dear father."

All except the very youngest bowed their heads, tears gathering in the corners of their eyes.

"Lord our God, king of heaven, please accept into your kingdom today Douglas Covington, a fine and good man, a good Christian who lived his life by loving those he valued the most, his dear wife of twelve years, his seven strong sons, and his two beautiful daughters.

"Dear Lord, give Douglas's loved ones the

strength to carry on without their beloved husband and father. Give them the assurance their loved one has found his place with You in heaven."

When she finished, she looked up at them. There was not a dry eye.

"I don't mean to make you sad," she said softly. "I want you to rejoice that your father has found his place beside his Lord in heaven. He has been reunited with his little lost Mary. He's free of coal dust and long hours of hard labor. He can rest at last."

She looked up to see that the eldest boy's lip curled into a crooked smile, though his eyes were still moist.

"Now," Carlotta said, "I want each of you to think of a special thing about your father. Something he did which was special to you. My son Stevie and his nurse will come here with paper and pen to write down your remembrances and put them in a book. A book just for memories of your papa. And one day each of you will learn to read that book." She paused. "And I think your father would have been very happy to know his children had learned to read."

By now they had stopped crying. All of them. She could almost see the thoughts churning through their little brains. "Now go sit by the brook and think of a story about your papa. The brook is an appropriate place to remember him. Running water is a sign of life. You're to remember your father's life."

As Carlotta and her husband returned to Yarmouth, he said, "I've got to close the mines."

She nodded. "You'll be losing your major source of income, too."

He whirled at her. "That matters to you?"

She shook her head. "Not at all. I believe I could be happy with you in a cottage no bigger than the Covingtons'."

A smile crept over his face. He was choked with emotion—as well as an overwhelming urge to draw her into his arms. Instead, he attempted to act casually. "We'll be fine. I have many profitable investments, and I can raise sheep and cattle on my land."

"We'll need to provide a means of livelihood for the misplaced miners."

He nodded.

"Please don't be angry, dearest, but I promised the Covington children they would learn to read." She related what she had just told the youngsters.

"We can manage that, I suppose," he said.

"James, I want to help the miners' families."

"I can't have the Countess of Rutledge being a schoolmaster," he said with a laugh.

"Not that," she protested. "I have managed to hang on to some very valuable diamonds that used to be meaningful to me. Since they are no longer meaningful, I wish to sell them and use the money to establish the miners with their own stock to start sheep farming—or something that you think will be suitable to replace their lost income."

James squeezed her hand. "I can afford to do that."

"But I want to! Besides, you have your own income replacement to demand your money."

He lifted her hand to kiss it. "If it will make you happy, I'll try to sell the diamonds for you."

When Carlotta got back to Yarmouth, she raced to her chambers to fetch the diamond necklace and came back down to the library and proudly presented the necklace to James.

He looked at the distinctive necklace. There was only one in the kingdom made like it. Mr. Rundel himself had told James the necklace would never be duplicated. Its setting, constructed entirely of diamonds, formed a perfect square frame upon which a heart was centered.

James stiffened. The necklace had been commissioned by Gregory Blankenship for his mistress.

Twenty-seven

James had gone to London a short time after ascending to the earldom. At Boodles he had met the wealthy Gregory Blankenship and had been told that women threw themselves at the handsome Blankenship's feet. For his part, James had found the man amiable and easy to admire. James thought he was a bit too free with his spending, even if he could buy half the men at Boodles. Or so the rumor mill had it.

During that stay in London, James had cause to go to Rundel and Bridges at Ludgate Hill to have some stones reset on some of the Rutledge jewels. It was while he was bringing in the jewels that he happened to run into Blankenship. Having made each other's acquaintance at their club, they nodded to one another, then James continued on to the next clerk.

It was Mr. Rundel himself who assisted the enormously wealthy Blankenship. When Mr. Rundel had held up the distinctive diamond necklace, James could not help but look at it. Indeed, everyone who was then in the shop gathered around the stunning necklace and made exclamations over its magnificence.

One of the customers had the bad manners to say, "How happy your wife will be to receive that!"

To which Gregory Blankenship quipped—after directing a haughty stare at the woman—"But I have no wife."

That was when James remembered being told that Blankenship had for a mistress the most beautiful woman—a woman with eyes the color of violets.

Thinking on it now sent stabs of pain directly to his heart. His Carlotta had been Gregory Blankenship's mistress. He thought back on all the things she had told him about her failed efforts to remarry after Captain Ennis died. *She had wanted to remarry and had given her heart to a man who did not offer marriage.* Gregory Blankenship.

Had Carlotta been felled by a bullet, James doubted his pain could have been greater than it was at this very moment.

He didn't know which hurt most, the fact that she had been a mistress or that she had loved Blankenship so greatly she could have sunk to such depths.

Unsummoned, visions of his beautiful wife in bed with the paragon, Gregory Blankenship, slammed into James. He was going to be sick.

He could not meet his wife's gaze. "Please excuse me," he managed. "I've become ill." He turned to return to his chambers.

"Darling, what's wrong?" she asked, setting a hand to his arm and starting after him.

Shaking his head, he shoved her away, then entered his room, slamming the door on her.

He was sick for a very long time. Even when there was nothing left in his stomach, he lay across his bed in the dark room, unable to move. A lifetime of uncommonly good luck now mattered for naught. He gave a bitter laugh. Would that he could have suffered a lifetime of strife to enjoy marital bliss now.

His life had not been without pain. Captain Ennis's death had hit him hard. He had been bereft when he had lost his dear mother. But neither of those losses could prepare him for the grief of losing his cherished wife.

For he had lost her. The beautiful widow he had fallen in love with had never existed. The loving attributes he had imbued her with were nothing but figments of his imagination. Even the passionate way she had given herself to him meant nothing now. For such amorous charms came naturally to a courtesan. And his wife had been a courtesan.

He had never felt more bereft. In the span of a single second, his life had been irrevocably altered. Instead of being possessed of a loving family and looking toward a future with a loving wife and several children, he had nothing.

For he could not accept a whore for a wife.

He could not continue living at Yarmouth with her. He must get away from her. As much as he hated her at this moment, he could not send her away. There was the lad to consider. As much as he disliked the mother, he could not penalize the child. No, James thought, he would have to leave. Nothing would change for the boy. James would still provide for them. He would just not be around.

He stood up to test his stomach and found that he could move about without ill effects. He would have to find Carlotta and tell her.

First, he told Mannington to pack all his clothing. "We go to Bath today," he informed his valet.

James found Carlotta in her study. When he flung open the door, she stood up and came forward to greet him, concern etched on her beautiful face. "Are you all right, dearest?"

As she went to secure his hands, he pushed her away and walked over to the fire, turning his back on her. "As good as can be expected."

"Pray, love, what do you think is the matter?"

He took a deep sigh. "I find I cannot accept your diamonds."

"Why? I told you I have no use for them. I shall never wear them as long as I live."

At least she was over Blankenship, he thought bitterly. James finally had secured that which he thought he wanted above everything, only to learn he now wanted no part of it.

"I will not have the necklace because Gregory Blankenship bought it." He whirled around to face her. "Bought it for his mistress."

Her face drained of all color as she slumped into her chair, her great eyes filling with tears.

His hands coiled into fists as he glared at her. "Why did you not tell me?"

"Because you never would have married me—" She burst into tears.

"No, I wouldn't have, but I should have been told, Carlotta."

She made no move to wipe her tears or to keep the agonizing tremble from her voice when she spoke. "I would have preferred dying over admitting the truth."

As much as he had come to loathe her, it was difficult to stand there and watch her suffering and not move to take her in his arms. "I don't understand, Carlotta, how could you have allowed yourself . . . ?"

Her voice shook when she spoke. "My love made

me a fool." Deep sobs racked her. "I . . . I thought he w-w-w-would offer marriage."

It was painful to hear her admit to loving Blankenship. Finally, he found his voice. "I must leave, you know," he said simply, avoiding her gaze.

She nodded, then buried her face in her hands as her shoulders shook with sobs.

He strode across the room, let himself out, and slammed the door behind him.

Carlotta was not unprepared for her great heartache. She had never been confident her dark secret would remain hidden. Gregory, though she was certain of his discretion, was far too well known to hide an affair of such long standing from his prying friends, of which the man had far too many.

Deep within her breast, Carlotta had always known James would discover her great shame. He was bound to learn he had given his name and his title to a fallen woman.

She had always known happiness would elude her. Whenever she'd had a glimpse of it, it had been brutally snatched from her. She had been orphaned at an early age. She had become a widow when she was but nineteen. And she had loved with all her heart a man who wanted only her body.

None of those hurts, though, could compare to today's devastation, she thought as she slumped over her desk, weeping bitterly. Complete happiness had been so close—nay, she had held it in her hand. She could live a thousand lifetimes and never find James's equal. He not only had her heart, he had possessed her soul. Just being in the same room with him could cause her eyes to tear from her boundless love. Every time he held her in his arms, something deep and profound had stirred within her.

He was the most unselfish man she had ever known. Even in his leaving, he had been unselfish. It was he who would give up the comforts of his home and servants in order for Stevie and her to keep them.

Fresh tears slid down her face.

She remembered the devastation she had felt when Gregory married. As wrenching as it had been, it diminished when compared to losing her beloved husband.

For she knew she had lost James. He was too fine a man to sully himself with a woman like her.

She remembered, too, how she had sulked and fretted and wished herself dead when she had lost Gregory. For months, she had not left her lodgings, except once—to move from a grand house when her settlement from Gregory began to run out.

Her eyes swollen, her heart irreparably bruised, she rose from her desk and walked to the window. Her glance fell on the parkland in front of Yarmouth and upon the broad avenue that led up to the home James loved so dearly. She watched as Jeremy brought Ebony around. Her breath caught and she cinched in her breath to keep from weeping as she saw James climb upon his mount.

Tears clouded her vision as her eyes followed James while he rode away from Yarmouth, away from the place where they had shared such total happiness. As painful as it was to watch, she refused to look away until she could no longer see him.

Great tears sliding down her face, Carlotta turned away from the window. It was as if her very heart had been wrenched from her. Were it not for her son, she would wish to die. But, by God, she *did* have a son. A son who needed her. No longer could she allow herself to wallow in pity, to forget there were others who depended upon her.

All the goodness James had imparted to her would matter for naught if she shirked her obligations. She would not demonstrate her love for James by weeping prostrate on her bed; she could demonstrate her love for him by putting aside her own heartache and giving of herself as James had so willingly given of himself to so many who needed him.

Now, though, she squared her shoulders and sat up straight in front of her desk. She refused to cripple herself over this. Not because she did not want to. Oh, she wanted to lie down and die. But she could not allow herself to. Too many people now depended upon her.

Her first concern had to be Stevie. For his sake she would be strong, even if her heart were bleeding. With James gone, there would be many other people who would look to her for counsel, and she meant to pull herself up from despair and take on all the responsibilities of the Countess of Rutledge.

Despite being a fallen woman, she would conduct her many duties with the dignity of a countess. Her shame was behind her. Her future lay in service to others. Especially those less fortunate than she. She must do that which James would have done, that which, by his example, he had taught her to do.

By day she would provide potent leadership and administer love to Stevie and those she cared for. By night, she would allow herself to ache for her lost James.

She cleared away her tears that very minute and stood up. She was determined to fill James's sturdy shoes to the best of her abilities. But what would she tell people when they asked about her husband?

She moved to the basin and put some cold water on her swollen eyes. She would have to cross that bridge when she came to it. One thing was sure: she would never lie again.

What could she say when weeks had passed and still Lord Rutledge had not returned? For she knew he would not.

Since the skies were clear, James had decided he would ride Ebony to Bath. Because of his late start, he was relatively certain he might have to put up at an inn for the night. That was preferable to staying at Yarmouth. How could a place which had brought him such happiness now hold such crippling grief?

The wind to their backs, he and Ebony rode over moors and glens and sweeping hills. By the time they were two hours from Exmoor, the skies overhead clouded. James looked up and realized rain was imminent. Which would be in keeping with this dreadful day. Let the rains come! What did he care? What did he care about anything?

Just the night before he had come to realize he possessed his heart's desire: the love of his wife. Now he had nothing. The woman he had married apparently gave her love—and her magnificent body—far too readily. Despite his sudden hatred for her, he grew aroused just remembering the sexual delights she had offered him the night before. *Damn her!*

He tried to reason with himself. Loving one man—though that one man was not her husband—did not make a woman a whore. For, as much as it hurt him to admit it, Carlotta had been in love with Blankenship. *Damn him!* She had been honest about that. And about wanting marriage—which the blackguard Blankenship refused to offer. How could the man have ruined her so? Would that James could punch away at the man's handsome face. Better not that, though, for James was not at all convinced he would not kill Blankenship if he were given the opportunity.

A light mist began to fall, and James hoped he could make it to the next village. He gathered his coat tightly around him to block the gathering wind. Before he had gone a mile, the sky grew darker and the mist turned into a drizzle; then the drizzle quickly became a pounding rain that beat down upon him relentlessly. Huge, gaping puddles began to mire Ebony's way, and he could hardly see three feet in front of him.

James leaned forward and stroked Ebony, speaking soothingly to him. He only hoped the lightning he saw in the distance would stay away because his horse was terrified of thunder and lightning.

Again, James's famous good luck did not hold. Thunderclaps came ever closer until it seemed as if the heavens roared directly above them. Ebony's great hind legs collapsed under him as his front legs soared upward. Because of the wetness, James slipped from the saddle. He fell backward, and as his head hit the ground, he felt it come into contact with something hard and sharp. Then all James knew was a great, vast blackness.

Twenty-eight

How many hours he had lain in the wet, pounding rain, James had no idea. Several hours, he knew. When he came to, the night was black, and the rain had subsided though James looked and felt as if he'd been swimming in a raging river, his back dragged across the its rocky bed. There was no sign of the thunder and lightning that had so frightened Ebony.

As James went to raise himself, pain shot through his head. Unable to ignore the headache and unwilling to give in to it, he struggled to his feet. He heard a stirring in the woods behind him and spun around. Despite the throbbing in his head, a smile slid across his face. Ebony had not run away but must have stayed beside his master's body for hours. Bloody horse probably felt guilty.

Shivering with cold, James went forward to sweet-talk and stroke the beast.

What James needed now was a warm room at an inn. He had no idea where he was or how long it would be before he would reach an inn. Not without pain, he mounted Ebony and headed east.

Squinting against the noonday sun, Carlotta rode her filly across the lonely moors. This morning's business had been most unpleasant, indeed. She had gone to console the widow and children of the other deceased miner, Matthew Linderman. Her heart had gone out to the poor widow. She was so young—not more than two and twenty—and was now left with four young'uns to care for alone. And judging from her swollen belly, she was due to deliver another before the summer solstice.

Carlotta had immediately admired the young mother, who had made an effort to brush aside her grief in order to welcome Lady Rutledge into her modest cottage. The girl had beamed with pride when she had introduced her children to Lady Rutledge. The eldest—a sturdy lad—could not have seen more than four summers.

Mrs. Linderman would not leave the side of her husband's coffin, which sat waist-level on a bier.

The grateful, sobbing widow could have kissed Carlotta's skirts when the countess assured her Lord Rutledge would provide for her and her children.

Leaving the sadness of the Linderman cottage, Carlotta realized her own fate could have been worse. At least the man she loved so dearly was still alive. She could not have borne the sight of her beloved James gray and lifeless in a coffin. It was bad enough that she would never again be held in his arms, never meet his teasing gaze nor hear his whispered words of love.

After so agonizing a morning and so wretched a night, Carlotta was ready for a glimmer of brightness, and who better to bring her this than her sweet little son?

Back at Yarmouth, she found him in the nursery with Miss Kenworth. "I've come to hear Stevie read," Carlotta announced as she strolled into the room and bent to kiss her son.

He shot an embarrassed look at his nurse.

"Why do you not read her your newly learned poem, lad? Your mother is uncommonly fond of poetry."

He began to fumble through a pile of thin books at his desk until he came to the one he sought. "Here it is!" he exclaimed, looking up happily at Carlotta.

"I should love for you to read it to me, lamb." She pulled a child-sized wooden chair up beside her son and sat down, beaming at his serious little face.

He took the slim book and stood up. "It's called *The Wife of Usher's Well.*"

She nodded.

" 'There lived a wife at Usher's Well and a wealthy wife was she; She had three stout and stalwart sons and sent them o'er the sea.' "

He stumbled only at the word *stalwart.*

When he got to the final stanza of the old ballad and read, " 'Fare ye weel, my mother dear; Fareweel to barn and byre; And fare ye weel, the bonny lass that kindles my mother's fire,' " a tear slipped from Carlotta's eye.

"You read that very well, my sweet. I'm very proud of you."

He looked up and smiled. "Just like *The Wife of Usher's Well.*"

"She did so love those sons," Carlotta said. "Just as I love my son."

"Mama?"

"Yes, love?"

"I heard the servants say Papa has gone away. Can that be true?"

Her breathing ceased. "Yes, he has gone. I shall miss him greatly, as I'm sure you shall." She tried to sound casual, to belie the crushing pain in her heart.

"When's he coming home?"

She shrugged. "I don't actually know, love. Soon, I hope." Her poor son had undergone enough change. She must allow him to be accustomed to not having James around before she dared to tell him how unlikely it was that he would ever see his stepfather again.

With a forced smile, she left the nursery and trudged to her study. What was she to do? She had unfinished work here at Yarmouth. For the first time in her life, she actually felt needed, felt as if she had a contribution to make. Furthermore, she vehemently objected to displacing her son once more.

Yet, underlying all the reasons why she *should* stay at Yarmouth was the single reason why she should leave: *Yarmouth wasn't hers.* It was James's. He had done nothing in *his* past to warrant his expulsion from his beloved home. Why should he live the life of a vagabond because of her great sin?

She also felt guilty about accepting his generosity. She and Stevie were enjoying the lavish life afforded them by James. She felt ashamed to keep accepting it. Then she placated herself with the memory of the great debt James owed her and Stevie for having deprived them of a husband and father. And it wasn't as if James couldn't afford it. Had it only been her, though, she would have left Yarmouth with nothing. But she had to provide for her son.

Had it not been for Stevie, she realized, she would have lain in her bed lamenting James's loss and hoping for death to release her from her woeful life. But because her son needed her, she refused to give in to her grief.

She finished penning a dutiful letter to her grandmother, giving the poor old woman no hint that all was not well at Yarmouth Hall; then she went downstairs to post the letter.

Mr. Fordyce was just walking into the hall with several items he intended to post. "Oh, there you are, my lady," he said, nudging his spectacles up the bridge of his nose. "Could I have a word with you?"

Carlotta cocked her head. "Certainly."

He set the letters down on the demilune table and lowered his voice. "In my office, if you please."

She followed him into the library and into his adjacent office, taking a seat before his desk.

He remained standing. "It's about his lordship," he began. "I've been told he suddenly left yesterday, but that is most unlike Lord Rutledge. I've never known a more conscientious man than he. We—the steward and I—had many projects that demanded his attention. Surely he's not gone off?"

"Oh, dear," Carlotta said lightly in an effort to conceal her grief, "he has gone off. I daresay he's convinced you and the steward are well able to make decisions without him."

Fordyce's forehead collapsed into a scowl. "When will Lord Rutledge return?"

She shrugged. "I'm not really sure I know."

"If you could give me his direction, I will endeavor to communicate with him by post, then."

Carlotta's chest tightened. On the one hand she did not wish to lie; on the other, she was not sure her husband would like it known that he had fled in anger. What was she to do? "It will be extremely difficult to communicate with him as his destination is rather uncertain." At least she had not lied.

"But what if you need to communicate with him?"

"Oh, I don't need to," she said breezily.

The secretary began to pace his office from one end to the other, pausing once to peer from the window. "Did his lordship authorize you to act in his behalf?"

Oh, dear. She really did not want to lie. "I *can* act on his behalf." *Even if he didn't authorize me to do so.*

Mr. Fordyce's face cleared. "Yesterday Lord Rutledge told me to establish trusts for the families of the two miners who were killed. They are to receive funds indefinitely the first of every quarter."

Carlotta nodded.

"But his lordship did not tell me how much money is involved."

"That's a simple enough matter to solve," she said decidedly. "You need only determine how much the collier's wages were and see to it that the family continues to receive the same amount of money."

Mr. Fordyce chuckled. " 'Twas so easy, I can't believe I didn't think of it myself."

"I believe, Mr. Fordyce, I should like the miners to gain a new means of livelihood in the event my husband decides to close the mine."

"You, my dear Lady Rutledge, may not be aware of it, but you are reform minded."

"I believe I shall take that as a compliment." She paused. "Mr. Fordyce?"

"Yes?"

"I would wish to send you to London on a mission for me."

"To London?"

"Yes. Surely you've been there?"

— "Many times."

"I should like you to go to Rundel and Bridges and sell a hideously gaudy necklace of mine for me. I should like to use the money it fetches to, perhaps, allow the miners to foray into sheep farming—or some such endeavor that would allow them to replace their income."

"Does his lordship approve of you disposing of your jewels in such a manner?"

"Of course he approves—though these are *not* Rutledge jewels. They were in my possession before I married. And, I assure you, my husband is a most generous man, as you must know. It's just that if he closes the mine, I fear his own income will be substantially reduced. I shouldn't wish him to suffer on any account. Especially when I have in my possession so valuable a necklace."

"When should you like me to leave?"

"If you have no objections, tomorrow morning should be fine."

Each time Ebony shifted his weight, James's head throbbed with pain. He was cold. His body was weary. They rode and rode and still did not come to an inn. Finally, a light in the window of a stone farmhouse beckoned. He had to take refuge there before he slid once again from Ebony's back in his aching exhaustion.

A moment later, James limped to the farmhouse door and knocked.

A white-headed man in homespun answered, a curious look on his face.

"Forgive me for disturbing you," James croaked, "but I've been injured in a fall from my horse and would like to pay for a night's lodging at your home."

The farmer swept the door open wider. "Yer welcome to it, sir, though I cannot vouch for the cleanliness of the linens. The children's room ain't been used since me missus died. 'Course, our children are old enough to have sired ye," he said with a laugh.

James stumbled through the doorway.

"Can I help see to yer wounds?" the old man asked.

James shook his head. "If you'll just direct me to the bed . . ." He had barely enough energy to talk.

"This way," the man said, leading James up the dark, narrow stairway.

When the man lit a candle and set it beside the bed in "the children's room," James thanked him and collapsed onto the bed.

He slept like the dead until morning and woke up feeling refreshed and a great deal better than he had the night before. Then he moved. The bruises on his back and head screamed. Bracing against the pain, he removed himself from the damp, lumpy bed and went downstairs.

There, the farmer was preparing a breakfast of tongue, trout, and toast—as he informed James.

James could eat a horse. "May I lend you a hand?" he asked the farmer.

"Not a gent like yerself. Daresay ye've never been in no kitchen in yer life."

James chuckled. "I've been in a kitchen, though I daresay I don't know my way around one."

The old man sighed. "Day was when I didn't. But then me Betty died. Married eight and thirty years, we were."

"You must miss her very much."

"That I do." The farmer scooped up the trout and set it on two plates, then glanced at James. "You married?"

James's stomach plummeted as he barely nodded. The host filled the plates and set them on the table in front of James. "Not fancy food like a gentleman of quality such as yerself is used to," he said apologetically.

"My dear man, this is the most welcome meal I've ever had." Then James set about stabbing the trout with his fork.

The farmer's appetite was not nearly as great as James's. A glance over his rail-thin frame confirmed the likelihood that this morning's feast was not customary.

"Allow me to introduce myself," James said after a sip of cold cream. "I'm James Moore." No sense flustering the man with his title.

The farmer nodded. "Me name's Tilburn. Michael Tilburn."

"Where are we?"

"Two hours from Bath."

He never would have lasted those two hours last night, James thought. He dove back into his plate. Once it was clean, he directed his attention to his host. "I thank you for your generosity, Mr. Tilburn. That was the best breakfast I've ever had."

The old man chuckled. "Ye must have been sorely hungry. A pity me Betty passed. Now there was a cook." He eyed James. "How long ye been wed?"

James gave a bitter laugh. "Only a few months."

The farmer's eyes scanned James. "Allow an old man to give advice. When me Betty died, I was filled with regrets. All the words I wanted to tell her I would never be allowed to say. The petty little arguments had caused a friction that I'd allowed to fester. Then before I knew it, she was gone, and I realized none of those disagreements mattered. All that mattered was that I had loved her with all me heart and had never told her."

He gazed solemnly at James. "Don't ever go to bed mad with yer wife."

The man's eyes moistened, and James knew he had better look away, or he would end up exactly like his host.

Before he left Mr. Tilburn's house, James gave him a sovereign with profound thanks.

By the time James reached the Sheridan Arms Hotel in Bath, Mannington, who had brought James's clothing in the coach, was beside himself with worry and extremely relieved when his master at last arrived.

The first thing James did upon his arrival was to crash into the fat feather mattress and sleep like the dead for nearly a full day. When he finally awoke, pain surged through him. Not just the pain from the bruises on his back or the swelling on his head, but the unending pain of knowing the Carlotta he had fallen in love with was lost to him forever.

James was in Bath for several days, venturing no further than the public houses which offered the spirits he had come to require.

Two days' distance separated him from Carlotta and still thoughts of her stormed through him. He had been so blessedly close to perfect happiness—he had touched it, tasted it, but it was too elusive.

James had been woefully inept in thinking he could purge Carlotta from his thoughts merely by removing himself from her presence. Her hold on him was strong. Barely a moment passed without him remembering her sweet lavender scent, or the purring sound of her seductive voice, or the smooth feel of her bare flesh. She had penetrated his mind and body like ink on a blotter.

When night would come he would lie in his bed and torture himself with visions of Carlotta writhing beneath Gregory Blankenship. He came to loathe both of them.

During his second week in Bath, he ventured into the Pump Room and signed the book, not that he expected anything to come of it. After all, he was not a social creature. He had been content to retire to the country with the woman he loved.

Rage swept over him. Now he knew why Carlotta had no friends in Bath, why she had been so anxious to remove him from the city. He felt utterly duped.

While he was perusing the names in the book, Gregory Blankenship strolled up to him. It was all James could do not to send his fist crashing into the man's face.

"Lord Rutledge!" Blankenship said. "I don't suppose you remember me." He swept into a bow. "Gregory Blankenship—from Boodles."

James's eyes could have burned through the scoundrel. "I do."

"Felicitations on your recent nuptials. I read the announcement in the *Times.*"

"I also remember you from Rundel and Bridges," James said viciously.

"The necklace!"

"Exactly." James spit out the words.

Blankenship looked behind him, then turned back to Gregory. "Where can we speak?"

"I have nothing to say to you."

"Then you know . . ."

"I know I should like to run a sword through you."

Blankenship hung his head. "It's not what you think, my lord. Mrs. Ennis was a virtuous woman," he almost whispered.

"You will never force me to believe the great womanizer Gregory Blankenship did not bed my wife," James said icily.

Blankenship looked around nervously once more. "From the beginning, she made it clear she would settle for nothing less than marriage. It wasn't what you think."

God, but James wanted to believe the man, but Carlotta herself had admitted her culpability. "I refuse to discuss my wife with you," James said, then spun on his heel and left the lofty chamber.

Twenty-nine

Her son accompanying her, Carlotta attended Sunday services at the little church located on the other side of Bagworthy Wood. It was the only time she got a glimpse of the miners with their faces clean. During the service, Carlotta was prohibited from viewing many other churchgoers because the Rutledge family pew was at the front of the church.

Afterwards, she joined those who had gathered outside in front of the church doors. Her eyes fell on Mrs. Covington's toddler son, who held up his arms for his mother to hold him, but his mother's hands were already full with Daniel.

Carlotta bent to pick up the boy, who was still a baby, but he was frightened of her. She then held out her arms to Mrs. Covington, "Allow me to hold Daniel."

After giving the infant to Carlotta, Mrs. Covington picked up the little lad, who could not yet be two. Despite the sorrow on the widow's face and the pain she had to be going through, Carlotta was strangely jealous of her, for Mrs. Covington had borne nine children—nine wonderful children—for the man she had loved. Her riches were far greater than Carlotta's. Carlotta hugged Daniel to her.

Affectionately stroking the infant and planting

soft kisses on the downy hair on top of his head, Carlotta made it a point to greet as many miners as she knew by name and others she knew only by sight.

"Tell me it ain't so that Lord Rutledge has left Exmoor," one of the miners said to her.

"Lord Rutledge may not be here physically, but be assured my husband's here in spirit. The miners are never far from his heart. If it were at all possible for him to be here, he would." Another evasive answer, which she had become so adept at giving of late.

After visiting with the parishioners, she and Stevie got into the carriage. Though they had walked to church the week before, Carlotta thought not to today in order to keep Stevie from being outdoors more than necessary. He had been coughing and sneezing, and—fearing he would take a chill—she meant to keep him indoors.

He sat on the opposite seat from her. "Come sit by your mama, love," she said soothingly.

He came and sat close to her, tucking his head into her bosom. Her arm slipped around him. Was there anything on earth as fulfilling as feeling your arms around your child? she wondered. She went to stroke the hair from his forehead, and her hand came into contact with skin as hot as a fire screen. "Oh, dear, you're burning up, lad! Why did you not tell me how sick you were?"

"I'm not sick," he protested, his teeth chattering. "J-j-just cold."

She swept off her own cloak and wrapped him in it, taking his little hand into hers. "We need to get you home and into bed, lamb." Her hands rubbed up and down his thin arms in an effort to warm him.

She glanced down at his listless face and his drooping lashes, and she became frightened. She had never seen Stevie when he did not have boundless energy.

The ride back to Yarmouth seemed interminable. She kept patting his arm, his shoulder, kept kissing the top of his head, all the while a sick feeling gnawing in the pit of her stomach. Other, more experienced, mothers might not react as she did, but since this was her first time to care for her own sick child, she was, perhaps, unnecessarily worried. Was it normal for her poor little one to run a fever? What a wretched mother she had been not to know more of her child's background.

When the coach pulled up in front of Yarmouth, Carlotta did not wait for the footman to open the carriage door. She swept it open and reached back to lift up her son. She carried him into the house and up the stairs to his chamber, ignoring pleas from the footmen, who wished to take the lad off her hands.

She set Stevie on his new red bedcovering and stooped to remove his shoes, then his clothes. She tucked him beneath the covers and kissed him. "What you need, lamb, is sleep. By tomorrow, you'll likely be back to your normal self."

"Mama?" he whispered in a croak.

She leaned into him. "What, my love?"

"It feels so good to be lying here."

"I know, my sweet." *If only it could be I.* It was far too painful to see her son so incapacitated. Especially now that she had already lost James. James, who would have been such a help at a time like this. She must not allow herself to think of James. She had schooled herself to push thoughts of him from her mind to enable herself to function here at Yarmouth in his absence. If she had allowed herself to remember the love she felt for James or the bliss he had given her or the emptiness she felt now, she would never have been able to perform her duties.

Carlotta could not bring herself to leave Stevie's bedside. The footmen must have talked about her dramatic entry, for soon Miss Kenworth flew into the room, concern on her face. "My lady! What's wrong with Master Stephen?"

It felt good to share her concerns with another adult. "He's burning with fever, even though I made him take the carriage to church—because of his cough. I daresay he'll be back to his old rambunctious self by tomorrow."

Miss Kenworth's brows lowered as she stepped closer. "I told him he needed a coat yesterday, but he would have no part of one." Her face clouded. "Oh, 'tis my fault, I fear."

"It's no one's fault," Carlotta said sternly. "The child has merely taken a chill."

Miss Kenworth turned to Carlotta. "Don't worry about Master Stephen, my lady. I'll stay here with him."

Carlotta nodded, kissed her son, and left his newly painted chamber, smiling at his color choice of ruby red.

Since it was Sunday, she could not even indulge herself by working in the garden, but she could at least walk its paths. And hope that James did not converge upon her thoughts too greatly. Sweet Jesus, but she missed him. Not a day had passed that she did not think of something she wanted to share with him. And she dared not allow herself to remember his voice or his smile or his sensual touch.

She strolled the myriad dissecting paths, unable to purge the man who had been her husband from her thoughts. Where was he? Was he ever going to return to Yarmouth? Did he ever spare a thought for her or for Stevie? Her stomach tumbled. Would she ever see him again?

Even if they could never recapture what they had shared, she yearned to see him once more. It would be balm to her soul.

In the event he did not return, she needed to start making arrangements for the running of Yarmouth and the mines, even if it was not her place to do so. But it would be better were he to come home.

When he returned—if he did—she knew she would have to leave Yarmouth. She and Stevie both. For Yarmouth wasn't theirs, even if they had grown to think of it as their home. She and Stevie would find a little cottage somewhere and accept a modest settlement from the man who had caused Stephen Ennis's death.

If only they could find a way not to miss James so horribly.

"Good afternoon, my lady."

She turned to see Mr. Fordyce. She had not even heard him approach. "Hello, Mr. Fordyce."

"Would you object if I walked with you?"

"Please do. I always love sharing my garden, and I daresay I could use the company, too. Things have grown rather lonely here at Yarmouth without my husband."

Fordyce fell into step beside her. "Any word when Lord Rutledge is coming home?"

She shook her head. She had grown so tired of hearing that same question.

"I must commend you on your wisdom in selecting Miss Kenworth. She's extremely capable," he said.

"I cannot deny she is well qualified. What has been serendipitous—for Stevie, especially—is her unequaled good nature. Finding Miss Kenworth has, indeed, been a blessing for all of us."

"By Jove! That's it!" he exclaimed. "She's gifted with uncommon good nature."

Carlotta stole a glance at him. Could Mr. Fordyce be falling in love with the pleasant nurse? *How devilishly wonderful!* " 'Twould be difficult to imagine Miss Kenworth ever being in an ill humor."

"And she is singularly intelligent," he added. "Especially for one as young, as delicate, as Miss Kenworth."

Miss Kenworth delicate! Carlotta willed herself not to laugh.

Mr. Fordyce slowed his pace. "It was obvious to me when Lord Rutledge was here that you love him very much."

She sighed. "I do."

He cleared his throat. "Such an observation came to me because I seem to have love and marriage on my own mind a great deal of late."

She kept walking and spoke calmly. "Since Miss Kenworth has come to Yarmouth?"

"Exactly."

"Methinks, perhaps, you've fallen in love, Mr. Fordyce."

"I believe you to be right, my lady. The question is, what shall I do about it?"

She slowed her step. "Should you wish to marry the lady?"

"I do, indeed."

Carlotta slowed her step and directed a smile at him. "Why, then, you've only to ask her!"

"But I should be ever so humiliated were she to

turn me down. After all, it's not as if I don't have to see her every day of my life."

Carlotta stopped and looked up at him. "But, Mr. Fordyce, I really don't believe Miss Kenworth *will* turn you down."

"She's spoken to you?" he asked hopefully.

Her shoulders slumped. "No, but I can tell by her demeanor, the same way you could tell from mine how greatly I love James." *Even if he does not love me.* She would always love James.

He looked at her suspiciously. "Would that I could believe you."

Carlotta set a hand on his arm. "Trust in me."

Then, without talking, the two of them set off walking again.

At length, Carlotta said, "Why do you not ask her?"

"I'm not very knowledgeable about matters of the heart. I know one is supposed to ask the maiden's father, but since Miss Kenworth's father is deceased, I'm not sure how I should go about this."

"Just ask her. Miss Kenworth's mature enough to know her own mind."

"I've never been so nervous."

"Allow me to send her down. The quicker you do it, the sooner it will be over with."

"Do you really believe she will favor my suit?"

Carlotta had turned to walk away. She stopped and pivoted back to him. "I know not what Miss Kenworth's opinions are on marriage, but I believe she would entertain your suit above all others."

He sighed. "Very well."

Carlotta tiptoed into her son's room, where Miss Kenworth, reading a book, sat beside his bed. "How is he?" Carlotta whispered.

"There's been no change, my lady," Miss Kenworth answered.

"Allow me to relieve you now," Carlotta said. "Mr. Fordyce is in the parterre garden, and has asked me to ask you to join him."

Miss Kenworth's hand automatically flew to her hair. "Me, my lady?" she asked with surprise.

It was all Carlotta could do not to blurt out the secretary's intentions, but she dared not relieve him of that pleasure. "Yes. You two have become rather good friends, have you not?"

Miss Kenworth spoke shyly. "I should like to think we have."

"Then go on with you!"

"Are you sure you can spare me?"

"I'm sure."

For a long time Carlotta sat there watching her son. He was so beautiful with his tawny hair and tawny skin and perfect little face. A pity he felt so wretched today. He continuously tossed and turned, throwing off his covers, sweat drenching his head. Then he would alternately begin to shiver and beg for the counterpane. She grew quite concerned, and finally rang for a servant.

Adams himself answered her ring.

"I need the doctor fetched," she said, not without worry. "Master Stevie's quite ill."

"I shall dispatch a man immediately, my lady," Adams told her before he slipped quietly from the sickroom.

No sooner had Adams left the room when Miss Kenworth—along with Mr. Fordyce—entered.

Carlotta glanced at their beaming faces and knew they came with good news. She stood up and, with her hands outstretched, went to greet them.

"I wanted you to be the first to know, my lady," Miss Kenworth said.

Mr. Fordyce stepped forward. "Miss Kenworth has done me the goodness of accepting my offer of marriage."

Carlotta smiled from one to the other. "I have every confidence you two will suit each other extremely well. Please accept my felicitations." She took both their hands. "Will you marry in Middlesex, do you think?"

The betrothed couple looked at each other, and Miss Kenworth shrugged.

"You are welcome to marry at Yarmouth Hall," Carlotta said.

"We have many decisions to make," Mr. Fordyce said.

Carlotta shooed them toward the door. "Then you two run along now. I shan't be needing Miss Kenworth the remainder of the day."

"But, my lady . . ." Miss Kenworth protested.

"The doctor's coming, and I should like to stay here with my son."

After they left, Carlotta once again took up her position at Stevie's bedside. He broke into a fit of coughing, and she felt completely powerless to help him. *Poor little lamb.*

Soon Adams showed the doctor to Stevie's bedchamber. The middle-aged man, his medical bag in hand, entered the room.

"What are the lad's symptoms?" he asked gruffly.

"I thought yesterday he might be taking a chill for he began to cough. Then after church today, he began to run a fever."

The doctor set his hand on Stevie's forehead. "Has he eaten?"

She shook her head.

"What about liquids?"

"He has not wanted anything at all."

"The lad's obviously suffering from a lung complaint," the doctor said. "I shall give him an aqua cordial to cool the blood. He needs rest, of course—not that he's likely to go anywhere, as wretched as he feels—and day after tomorrow he should be as good as new."

"I hope you're right," Carlotta said in a somber voice.

"The lad's too thin," the doctor snapped, his eyes meeting Carlotta's. "When he gets well, you need to fatten him up."

Her eyes somber, Carlotta nodded.

After administering the cordial, the doctor repacked his bag and moved toward the door. "If he's not well day after tomorrow, send for me."

Thirty

James's journey back to Yarmouth was free of disturbances. It had seemed that every step of the way made him hunger more for the sight of Carlotta. But she was not the reason he was returning. Her son was.

When he had married Carlotta, he had agreed to raise Stevie as he would a son of his own. It wasn't fair to the lad to abandon him now that James had won his trust. It wasn't Stevie's fault his mother had misrepresented herself. James had never subscribed to the school of thought which blamed sons for the sins of their fathers. He had always been puzzled over the way bastards were ostracized, when it was not they—but their parents—who had sinned.

He dreaded facing Carlotta. James would be happy if he never had to see her again. Perhaps *happy* was not the correct word.

The pull of Yarmouth Hall was strong. He had grown hungry for the sight of the hall and the Bagworthy Wood and River Barle and the heather on the moors.

Also, he had made a decision to close the mine, and it should be he—and not someone else—who should break the news to the colliers. He planned to adopt Carlotta's plan to reestablish the men in other professions.

Which brought to his mind those wretched diamonds. He wished Blankenship had died in the womb and never blackened Carlotta's life.

It was dusk when James rode Ebony up the broad avenue to Yarmouth. He thought it had never been more lovely. The rhododendrons were in full bloom, and ribbons of bright yellow daffodils twisted about the entire landscape. Pride swept over him.

He went first to his secretary's office.

"My lord! You've returned," the secretary said, springing to his feet to bow to his employer.

James picked up some papers off Fordyce's desk. "How have things gone since I left?"

Fordyce was quick to tell his employer that Yarmouth had prospered in the countess's capable hands. He apprised James of the settlements made on the dead miners' families and of how much money her ladyship's unwanted diamond necklace had fetched.

"At first," Fordyce told James, "everyone was distraught when you left, but they soon came to rely upon Lady Rutledge. If I might be so bold as to say it, I believe you could have searched the world over and never found another woman who so well blended with your own views, especially when dealing with underlings. Lady Rutledge is greatly admired by all who are employed by you."

James had to admit he had done well when he selected Carlotta for his bride. How was he to have guessed the dark secret she had kept hidden from him?

He felt as if he could slam his first into Fordyce's sturdy desk.

James nodded at his secretary and started to walk away.

"My lord?"

James turned back, a single brow cocked.

"Is her ladyship correct in her assumption that you will close the mine?"

Damn! Fordyce was right! No other woman on the planet knew his thoughts like Carlotta. James slowly nodded. "It's what's right."

Fordyce gazed somberly at him for a moment, then broke into a smile. "By the by, my lord, I have an announcement to make. Miss Kenworth has done me the goodness of accepting my offer of marriage."

So Carlotta had been right about that, too. James answered with a smile. "Miss Kenworth is, indeed, a most fortunate young lady. When is the ceremony to occur?"

"We have not gotten that far. I only declared myself yesterday. Lady Rutledge, kind, unselfish soul that she is, gave me the encouragement I needed."

James's chest tightened at the mention of his wife. He supposed he could not put off his meeting with her any longer. "Do you happen to know where my wife is?"

Fordyce's eyes widened. "You have not seen her yet?"

"No."

"She's in Master Stevie's room. He's taken ill."

James's heart and lungs and stomach churning, he mounted the stairs to Stevie's room.

Carlotta stood by her son's bed, one hand stroking his fevered forehead, the other gripping his little fist. Her muslin day dress was a mass of wrinkles, and wisps of her midnight hair hung loose. She looked completely worn out, but more than that, grim worry was etched on her face, the face he had always loved to behold.

This was not how James had been picturing her. She was a seductress, not a loving mother.

She turned and looked at him, no emotion save grief on her face. "You've come home." She said it simply, almost forlornly.

He nodded. "I cannot turn my back on my responsibilities here. I pledged to be a father to your son. I have returned because of him." He stepped closer. "How is he?"

Her eyes watery, she glanced back to her son. "He's no better."

James came to Carlotta's side. "Has he eaten?"

She shook her head woefully. "Food, even drink, is the last thing he wants."

"When did he get sick?"

"Just yesterday—as we came from church in the carriage. Normally we walk, but I had thought to order the carriage because I perceived he had the beginnings of a lung complaint which, I thought, should necessitate being indoors."

Carlotta had even begun to attend church services—something she had seldom done in Bath, he thought.

She looked up at James. "When Stevie gets well, we'll leave."

"That won't be necessary," he said curtly. "I'll have my things moved to the south wing. We shan't live together as man and wife, but I have no intention of releasing my claims to the lad."

" 'Tis very kind of you, given the . . . circumstances of your estrangement from me."

As he stood there glaring at her, with no more

than a foot separating them, he could smell her lavender scent and take in her somber countenance, hear her gentle voice, and he would never have believed such a lady could have been mistress to a rake. He could almost believe Blankenship's claims. *Mrs. Ennis is a virtuous woman.* Almost. Were it not for Carlotta's own admission.

"You need to rest now," he said. "I'll sit with the lad."

She shook her head. "I'll not leave him."

James shrugged. "As you wish." Then he turned and left the room.

It was too dark now to go to the mines. He would do that in the morning. He would have to tell the miners the fate of the old mine. He took some consolation in the fact that the money Carlotta's necklace had fetched should go a long way toward purchasing livestock for the farms Carlotta had hoped the miners would establish. He paused, a grin pinching at his somber face. The necklace, at least, had meant nothing to her.

During the agony of those days he had spent in Bath, he had tortured himself with the memory of Carlotta's words of love. They had come neither easily nor readily but when at last they came, they had come from the depths of her heart. More the pity.

In the hallway he passed Miss Kenworth, who appeared to be bringing a tray of Stevie's favorite sweets to his chamber. "I'll wager the lad's too sick to desire those."

Her plump face fell. "I daresay you're right, my lord, but I had to make the effort. Poor lamb."

James nodded. "By the way, Miss Kenworth, allow

me to offer felicitations on your forthcoming marriage."

It was as if his words sent the stars from the skies to her shimmering eyes and the blush from the rose to her cheeks. "Thank you, my lord."

Now that was a woman in love, James decided.

That first night back at Yarmouth he saw no need to relocate his chamber since his estranged wife had no intention of leaving her son's side. Perhaps tomorrow, he thought, assured Stevie would return to prime good health.

James returned to Fordyce's office, secured armfuls of papers that demanded his attention, and planned to spend the night in his library catching up with his duties.

The sight of James had brought a peculiar mixture of pleasure and pain. Mostly the numbing pain of knowing they would never again be intimate. He would never again find anything to admire in her. She had not only lost her lover, she had lost her dearest friend.

Knowing she could stay at Yarmouth was a mixed blessing. On the one hand, she and Stevie had come to love the rugged Exmoor landscape and its people; on the other, she would have to endure the pain of James's torturing presence day after somber day.

But she could not trouble herself to think of James tonight. She was far too worried about her listless son. A hand pressed to his warm flesh told her his fever had climbed. He no longer seemed cognizant of anything around him, which caused her heart to trip.

How she had come to hate the woman she had been. If only she had spent his short lifetime with Stevie, she would have known if such a complaint was common to him or if it was something to give her concern. Oh, dear God, why had she not paid more attention to him? She had lived such a wretched, wicked existence before . . . before James.

Peggy brought her dinner, but Carlotta refused it. Miss Kenworth tried several times to relieve Carlotta, but Carlotta did not wish to leave Stevie. "What if he calls for me?" she had said wistfully.

Except for Carlotta's elderly grandmother, who was a stern taskmaster with the lad, Stevie had only his mother. James was doing an admirable job attempting to replace the boy's father, but the fact was, he wasn't the boy's father.

Later that night, as the sounds of the busy house began to die down and one after another of the servants had retired, the only sound that could be heard was Stevie's rumbling cough. James entered the boy's chamber. "I thought perhaps I could relieve you now," he said to Carlotta.

She gazed at him with solemn eyes. "I don't need any relief. I shall sleep in the little bed where Miss Kenworth generally sleeps so I'll be close at hand if Stevie should need me."

James moved closer to the boy's bed. "How's he doing?"

Her eyes pooled. "I'm afraid he's worse as the night wears on."

"I have some knowledge of fevers," James said in

a gentle voice. "I've dealt with them in The Peninsula and in India. They're always worse at night. They're down in the mornings." He paused. "Be assured that once the fever passes, recovery can commence."

"Then I hope the fever passes soon, for I'm quite beside myself with worry!"

"Imagine Mrs. Covington! Nine children to worry about," he said, hoping to divert her.

"I'm such a wicked person, I've even envied the poor widow all those children." Carlotta looked up at James's somber face and colored. Why, in heaven's name, had she gone and blurted her innermost thoughts? It wasn't as if he were still a husband to her. What they had shared in the past could never be rekindled.

"It's not wicked to be a loving mother," he said with kindness in his voice. "I remember when I was a lad. I always enjoyed good health, except for once. I burned with fever, and my mother—like you—refused to leave my bedside. As my fever climbed, my mother's eyes grew more teary." He stopped and smiled. "And, as you can see, I completely recovered."

She nodded at him, but could barely see him through her tears.

The following morning, as James had foretold, Stevie's fever had abated, but he was still listless and refused to eat or drink. His coughing grew more frequent—and more wrenching.

Carlotta left him with Miss Kenworth long enough to change into fresh clothing.

"Oh, my lady," Peggy said excitedly as she

brushed out Carlotta's hair. "Isn't that wonderful news about Miss Kenworth and Mr. Fordyce?"

"That it is. 'Tis the only good news I've had."

"Aye. To think Miss Kenworth's been here but eight weeks and already claimed the man's love."

"Have patience, Peg. You'll win Jeremy's heart yet."

"Then ye know my feelings?"

Carlotta nodded. "As I knew Miss Kenworth's and Mr. Fordyce's."

"I declare! Ye must be clairvoyant."

Carlotta laughed. "Hardly that. I've got eyes in my head. That's all."

Peggy nodded. "Aye, that's ever so true. Remember back at Mrs. McKay's, I told ye his lordship had love in his eyes when he looked at ye?"

It was as if Peggy had kicked her mistress in the heart. Had James truly loved her then? She could cry a river for all she had lost.

Peggy pinned up Carlotta's hair. "Now, ye were much later to fall in love with him. Ye weren't in love with him when ye married Lord Rutledge. But by the . . . oh, I hates to speak of that tragic night. The night of the disaster at the mine, there wasn't a soul in Exmoor who was unaware of yer powerful love for Lord Rutledge."

Powerful it was. *And still is.*

"Enough talk of my marriage. I need to hurry back to my son."

By late afternoon, Stevie's fever had returned, and all through the night he coughed uncontrollably and thrashed about deliriously. Carlotta stood beside him, stroking him and trying to force water between his parched lips. More than once she changed him out of soaking clothing, but he was completely unaware of his mother's ministrations. When she was not tending to him, she watched the clock upon his mantel as the worrisome minutes grew into hours. And still her son was no better. The doctor had expected him to be recovered by today, but he not only had not recovered, he had worsened. Carlotta's doubts ballooned.

The following morning, when he showed no sign of improvement, she sent again for the doctor.

James, who was also becoming concerned about the lad, waited for the doctor and showed him up to Stevie's room.

Carlotta watched with hollowed eyes as the doctor examined her son.

"His lungs are much worse now," the doctor mumbled. "Were this a regular chest complaint, the fever should have abated by now."

"Then what is it?" Carlotta asked in trembling voice.

His spectacles sliding down his nose as he bent over Stevie, the doctor looked up at Carlotta, swallowed, and said, "I'm afraid it's the consumption."

For as long as he lived, James would never forget the howling cry that came from Carlotta's throat at the doctor's words. Then she collapsed, weeping, onto Stevie's bed. "Oh, dear God, why could it not have been me?" Great rivulets of tears slid down her creamy cheeks.

Dear God, why is there nothing I can do for her? Or for the lad? Though James wished to slam his fist through the window—something he had been extremely desirous of doing lately—he had to offer Carlotta hope. As long as he had lived, he had been acquainted with only one person who had ever recovered from consumption. Still, he had to offer Carlotta hope.

He put a hand on her shoulder as he leaned over her protectively.

"If I should lose Stevie, I shall die," she said mournfully.

Her words were like a bullet to his own heart. In one blindingly quick second, he realized he could not live without Carlotta. Even if she had been Gregory Blankenship's mistress.

"You won't lose him, Carlotta," James said sternly.

"But it's . . ." Sobs racking her, she looked up at the doctor. "Will bleeding help?"

"We can try," he said, unwilling to offer much encouragement.

Carlotta stood stoically beside Stevie's bed and did not flinch when the doctor slit the boy's thin arm, and great quantities of her son's blood began to stream forth.

James kept his arm about her, stirred by her strength.

After the doctor left, she turned to James and buried her face into his chest and sobbed uncontrollably.

He merely held her and whispered soothingly to her. When she finished, he held her at arm's length and spoke sternly. "Don't give up, Carlotta. He'll get better."

"Oh, James, I wish I could believe you, but 'tis such a horrible disease. No one ever conquers it."

He swallowed. "I did."

She whirled at him, hope in her swollen eyes.

"When I was seventeen. I was just as sick as Stevie. That's the fever I told you about."

She smiled and brushed away a tear. "When your mother cried at your bedside?"

He nodded.

"But . . ." She looked away from him. "Your mother was a righteous woman. The Lord answered her prayers." She buried her face in her hands and cried. "But he won't answer mine because . . . because I'm so great a sinner."

James jerked her into his arms and spoke firmly. "You're not a sinner, Carlotta. You've been the best thing that's ever happened to the yeomen of Exmoor. You're kind and generous and a loving mother. There's nothing wicked about you."

She quivered from her sobs. "But I duped you, James, and you deserved so much better."

"It angers me when you speak in such a manner about the Countess of Rutledge."

She tried to laugh, but succeeded only in bursting into fresh tears.

"I know you didn't sleep last night," he said. "Why do you not allow me to stay here tonight?"

She shook her head. "I can't."

"If he asks for you, I'll summon you at once."

She shook her head more vehemently. "I can't leave him. I would be unable to go to sleep, knowing how gravely ill he is." She burst into tears again.

"Then I'll stay with you."

What did she care if James stayed or not? Nothing mattered anymore. Save her precious son, who clung feebly to his life. She pulled a chair up to his bed and sat beside Stevie, clutching his limp hand in her own.

"Oh, dear God, spare him. Take me. I'm the one who's brought all this on."

"Carlotta, don't beat up on yourself so. Stevie's sick because he came into contact with someone who carried the disease. Not because of anything you did."

"But I've led such a wicked life."

"Since when is it wicked to love someone? You fell in love with a man. An unmarried man. You were not an adulteress."

"Only a mistress," she said bitterly.

"I spoke with Blankenship in Bath."

She whirled at him, her eyes flashing angrily.

"He denied that you shared his bed."

After all the heartache Gregory had caused her, at last he had done something good and decent. *Even if it was a lie.*

"I don't ever wish to hear Gregory's name again."

"Nor do I," he agreed.

Thirty-one

Day after agonizing day, Stevie's fever raged. Carlotta kept a constant vigil at her son's bedside, and the doctor visited daily. James became as concerned over Carlotta's well-being as he was over their son's. She'd had very little sleep, she'd completely lost her appetite, and she had taken to being sick every morning. Before his very eyes, she grew thinner, and the color left her hollowed cheeks.

Even when Stevie's fever broke—after two weeks—the prognosis was bleak. At least the poor lad was now cognizant of those around him, and he had begun to beg to have his favorite stories read to him. But his deep, racking cough grew hardier each day, and his ability to speak without gasping for breath diminished. Adding to the severity of his condition was the fact that he still had not eaten a single bite of food.

Carlotta continued to sleep in his chamber every night. She had neither been downstairs nor out of doors in over two weeks. She insisted the draperies in her son's room be open each day in the hope that the sun would burn away the damp air which was so culpable for consumption. Then, when night brought cooler air, she would close the draperies in hopes of keeping out the dampness.

The day after he had returned to Exmoor, James had announced the mine closing. Over the last two weeks he had met individually with each collier. To a man, each of them agreed to accept James's offer of setting them up in the business of sheep farming. More than one grateful wife had thanked James for keeping her loved one from having to go back down into the black pits.

James happened to be in Stevie's room one afternoon, vainly trying to offer Carlotta hope, when Adams informed them that Mrs. Covington had come to see Lady Rutledge.

"Should you wish to ask her in?" the butler inquired with a haughty air.

"Indeed I do," Carlotta said, standing and walking toward the door. "I shall meet her in the saloon."

Once Adams was gone, Carlotta cast an impatient glance at her scowling husband.

"Don't be angry at Adams. He's aware that Mrs. Covington is not of our class. He's merely doing his job."

Carlotta's lack of snobbery filled James with pride. Indeed, every step she had taken since she had become his countess was faultless, and his pride in her continued to escalate.

In the saloon Carlotta forced a smile, held out both hands, and walked to Mrs. Covington. It was obvious that the woman had come in her Sunday finest. Of course, her dress was black. Homespun. And she had neatly pinned back her lackluster brown tresses.

"To what do I owe the pleasure?" Carlotta asked after the widow had dipped her a curtsy.

Mrs. Covington continued to grasp Carlotta's hand. "I've heard your young'un is ailing."

A look of sorrow swept over Carlotta's face, and her eyes filled with tears. "Indeed he is. I should appreciate your prayers."

"All ten of us is praying for the little lad to return to good health."

"Then that's all I can ask," a somber Carlotta said with trembling voice.

The widow held out a small bottle. "I've brought this distillation of motherwort for ye lad. It's said to aid in the recovery of all lung complaints. I extract it from the stalk what grows only behind me parents' cottage in Porlock. Two spoons three times a day and it's never failed to work."

"You went all the way to Porlock to procure this for Stevie?"

" 'Twas nothing after all yer kindness to me and mine. I only wish I'd had it when me little Mary came down sick. She was gone less than two days after her symptoms arrived."

Carlotta took the bottle, tears spilling down her cheeks. "I'm much indebted to you, Mrs. Covington."

"You go on now and give it to the lad. I've got to return to my own young'uns."

Carlotta stepped forward and hugged her, then turned around, left the room, and fairly flew up the stairs.

"You dispatched the widow rather quickly," James said.

"She brought me a concoction for Stevie. She swears by its success."

"That was very thoughtful of her. Let's hope she's right."

Carlotta poured the liquid into a spoon and coaxed Stevie into swallowing it. "Come love, you must get well. Brownie misses you very much. It's not fair to your pony that he's not been exercised in three weeks."

The boy grimaced, but took the concoction. "Poor Bwownie," he said.

She ruffled her son's hair.

The lad did not have the strength to play soldiers. Any activity with his arms robbed him of breath. Therefore, James sat by his side hour upon hour, spinning yarns of life in the military.

"I'm going to be a soldier when I gwow up," the boy proclaimed.

To which Carlotta's eyes would fill with tears. Her son would not see the next year, much less grow to manhood. Nothing had ever hurt with such ruthlessness. It was as if her heart were being wrenched from her body. Yet, she refused to allow him to see her cry. For the time he had left, she had vowed to bring him as much happiness as she could.

The word *no* was not in her vocabulary. If Stevie desired her to lie beside him as he went to sleep, she would oblige. Were he to express an interest in the scullery maid's kitten, his mother would procure the creature. Whatever story he desired to have read, she would read to him.

A pity, she thought, she could not find any food that would entice him to eat. Nothing she suggested stimulated any appetite in him. It had been three weeks now since he had eaten. If the doctor had found him thin three weeks ago, he must find the child emaciated now.

Whenever she would chide her son for not eating,

her husband would admonish her on the same grounds. "You have no room to talk, Carlotta," James would say sternly. "You're eating no better than Stevie."

Her husband's apparent forgiveness of her went almost unnoticed in her grieving state. Her own happiness now rested solely on the prospect of her son's health. That James cared for her was not something she could contemplate now. Her mind was too fogged with grief. There was no way she could burden it with anything else. Especially something that pertained to her wicked self.

Like a religious ritual, she administered to Stevie Mrs. Covington's motherwort three times every day. She did not know if it were her hopeful mind or if it were fact, but it seemed to her that after three days Stevie's cough seemed less severe.

"James?" she called.

He sat in the chair next to hers beside Stevie's bed. "Yes?"

"Do you not agree that Stevie's cough is improving?"

"I do. I had not wanted to get your hopes up, but I've been thinking the same thing."

For the first time in three weeks, a smile flashed across Carlotta's face.

The next day she was convinced her son's cough had improved.

The day after that he sat up in bed. "Mama?"

She stood up and came to his side. "What, my sweet?"

"Do you think I might have some plum pudding?"

Unable to speak because she was weeping so hard, Carlotta turned to meet James's twinkling eyes then she fell into her husband's embrace, sobbing tears of joy.

"Oh, my love," she said to James, "he's going to make it!"

Those were the most wonderful words James had ever heard. He picked up her hand and pressed a kiss into the hollow of her palm. "I believe you're right, dearest."

With eyes wet yet happy, she looked up and stroked the planes of his cheekbones. "I don't deserve such happiness."

He gathered her into his arms. "I'd say your happiness is long overdue, sweetheart of mine."

She lifted her face to his for a kiss.

"Mama?" Stevie said.

She withdrew from her husband. "What, lamb?"

"How come you and Papa have not been kissing each other since he came back?"

Carlotta began to giggle. "I daresay because your papa was gone for so long I forgot how!"

"I'm glad he's back," Stevie said, his eyelids growing heavy.

Carlotta looked back at James. "I am, too."

All told, Stevie was sick for six weeks. Even after his cough was gone, Carlotta refused to allow him outdoors. The word *no* had returned to her vocabulary. After another two weeks she relented and allowed him to ride his pony, provided that his mama and papa accompany him, and provided it was a sunny day and provided he dressed warmly.

Miss Kenworth, having grown utterly attached to her charge, decided not to return to Middlesex for her wedding but to have it in Exmoor so she would not have to leave Master Stephen.

"But once you begin to have children of your own," Carlotta pointed out, "you'll be leaving him."

"Mr. Fordyce and I have discussed the matter, and he agrees that I can continue with Master Stephen even after we have children of our own, provided that you don't object to our children being raised alongside of yours."

"It's a rather unorthodox scheme, but we can try it since none of us should care to lose you." Carlotta's eyes danced. "Of course, I daresay Mr. Fordyce won't allow you to continue sleeping in Master Stevie's room once you are married."

The poor nurse's face grew scarlet as she scurried from the chamber.

Carlotta's own breath grew short when she thought of lying with her husband. She had not lain with him in many, many weeks. She was still too worried about Stevie to leave him at night, for sometimes at night, Stevie's coughing returned.

One of the first places Carlotta went upon Stevie's recovery was to the Covingtons' cottage. It looked so different than it had the first time she had come when winter's frost had only recently left. Now geraniums bloomed from window boxes, and a bank of daffodils separated the kitchen garden from the pasture where a hundred sheep grazed.

Two of the younger lads were gathering eggs from the hen house, and the little toddler sat in rich, dark dirt, spooning it into a cup.

Stevie had instantly run off to shadow the older Covington lads, whom he greatly looked up to, and who were very kind to him in return.

Carlotta knocked on the door and entered at Mrs. Covington's command. Especially different was the inside of the house. All signs of the coal dust were gone. No more grayness. Things looked clean and bright. Daniel, now too big for his cradle, was crawling around the wooden floors.

"Ah, me lady," Mrs. Covington said. "I'd hoped ye'd be a comin'. I've procured tea especially for yer visit."

"How very considerate of you," Carlotta said, sitting at the kitchen table.

"Not here, my lady. No fine ladies like yerself belong in kitchens."

Carlotta laughed. "I wasn't always a lady, Mrs. Covington. When I was growing up, I was allowed to actually help our cook in the kitchen. I'm a most accomplished potato peeler, if you must know."

Mrs. Covington broke into laughter.

"Seriously, Mrs. Covington, I had to come today to tell you how grateful I am that you came to us that day and kindly brought the elixir. I can date my son's recovery to that day. I don't suppose we'll ever know if it was all our prayers or your elixir that spared my lad, but I'm powerfully thankful."

Now it was the widow who teared up. "It broke me heart to think of ye losing yer only child. I kept rememberin' as how ye told me what riches I had in me children. Yer words helped me when I needed help the most." Then the widow looked askance at Carlotta. "I declare, my lady, I can tell by lookin' at ye. Ye are increasing, are ye not?"

Carlotta's lashes lowered, and she began to blush. "I am."

Mrs. Covington broke into a smile. "I'm so happy for ye. What does his lordship have to say 'bout the babe?"

"I haven't told him yet."

The widow set the kettle on the hook over the open fire and spun around to face Carlotta. "How could ye withhold such wondrous news from him?"

"I only learned of it during Stevie's sickness, and, quite naturally, I was not excited about anything at the time."

"And now?"

Carlotta shrugged. "Would that I could think of a special way to tell him."

"Ye will. Ye will."

That very night at the dinner table, James began to admonish his wife for her lack of appetite. "It wouldn't be fair to Stevie and me, Carlotta, for you to allow yourself to waste away."

"Nor would it be fair to the babe, either, I dare-say," she said rather nonchalantly.

He glared at her for a moment, as if he were trying to understand the enormous impact of her words. "The babe?" he finally asked hopefully.

She nodded.

"Then . . . then you've known since . . ."

"Since you went away, actually. I became certain when Stevie was sick."

She watched as a smile warmed his cherished face. "I may very well be the luckiest man on English soil."

Thirty-two

He woke up to bright sunlight and looked down at Carlotta, curled up asleep beside him. His hand went to her bare back, to glide over it. Here—here in the Earl of Rutledge's bed—is where she belonged. Here, their babe would be born. He could burst with his happiness, with his pride.

He had returned because Yarmouth's pull was strong. He'd come to understand his fate was intermingled with this moorland wilderness as inevitably as his ascension to the title. This is where he belonged. This is where his heart was. This is where he wished to put down roots.

When he had returned to Yarmouth after his absence he had been blinded by his rage against Carlotta. She had withheld the truth from him. She had deprived him of the happiness he so hungered for. She had been mistress to a rake. She had shattered the heart James had given her.

His anger toward her had been unwavering—as long as he did not have to behold those violet eyes or smell her lavender or hear her husky voice. If it weren't for seeing her again, he could have denied all that had once been in his heart.

But he had not been prepared for the potent effect she would have on him.

She was merely Carlotta. A woman who had been widowed. A woman who had made a wrong choice. A woman who had learned to give of herself unselfishly. A woman who once loved him.

As soon as he had seen her with her heart laid bare, he forgot his anger. She hurt, therefore he hurt. It was that simple. He had been an imbecile to think he could stop loving her because of something that had occurred long ago.

He came to realize it did not matter if Blankenship had bedded her or not. What mattered was their future.

When he had returned, it had not taken long before he had come to realize Yarmouth had taken possession of Carlotta as it had him. Everywhere he turned, he was inundated with praise over his wife's allegiance to the people of Exmoor.

"If anything ever happened to Lord Rutledge," one of the miners had said, "we'd be in her ladyship's capable hands. Never was a lady such as her who understands the land and the people of Exmoor."

His pride for her was a talisman he wore each day with growing appreciation.

When he had come to realize they could very well lose Stevie, Carlotta's past meant nothing to him. Yes, she had been a poor mother, but those days were as buried as Stephen Ennis. Hadn't her recent actions, her recent unselfishness, more than compensated for any past sins?

All James had ever wanted—a wife, a child, a happy family—he was allowing to be snatched from him.

When Carlotta bemoaned her evil past, it was more than he could bear. How dare she disparage herself! She was loving and kind and the perfect woman to be his countess. How could he have not realized how blessed he had been? Even if she had loved Blankenship, he knew that love was now dead. That she could love so powerfully was merely a demonstration of her ability to love without inhibition. As he liked to think she had loved him.

He only hoped he had not killed that love.

During the boy's sickness, James had only spared a brief thought to his own plight, so concerned was he over the lad. As was Carlotta.

But once Stevie's recovery commenced, it became clear that not only did Carlotta still hold James with some affection, but she also had no rancor over his flight. To the contrary, she blamed herself totally for everything.

In a few short months his beloved Carlotta had completely metamorphosed from hedonist to devoted mother. His pride in her rushed over him like a morning breeze, fresh and welcome.

All that mattered was the future. A future in which he was assured Carlotta would dedicate herself to good works. A future which would, hopefully, fill Yarmouth Hall with their children.

As he gazed down at her, his hands gliding over her smooth, bare flesh, she began to stir. Her eyes opened and she looked up at him. "Good morning, my love," she said sweetly, reaching out for him.

"How are you feeling this morning?" he asked with concern.

"A bit queasy, but it will pass."

He traced her nose with a finger. "I could stay here with you for the rest of my days."

"As could I," she whispered. "Oh, James, I regret that I was blind to my love for you for so long, but I vow I've never loved so deeply." She lifted her face to his.

He kissed her softly. "I have a confession."

She raised up on her elbow, her brows lowered.

"I've never loved anyone but you, Carlotta. I think I even loved you when . . . when we were on The Peninsula."

She threw herself into his arms. "Then you *did* ask me to marry you because you really loved me?"

"I'd hardly wish to spend the rest of my life with a woman I did not love."

"I was so worried that the only reason you married me was out of responsibility toward Stevie."

"I need hardly have shackled myself to exercise my responsibilities."

Contentedly, she laid her face against his chest. "I am so happy you've shackled yourself to me."

"Speaking of shackles, Jeremy has offered for Peggy."

Carlotta squealed with delight. "It seems Cupid is in danger of injuring his arm from all the arrows he's been shooting of late." As she spoke, she was careful not to disengage her arms from around her husband's back.

"When you left," she said, "I wanted to die. Then I scolded myself. *What would James want you to do?* I asked myself. I knew you would have wanted me to be strong and minister to your yeomen's needs, to take your place in your absence. It gave me strength. For the first time in my life I was strong and capable."

"You've made me very proud, but nothing has ever made me more proud or more happy than the news you imparted to me last night."

She tightened her hold on him. "I'm happy, too."

"But I do so worry about you," he said gently. "Are you sure it's all right to . . . to allow me access?"

She laughed. "I am most sure. Now, could I, perchance, persuade you . . . ?"

Epilogue

Eighteen months later

After an unusually warm summer, Carlotta was happy to welcome autumn. Stevie especially enjoyed jumping on the heaps of russet leaves in an attempt to smash them.

"I believe I'll have you carry one of these baskets of apples, lamb," Carlotta said to her son, "for, I declare, my arms are aching."

"Papa says your arms should ache right off from constantly holding the baby."

"Your papa's a fine one to talk," she mumbled. "There never was a more coddled babe than that brother of yours."

"I wish he were bigger so he could have come with us today."

"We must learn to be happy with what we have and not go wishing our lives—or Jimmy's life—away."

He took the smaller basket of apples from his mother. "Can I have one?"

"May you?"

"May I?"

"Not now, lamb. Yours are at home. These are for the Covington family."

She heard a clapping sound behind them and turned to see her husband, flicking the ribbons to his tilbury. He drove it up to within a few feet of her.

"And what brings you this way?" she asked.

"I learned that you were carrying two rather large baskets of apples and decided I should have to relieve you, my lady. Have I not scolded you often enough about curtailing your activity . . . in your condition?"

"But, my darling man, 'tis merely a basket of apples. Stevie took the other. And I assure you I feel fine."

"Here, Stevie, take the ribbons," James said, handing the reins to the boy as he jumped down. He gave his wife a hand up. "I must insist you ride, not walk."

She pouted, but obliged him.

Once they were on the road, she asked James if the wool fetched a good price.

"Indeed it has. The best ever, I'm told. That, of course, I expected. I'm not known as the luckiest man alive for nothing." He lifted his wife's hand and kissed it. "My lucky star was shining the day you agreed to become my wife."

"You know what, Papa?" Stevie chimed in.

"What, son?"

"My lucky star was shining the day you became my father."

ABOUT THE AUTHOR

After careers in journalism and teaching English, Cheryl Bolen published her first novel (*A Duke Deceived,* with Harlequin Historical) in 1998 and was named Notable New Author.

Cheryl lives in a suburb of Houston with her husband, a professor. They are the parents of two sons. An antiques dealer, she enjoys traveling to England whenever her writing deadlines permit.

Readers can write to her at Kensington Books or through her Web site at www.cherylbolen.com.

If you enjoyed A FALLEN WOMAN, be sure to look for AN IMPERFECT PROPOSAL, the next book in award-winning author Cheryl Bolen's fabulous *Brides of Bath* series, available wherever books are sold in May 2003.

It's been two years since George Pembroke lost his beloved wife, and he's not recovering the way family and friends think he should. His sister Glee's friend Sally Sullivan is concerned about him, but with her father dead and her brother too outspoken and meddling for her taste, she's also uncertain about her own future. When Glee proposes that she move in with George to care for his children, Sally is wary—it seems highly improper, even if she didn't cherish a *tendre* for the melancholy widower. Of course, there's no question that he would ever return her feelings. Or would he . . . ?